TWENTIETH CENTURY
EUROPEAN
SHORT STORY

THE
MAGILL
BIBLIOGRAPHIES

Other Magill Bibliographies:

The American Presidents—Norman S. Cohen
Black American Women Novelists—Craig Werner
Classical Greek and Roman Drama—Robert J. Forman
Contemporary Latin American Fiction—Keith H. Brower
Masters of Mystery and Detective Fiction—J. Randolph Cox
Nineteenth Century American Poetry—Philip K. Jason
Restoration Drama—Thomas J. Taylor
The Victorian Novel—Laurence W. Mazzeno
Women's Issues—Laura Stempel Mumford

TWENTIETH CENTURY EUROPEAN SHORT STORY

An Annotated Bibliography

CHARLES E. MAY
Professor of English
California State University, Long Beach

SALEM PRESS

Pasadena, California   Englewood Cliffs, New Jersey

Library of Congress Cataloging-in-Publication Data

May, Charles E. (Charles Edward). 1941–
   Twentieth century European short story / Charles
   E. May.
      p.   cm. —(Magill bibliographies)
     ISBN 0-89356-656-X
     1. Short stories, European—History and criti-
cism—Bio-bibliography. 2. European fiction—20th
century—History and criticism—Bio-bibliography.
I. Title. II. Series.
Z5917.S5M39 1989
[PN3335]
016.8093′1—dc20   89-10853
                                CIP

To Mom and Dad, with gratitude.

CONTENTS

TWENTIETH CENTURY EUROPEAN SHORT STORY

CONTENTS

CONTENTS

EDITORIAL STAFF

INTRODUCTION

The short story is both mankind's oldest form of narrative communication, dating back to the dawn of the human need to recount an event, and Western culture's most modern aesthetic form, coming into its own as a unique genre as late as the mid-nineteenth century. It is an ambiguous form, fraught with controversy, for it has been termed the most natural medium of narrative communication as well as the most self-conscious aesthetic form. With its focus on sacred moments of revelation as well as secular moments of isolation, it is a form that seems particularly suited to the modern world of relativistic reality.

The European tradition of short fiction began in Italy in the fourteenth century with the *novella* form, best represented by the short tales in Giovanni Boccaccio's *The Decameron*. Derived from the Latin *novellus*, a diminutive of the word *novus*, meaning "new," the term *novella* was used to designate stories that were fresh, strange, and unusual. Cognate terms, such as *novela* in Spain and *nouvelle* in France, continued through the eighteenth century to denote short tales that were "new" and interesting in much the same way that contemporary human-interest "news" stories are interesting. In Germany, in the early nineteenth century, another cognate term, *novelle*, was used to designate both the very short stories of Johann Wolfgang von Goethe and the somewhat longer stories of E. T. A. Hoffmann.

The modern European short story began at the end of the nineteenth century with the stories of Russian writer Anton Chekhov. The major difference between Chekhov's short prose fictions and those that preceded him was that whereas such nineteenth century European writers as Goethe, Nikoli Gogol, Prosper Mérimée, and Hoffmann transformed the folk- and fairy-tale forms of their village cultures into projective psychological stories of the grotesque, Chekhov focused on characters caught in realistic dilemmas and conflicts. After Chekhov, short fiction began to gain new respect and was further refined by such American, British, and Irish writers as Sherwood Anderson, Katherine Mansfield, and James Joyce.

In the twentieth century, the short story developed from previous dominant literary traditions in their respective countries. The modern Italian short story still owes much to the realistic tradition of the Boccaccio *novella*, as the term "neorealism," often used to discuss modern Italian fiction, reflects. The contemporary French short story is indebted to the romantic-realistic folktale modernized by Mérimée and the psychorealistic *conte* perfected by Guy de Maupassant. Spanish short fiction derives primarily from the Renaissance *novelas* of Miguel de Cervantes. German short fiction springs from the romantic *novelle* form of Goethe, Heinrich von Kleist, and Hoffmann. The modern Russian short story comes from both the lyrical stories of Ivan Turgenev and the grotesque tales of Gogol.

This annotated bibliography covers European writers of short fiction since Chekhov; although he has had the most significant influence on all twentieth-century short-story writers, his works were published primarily in the late nineteenth century. The earliest figure covered is Maxim Gorky, who sought Chekhov's advice on the art of short-story writing. The most predominant figure is Franz Kafka, who has had an influence on subsequent writers trying to imitate his style and an impact on modern critics eager to understand his puzzling stories.

To give the individual annotations of this bibliography a context, it is necessary to make some suggestions about basic differences between the novel and the short story. For example, the novel form thrives in a cultural setting that is relatively stable and socially organized (precisely the kind of culture where people read), whereas the short story is often the fictional form of choice for a culture that still owes much to village and folk life (an oral culture). This difference may explain, for example, why the novel is the predominant form in England, whereas the short story is favored in Ireland.

Furthermore, the novel form is better able to deal with abstract philosophic issues than the short story is; thus, the novel is a structure of ideas, whereas the short story is more lyrical in its focus and thus likely to be based on an emotional response or a spiritual discovery. For this reason, so-called philosophic writers such as Thomas Mann and Fyodor Dostoevski have had more influence through their novels than through their short fiction works. Thus, in general, the novel deals primarily with organized society or organized ideas; the short story, on the other hand, often focuses on a disruption of, or challenge to, the smug assumption that structured ideology or organized society can cope with the mysterious fears and desires of humankind.

One can see the distinction between the ideological structure of the novel and the aesthetic or lyrical structure of the short story by examining the works of Albert Camus and Jean-Paul Sartre. Most influential for their contributions to the framework of existentialism, Sartre and Camus primarily expressed their ideas in novels, dramas, and philosophic treatises. Yet both wrote a small number of short stories, which most critics agree are more personal and poetic than their longer fictional works and thus not as dependent on philosophic ideas. Although the best-known and most anthologized stories of both authors—Camus' "The Guest" and Sartre's "The Wall"—do focus on existential choice, they do so not within an elaborate philosophic framework, but rather in terms of an isolated moment of confrontation with death and brotherhood.

Other modern European writers best known for their ideas are also best known for their novels. Hermann Hesse and Thomas Mann are the most obvious examples. Hesse's impact on the American student movement of the 1960's was made with such novels as *Siddhartha*, *Demian*, and *Steppenwolf*, not with the short stories, which have a more lyrical, poetic, and elliptical style than the novels. Although much has been written about Mann's short stories, it is his novels that most clearly outline his philosophic ideas and create the similitude of a highly developed social structure. In his short stories he is more concerned with antisocial and nonconceptual aesthetic experiences and structures.

Although such short fiction works as "Death in Venice" and "Mario and the

Magician" deal with both social and philosophic ideas, they focus on the ambiguity of the situation of the Romantic artist. Both short stories have an elaborate symbolic and poetic structure based on Mann's concept of the musical leitmotif as well as his use of preexistent mythic stories; the result is the spatialization of temporal reality, a distinguishing characteristic of the poetic structure of modern narrative.

Mann has had an influence on modern fiction because of his novels as well as his short stories. A number of writers are included in this bibliography, however, whose short fiction is either overshadowed by their work in other areas or who are so little translated and anthologized in English that they have not been discussed widely by English-speaking critics. First, there are those writers who are primarily known to American readers for only one or two short stories. The Austrian writer, Ilse Aichinger for example, has written several works of both short and long prose fiction; as far as American critics are concerned, however, she is the author of one well-known story, "The Bound Man." Moreover, her critical fame is primarily due to the story's stylistic and thematic similarities to Kafka's stories, especially "A Hunger Artist."

Similarly, Ivan Bunin, who was a very prolific writer, is primarily known to American students for his brilliant short story "The Gentleman from San Francisco," a work which is often compared to Leo Tolstoy's better known "The Death of Ivan Ilyich" because of its focus on one man's confrontation with death. "The Last Judgment" is virtually the only story by Karel Capek anthologized in English-language texts, whereas Gorky's "Twenty-six Men and a Girl" is practically the only familiar story in the English-speaking world by one of the most popular writers in Russia. Moreover, it is only the appearance of single stories in anthologies of short stories by such writers as Tommaso Landolfi ("Gogol's Wife") and Cesare Pavese ("Suicides") that makes them known to American students.

This bibliography also lists several modern European writers who are well known to English-speaking students, but primarily through their work in genres other than the short story. These include novelists Heinrich Böll, Italo Calvino, and Aleksandr Solzhenitsyn; playwrights Bertolt Brecht and Luigi Pirandello; and poet Boris Pasternak. Others who are less well known for their work in the short-story genre are the French writers Colette and Alain Robbe-Grillet. Most studies of Colette are biographies, and most criticism on Robbe-Grillet discuss his experiments with the *New Novel*.

The writers included in this volume who have made the short-story form their central genre and have had the most influence on it are Isaac Babel, Isak Dinesen, Franz Kafka, Isaac Bashevis Singer, and, in some respects—although the short story has not been their most dominant form—Thomas Mann and Vladimir Nabokov. What characterizes the work of these writers, as a survey of the criticism shows, are the following common denominators: a focus on the grotesque, the use of traditional folk-tale structures and motifs, a concern with the aesthetic experience, an obsession with the dream experience, the search for style and form, an insistence on the importance of language, the use of surrealistic imagery, and the development of a tightly unified poetic form.

Isaac Babel takes a rather narrow spectrum of experience for his subject matter, but his focus on the revelatory moment and his understanding of the short story as a form of aesthetic contemplation make him a powerful force in modern European short fiction. Similarly, Isak Dinesen, who derives her stories from medieval legends and tales and deals with life as an aesthetic game or a marionette theater, is primarily interested in stories that are about storytelling itself. Isaac Bashevis Singer is also a writer who "modernizes" the medieval, focusing on the inextricable relationship between middle-class realism and the archaic, prerational traditions of the supernatural and the demonic.

Although Thomas Mann and Vladimir Nabokov do not deal with the primitive folk-tale world of Dinesen, Babel, and Singer, they also are more interested in aesthetic or "story" reality than the so-called realistic world of everyday life. Whereas Mann deals with the artist as magician or the artist caught between Dionysian and Apollonian forces of raw experience and aesthetic control, Nabokov sees reality as an artistic game and focuses on characters who are self-consciously aware of themselves as fictional characters caught in the complexities of life as if it were an elaborate story.

Kafka's powerful place in modern European short fiction is a result of his ability to combine the primitive dream reality of Babel, Dinesen, and Singer with the complex aesthetic sophistication of Mann and Nabokov. Because his fictions are so evasive, so complex a mix of the world of everyday reality and the world of nightmare and fantasy, they lend themselves to a variety of critical approaches: formalist, Freudian, structuralist, and poststructuralist. Moreover, one can see virtually all the conventions of the European short fiction tradition in the short stories of Kafka—from the grotesque tragicomic style of Gogol to the intensified hyper-reality of Chekhov to the self-reflexive aesthetic games of Nabokov.

The short story is perhaps the narrative form most adequate to present the nature of reality as it is experienced in the modern world. Because of its fragmentary nature, its focus on the moment of epiphany, and its dependence on spatial, aesthetic form rather than on temporal, realistic structure, the short story may indeed be more reflective of modernist themes and techniques than its big brother, the novel.

This annotated bibliography attempts to bring together most of the criticism on the important European writers who have attempted to master the short story, and, as a result, to generate more interest in this frequently neglected form. By scanning the annotations, one can get an idea of the themes and techniques most commonly used by modern European short-story writers and thus discover areas of research not previously explored by critics. One can also determine which writers and stories have been most neglected by critics and which are most in need of further analysis and study. Furthermore, the individual annotations are, although not extensive, detailed enough to give the individual researcher some sense of the commonality that exists among twentieth century European short stories.

Perhaps the best way to proceed, after determining which author, typical theme, or generic type to explore further, is to begin reading, or skimming, the most general biographical/critical introductions to an author. After formulating a general critical context for an author, the student can read with inquisitive insight the more specialized studies of the author's thought and technique and the individual studies of separate stories. For certain authors, where there are no extended discussions of individual stories, the student will necessarily be limited to general studies.

The teacher or student may consider this book a critical map charting a still largely unexplored narrative territory. The bibliography is not meant to be an end in itself; it is not even intended to be a means to an end. Rather it is meant to be the means to the never-ending study of modern short fiction as a form that reflects human life as it is caught in moments of significant revelation.

General Studies

Arrowsmith, William. Introduction to *Six Modern Italian Novellas*. New York: Pocket Books, 1964.

A brief discussion of postwar neorealism in Italian literature. Argues that the best of Italian postwar fiction has taken the form of the long story or the short novel—an experimental form which often has a tendency to lyricism or the single-minded pursuit of a central idea.

Barzini, Luigi. "Italy." Translated by Helen Barolini. *The Kenyon Review* 32 (1970): 95-97.

Notes two basic characteristics of the modern Italian short story: They all follow the ancient pattern created by Giovanni Boccaccio of being pithy, realistic, and slightly cynical, and they continue to be quite brief, usually about two thousand words in length.

Bender, Hans. "West Germany." Translated by Peter Salm. *The Kenyon Review* 31 (1969): 85-92.

States that the short story became the most characteristic genre of the new beginning of German literature after World War II. Provides a brief survey of the postwar German short story, Quoting several definitions of the form by German writers. Notes that although younger authors reject previous forms and prefer the term "text" to designate their work, in their prose texts the short story continues to live unrecognized.

Bennett, E. K. *A History of the German Novelle*. 2d ed. Cambridge, England: Cambridge University Press, 1965.

The final chapter of this standard study of German short fiction, written by H. M. Waidson after Bennett's death, deals with the twentieth century *Novelle*.

Suggests that there is no way to distinguish the short story from the *Novelle*.
Discusses briefly the stories of Thomas Mann, Hermann Hesse, Franz Kafka,
and several lesser known German writers.

Brée, Germaine. Introduction to *Great French Short Stories*. New York: Dell Books,
1960.
Points out that the French short story either deals with the fantastic and the
supernatural or else, like the medieval fabliau, with anecdotes of events taking
place in the everyday world. A brief survey of French short fiction, including
the modern stories of Colette, Albert Camus, Jean-Paul Sartre, and Samuel
Beckett.

Cassola, Carlo. "Italy." *The Kenyon Review* 30 (1968): 486-490.
Discusses modern Italian short fiction as existentialist. According to Cassola,
what drives the modern Italian author to write is not psychological curiosity or
social interest, but a metaphysical need for the purity of perception which
enables him to express the emotion with which life fills him.

Connolly, Julian W. "The Russian Short Story: 1880-1917." In *The Russian Short
Story: A Critical History*, edited by Charles A. Moser. Boston: Twayne, 1986.
In the twentieth century section of this essay, Connolly summarizes the short
fiction of Maxim Gorky, Ivan Bunin, and others. Also discusses the influence
of Symbolism on the short story in early twentieth century Russian literature.

de Onís, Harriet. Introduction to *Spanish Stories and Tales*. New York: Washington
Square Press, 1956.
A brief survey of Spanish short fiction, including Spanish American short
fiction. Notes that after 1880 the short story's reputation rose in Spain. States
that the Spanish ideal of beauty expressed in the short story is less purely
aesthetic and more broadly humane.

Flores, Angel. Introduction to *Great Spanish Short Stories*. New York: Dell Books,
1962.
A brief survey of the development of Spanish short fiction from the sixteenth
century to the twentieth century. Discusses the trends of romanticism, realism,
local color, and magical realism in both Spanish and Spanish American short
fiction.

Halpern, Daniel. Introduction to *The Art of the Tale: An International Anthology of
Short Stories*. New York: Penguin Books, 1986.
A brief discussion of short fiction written since World War II. Discusses
different types of modern stories: fables, surrealistic tales, political stories,
stories with exotic settings, and conventional stories.

Houghton, Norris. Introduction to *Great Russian Short Stories*. New York: Dell Books, 1958.
Although most of this introduction deals with nineteenth century Russian short fiction, it does discuss briefly the transition from czarist Russia to the twentieth century with such writers as Maxim Gorky and Leonid Andreyev.

Huberman, Edward, and Elizabeth Huberman. Introduction to *Fifty Great European Short Stories*. New York: Bantam Books, 1971.
A discussion of some of the basic characteristics of European short fiction, such as the weight of time and history, a ritual structure built up over a long past, an inherited class structure, and a sense of inherited evil and guilt. Notes that the past continues to live even in the stories of the present.

Kŏs Erih. "Yugoslavia." *The Kenyon Review* 30 (1968): 454-457.
Argues that Yugoslavia is still under the influence of myths and only three generations removed from village life; thus, the people tell stories to one another. The short story is the most frequently used form of literary expression in the country, although because of laziness the modern reader has begun to favor the novel at the expense of the short story.

Lange, Victor. Introduction to *Great German Short Novels and Stories*. New York: Modern Library, 1952.
A discussion of the development of the German short story or *Novelle* from Johann Wolfgang von Goethe's use of it as a moral tale to Franz Kafka's and Thomas Mann's development of it for the embodiment of a poetic vision. Briefly discusses the modern sensibility that dominates the stories.

Matute, Ana María. "Spain." Translated by William Fifield. *The Kenyon Review* 31 (1969): 450-454.
Claims that the short story combines the mystery of poetry with the clarity of the novel and is thus the most responsive narrative form, but notes that there is little market for short stories in Spain. Yet, Matute believes that the short story in Spain is of a higher quality than the novel.

Maurino, Ferdinando D. "Italian Short Fiction." In *Critical Survey of Short Fiction*, edited by Frank N. Magill, vol. 2. Pasadena, Calif.: Salem Press, 1981.
A survey of Italian short fiction from the sixteenth century to the twentieth century. Notes that southern Italy has led in the production of short fiction in the twentieth century. Discusses Luigi Pirandello briefly and mentions Alberto Moravia, Cesare Pavese, Italo Calvino, and Dino Buzzati.

Nedreaas, Torborg. "Norway." Translated by Orm Oeverland. *The Kenyon Review* 31 (1969): 454-461.

Notes that although the short story is highly regarded by critics in Norway, it is not admired enough by the public for anyone to make a living writing short stories. Argues that the form often illuminates truth the way dreams do, for dreams may be truer than everyday truth.

Neuhäser, Rudolf. "The Russian Short Story: 1917-1980." In *The Russian Short Story: A Critical History*, edited by Charles A. Moser. Boston: Twayne, 1986.
A historical survey of Russian short fiction since the Russian Revolution. Includes brief comments on Isaac Babel, the Soviet Romantics, and others. Discusses short fiction during World War II and under Joseph Stalin, as well as during the thaw in the 1950's. Includes sections on women writers, village prose, and science prose.

Pasinetti, P. M. Introduction to *Great Italian Short Stories.* New York: Dell Books, 1959.
Points out that the Italian word for short story, *novella*, is related to the idea of novelty or news. States that the Italian short story is episodic and anecdotal and based on the assumption that the story should deal with a worthy piece of news about an actual and memorable event. Also notes fantasy as a minor feature of Italian art, especially when mixed with realism. Comments briefly on local color in modern Italian short fiction.

Picchi, Mario. "Italy." Translated by Adele Plotkin. *The Kenyon Review* 31 (1969): 486-492.
Surveys the tradition of the short story in Italy and discusses the basic differences between the short story and the novel. Suggests that in the modern world, in a time of change and expectation, the short story is better suited for contemporary existence than the novel.

Pick, Robert. Introduction to *German Stories and Tales*. New York: Pocket Books, 1955.
A short discussion of some of the generic characteristics of German short fiction. Notes that the story of the education and development of a young man is a common theme; discusses the use of irony as a characteristic of German storytelling.

Reeve, F. D. Introduction to *Great Soviet Short Stories*. New York: Dell Books, 1962.
A brief discussion of short stories that reflect the development of Soviet fiction after 1917. Focuses on the development of attitudes, tones, styles, subjects, techniques, and points of historical relevance.

Sayers, Raymond S. "Twenty-five Years of Portuguese Short Fiction." *Studies in Short Fiction* 3 (Winter, 1966): 253-264.

Points out that most Portuguese short fiction in the 1950's and 1960's has been influenced by neorealism and that the most common themes are the exploitation of the poor and the class struggle. Surveys the stories of several predominant Portuguese short-fiction writers, noting their typical styles and subjects.

Scandinavian Studies 49 (Spring, 1977).
A special issue devoted to the short story in Scandinavia. The essays provide brief surveys of modern short fiction in Denmark, Finland, Iceland, Norway, and Sweden. Most of the essays also include a representative short story and a brief analysis to illustrate the general points made.

Spender, Stephen. Introduction to *Great German Short Stories*. New York: Dell Books, 1960.
Brief discussion of some of the characteristics of German short fiction since Johann Wolfgang von Goethe. Notes that the stories often deal with the theme of the healthy and the unhealthy and that the German story, unless it is simply an anecdote, attempts to reflect a whole view of life and tends to be an extended parable. The emphasis is more on the twentieth century short story than on the nineteenth century form.

Stevick, Philip. Introduction to *Anti-Story*. New York: Free Press, 1971.
Many so-called antistories, such as those by Heinrich Böll, Tommaso Landolfi, Eugène Ionesco, Wolfgang Hildesheimer, and Alain Robbe-Grillet, are included here. Stevick discusses the stories as being against mimesis, event, reality, subject, analysis, meaning, scale, and the middle range of experience.

Strzetelski, Jerzy. "Explorers of the Heart and Mind: Short Fiction in Poland Today." *Studies in Short Fiction* 3 (Winter, 1966): 165-173.
Surveys the short fiction collections of eleven Polish writers publishing in the early 1960's. Comments on their themes, styles, and major characters. The discussion is organized in terms of the age of the writers: those who were mature at the outbreak of World War II, those who were adolescents at the time of the war, and those who are too young to remember the war.

Vlach, Robert. "Modern Slavic Short Fiction." *Studies in Short Fiction* 3 (Winter, 1966): 126-137.
Survey of twentieth century short-fiction writers in Yugoslavia, Poland, the Soviet Union, Czechoslovakia, and Bulgaria. Vlach provides a list of names, titles, and dates, with a few brief comments on the basic style and themes of the writers mentioned.

West, Theodora L. Introduction to *The Continental Short Story*. New York: Odyssey Press, 1969.

Lays out an existential approach to the themes of stories by Miguel de Unamuno, Luigi Pirandello, Thomas Mann, Franz Kafka, Jean-Paul Sartre, Albert
Camus, and Alberto Moravia. Also outlines aesthetic and technical approaches
to short fiction.

ILSE AICHINGER
(1921-   )
Austria

General Biographical and Critical Studies

Alldridge, J. C. *Ilse Aichinger*. London: Oswald Wolff, 1969.

A brief volume in the Modern German Authors series. In addition to the
thirty-five-page monograph on Aichinger's life and art, the book also contains
selected stories and poems as well as a bibliography of Aichinger's works. The
short summary analyses of the stories focus on Aichinger's use of the themes
of guilt and atonement and her use of the dream technique, both of which are
similar to the stories of Franz Kafka.

Selected Title

"The Bound Man"

Bedwell, Carol. "Who Is the Bound Man? Towards an Interpretation of Ilse
Aichinger's 'Der Gefesselte.' " *German Quarterly* 38 (1956): 30-37.

An analysis of the story in terms of its allegorical and symbolic nature. Bedwell suggests that Aichinger's characters, like Franz Kafka's, are symbols
rather than personalities and that they live in a world distant from that of
everyday reality. The difference between the two writers, says Bedwell, is that
whereas Kafka's works have an oppressive nightmare quality, Aichinger's have
a lyrical, dreamlike atmosphere. Moreover, for Kafka death is a degrading
termination; for Aichinger, it is a new beginning.

ISAAC BABEL
(1894-1941?)
Russia

General Biographical and Critical Studies

Babel, Isaac. "Babel Answers Questions About His Work." In *You Must Know Everything*, edited by Nathalie Babel. New York: Dell Books, 1969.
A transcript of a 1937 interview before the Union of Soviet Writers. Babel describes his fascination with the novella or short story, a form he is more comfortable with than any other. He notes that, with the exception of Anton Chekhov, it is not a form that Russian writers usually prefer. He says that a short-story writer must create a picture of his reader, noting that he aims at a reader who is intelligent and educated and has exacting taste.

Brown, Edward J. *Russian Literature Since the Revolution*. Cambridge, Mass.: Harvard University Press, 1982.
Primarily a discussion of *Red Cavalry* as typical of Russian Civil War literature, particularly in its depiction of Cossacks, peasants, Jews, Russians, and the cruel reality of war. Each story in the collection is built around a grim incongruity, says Brown; Babel did not intend to give a balanced view of either the Cavalry army or the Polish campaign. The goal of Babel's art, says Brown, is to reveal the reality of life by indirection, as if by accident.

Carden, Patricia. *The Art of Isaac Babel*. Ithaca, N.Y.: Cornell University Press, 1972.
Carden's focus is on Babel's "artfulness," his search for style and form, and his development of the short story as a form of aesthetic contemplation. Although there are chapters on each of the three major Babel story cycles, *Red Cavalry* rightfully receives more consideration than the Odessa stories or the stories of childhood. Carden includes detailed analyses of several important stories.

Clyman, Toby. "Babel as Colorist." *Slavic and East European Journal* 21 (Summer, 1977): 332-343.
A discussion of Babel's use of color imagery in his stories. According to Clyman, Babel uses color to create mood and to depict landscape much as an Expressionist painter might. From the Expressionists, Babel learned how to use color to communicate the most profound reality.

Ehre, Milton. *Isaac Babel*. Boston: Twayne, 1986.
A helpful introductory survey that includes a biographical sketch, a chronology

of events in Babel's life, and discussions of each of the major Babel short-story cycles. The most familiar Babel tales, such as "The Story of My Dovecot," receive the most attention. Although most of the analyses are simple plot summaries, the book is a good introduction to the most typical Babel themes.

Ehrenburg, Ilya. "A Speech at a Moscow Meeting in Honor of Babel, November 11, 1964." In *You Must Know Everything*, edited by Nathalie Babel. New York: Dell Books, 1969.

A speech given at a celebration honoring Babel's seventieth birthday at a meeting of the Union of Soviet Writers. Ehrenburg argues that Babel's so-called simplicity was born of complexity, that it is not a substitute for complexity. The speech is enlivened by Ehrenburg's report of conversations with Babel. He also notes conversations with Ernest Hemingway, who said that after having read Babel for the first time he found himself to be wordy by comparison.

Falen, James E. *Isaac Babel: Russian Master of the Short Story*. Knoxville: University of Tennessee Press, 1974.

This is the most detailed study of Babel to focus on the relationship between his life and his art. The early chapters deal with Babel's personality and his literary background. The core of the book consists of readings of *Odessa Tales* in terms of Babel's developing aesthetic and *Red Cavalry* in terms of the basic conflict between Cossack and Jew. Although Falen includes several detailed discussions of individual stories, they are not always the best-known stories.

Friedberg, Maurice. "Yiddish Folklore Motifs in Isaak Babel's *Red Cavalry*." In *American Contributions to the Eighth International Conference of Slavists*, edited by Victor Terras, vol. 2. Columbus, Ohio: Slavica, 1978.

Discusses how several stories in *Red Cavalry* deal with the world of the Hasidim in the Ukraine. Three stories— "The Rabbi," "Gedali," and "The Rabbi's Son"—in particular are linked together in their focus on the Hasidic rabbi and the Hasidic rebellion against overly intellectualized Judaism.

Hallett, Richard. *Isaac Babel*. New York: Frederick Ungar, 1973.

An introductory study, relatively short and sketchy, that integrates short discussions of the major stories with a brief summary of Babel's life. Most of the story commentaries focus on what Hallett considers to be typical Babel themes; however, the discussions are more often plot summaries than critical analyses. Little is noted of Babel's style or the characteristics of his development of the short-story genre.

Hyman, Stanley Edgar. "Identities of Isaac Babel." *The Hudson Review* 8 (Winter, 1956): 620-627.

An extended review of *The Collected Stories of Isaac Babel* (1955), this essay

14

Twentieth Century European Short Story

is important both because of Hyman's stature as a critic and because of his perceptive observations of the split in Babel's stories between culture and nature or between art and the life of action. Hyman argues tha: Babel's imagery has the shock effect of surrealism.

Lee, Alice. "Epiphany in Babel's *Red Cavalry*." *Russian Literature Triquarterly* 3 (May, 1972): 249-260.
Drawing on the definition of epiphany by James Joyce, Lee attempts to show that the basic structural and stylistic device in Babel's stories is the revelatory moment that sums up the whole story and contains an insight that has been hidden until that moment.

Lowe, David A. "A Generic Approach to Babel's *Red Cavalry*." *Modern Fiction Studies* 28 (Spring, 1982): 69-78.
Analysis of the stories in *Red Cavalry* as tales linked together in the manner of Giovanni Boccaccio's *novellas* in *The Decameron*. Lowe cites definitions of the *novella* from previous theorists of the form and shows how Babel's stories fit those definitions. In Lowe's opinion, *Red Cavalry* is a twentieth century version of a Renaissance *novella* cycle.

Luplow, Carol. *Isaac Babel's Red Cavalry*. Ann Arbor, Mich.: Ardis, 1982.
This detailed, full-length study of Babel's most famous collection focuses on the narrative perspective of the stories, the basic dialectic between the spiritual and the physical which they embody, their style and romantic vision, and the types of story structure and epiphanic vision they reflect. Although the study is not guided by a particular theoretical approach, it primarily makes use of formalist literary theory.

Harder, Herbert. "The Revolutionary Art of Isaac Babel." *Novel: A Forum on Fiction* 7 (Fall, 1973): 54-61.
Argues that Babel's stories are revolutionary both in their subject and in their style, reminiscent of modernist literature since T. S. Eliot's *The Waste Land*. Primarily a discussion of *Red Cavalry*, this essay argues strongly that Babel was an artist-revolutionary who wrote stories subversive not only of the Stalinist regime, but of all social orders as well; his works unite reality with the dream and folk fable with naturalism by means of surrealistic imagery.

Mendelson, Danuta. *Metaphor in Babel's Short Stories*. Ann Arbor, Mich.: Ardis, 1982.
A scholarly discussion, drawing from linguistic and psychological studies as well as structuralist studies of narrative. Because Mendelson is primarily interested in the theory of metaphoric expression and its effect on narrative, there is little detailed discussion here of the major Babel stories. However, the analysis

of *Red Cavalry* as an episodic novel in the modernist tradition, rather than as a strictly linear realist work, clarifies how the action of the book takes place on several poetic planes at once.

Mihailovich, Vasa D. "Assessments of Isaac Babel." *Papers in Language and Literature* 9 (Summer, 1973): 323-342.
A detailed analysis of criticism of Babel up to the early 1970's. Particularly valuable in providing information on Russian criticism not available in English translations. Includes a brief biographical sketch.

O'Connor, Frank. "The Romanticism of Violence." In his *The Lonely Voice*. Cleveland: World Publishing, 1962.
In his famous book on the short-story genre, O'Connor compares Babel to Ernest Hemingway because of their highly formalized styles and the unrealistic means by which both present physical violence. However, O'Connor is even more concerned with the split in Babel between the idealistic Jewish intellectual and the Soviet officer who admires the violence of his Cossack soldiers.

Poggioli, Renato. "Isaak Babel in Retrospect." In his *The Phoenix and the Spider*. Cambridge, Mass.: Harvard University Press, 1957.
Calling Babel's stories the best fiction to appear in Soviet Russia, Poggioli summarizes the major events of Babel's life, defends stories in *Red Cavalry* for their visionary epiphanies, and argues that *The Tales of Odessa* are the best introduction to his work, particularly the story "Guy de Maupassant," with its emphasis on style.

Sicher, Efraim. *Style and Structure in the Prose of Isaak Babel*. Columbus, Ohio: Slavica, 1986.
Because this is a formalist study of the style of Babel's stories, much of the discussion depends on Sicher's knowledge of the Russian language in which they were written. However, in addition to a discussion of Babel's lyrical prose, the book also analyzes setting, characterization, narrative structure, and point of view in Babel's stories.

Slonim, Marc. *Soviet Russian Literature*. New York: Oxford University Press, 1977.
A brief biographical and critical discussion that asserts that the foundation of Babel's art and style is the play on disparities between physical savagery and poetic revelations. Slonim argues that Babel is a master of the grotesque. He notes that although Babel's stories are compact and terse like those of his teachers Guy de Maupassant and Anton Chekhov, they have sharply developed plots and dynamic climaxes, unlike Chekhov's stories.

Stine, Peter. "Isaac Babel and Violence." *Modern Fiction Studies* 30 (Summer, 1984): 237-255.

A discussion of Babel as a passionate ironist, a stance that resulted from his psyche being divided between his moral and aesthetic consciousness on the one hand and his admiration of the Cossack ethos of violence on the other.

Struve, Gleb. *Russian Literature Under Lenin and Stalin, 1917- 1953.* Norman: University of Oklahoma Press, 1971.
A brief discussion of Babel's place in Russian postrevolutionary literature, particularly his importance in reviving the short story. Struve notes that Babel's favorite method is psychological and stylistic contrast and paradox; he also discusses the hyperbolism and romantic contrasts in *Red Cavalry*.

Trilling, Lionel. Introduction to *The Collected Stories of Isaac Babel*. Cleveland: World Publishing, 1960.
Trilling's introduction marks the first appearance of Babel's stories in a single collection for English-speaking readers. Trilling focuses on Babel's aesthetic preoccupation and his concern with style and form; as Trilling points out, however, for Babel style serves his moral vision. Much of Trilling's discussion deals with Babel's intellectual fascination with the violence of the world of the Cossacks.

Selected Titles

"The Awakening"
Carden, Patricia. *The Art of Isaac Babel*. Ithaca, N.Y.: Cornell University Press, 1972.
Carden calls this one of Babel's most deceptively simple stories and thus one of his most popular. The story belongs in the childhood cycle because in it the boy is introduced to the sensuous nature of reality. Thus, it is a portrait of the artist as a very young man and depicts the boy's movement from his bookishness, in which he is cut off from a direct relationship to the physical world, to a realization of the physical reality of the world.

Ehre, Milton. *Isaac Babel*. Boston: Twayne, 1986.
One of Babel's loveliest stories, "Awakening" ends the Dovecot cycle, says Ehre, on a note of acceptance, putting the final seal on childhood. As in other Babel stories of childhood, the youth is caught between two forces of violence: the anti-Semitic rioters and the Jewish father who tries to transform his son into a prodigy.

"Crossing into Poland"
Ehre, Milton. *Isaac Babel*. Boston: Twayne, 1986.
A brief discussion that examines the story as exemplary of *Red Cavalry* and as

a combination of the epic and the pathetic modes, both of which make rival claims to the reader's imagination. Instead of focusing on narrative, the story is part rhetoric and part lyric, moving toward an epiphany instead of a narrative denouement.

Falen, James E. *Isaac Babel: Russian Master of the Short Story*. Knoxville: University of Tennessee Press, 1974.
Argues that the story is representative of *Red Cavalry*. The story works by hiding large events behind the seemingly trivial, according to Falen. Both stylistically and structurally, "Crossing into Poland" suggests the pattern of ritual rebirth. As the opening story of an interconnected cycle, it states a number of Babel's central themes.

"Di Grasso"
Ehre, Milton. *Isaac Babel*. Boston: Twayne, 1986.
A brief discussion of how the story focuses on art's ability to open our eyes and free us from the blindness of habit. Ehre points out that the protagonist is the narrator; he comes to the realization that art is a paradoxical act of transcendence; it removes one from the usual only to bring one back. According to Ehre, the story suggests that perception is an act of choice that requires the freedom to be exercised.

Falen, James E. *Isaac Babel: Russian Master of the Short Story*. Knoxville: University of Tennessee Press, 1974.
Shows how the story makes use of a play within the tale as an instance of Babel's interest in motion within the static and as an embodiment of his theme of art as controlled violence. Explains Di Grasso's leap as a metaphor of Babel's belief in the heroic and in the redemptive nature of the aesthetic.

Freidin, Gregory. "Fat Tuesday in Odessa: Isaac Babel's 'Di Grasso' as Testament and Manifesto." *The Russian Review: An American Quarterly Devoted to Russian Past and Present* 40 (April, 1981): 101-121.
Cites many elements in the story which characterize it as a retrospective manifesto of Babel's work; for example, its use of the Carnival tradition, its epiphany structure, and its use of the decapitation motif in an erotic context. Notes the decapitation motif, to which most of this essay is devoted, in other Babel stories, such as "First Love."

"Guy de Maupassant"
Carden, Patricia. *The Art of Isaac Babel*. Ithaca, N.Y.: Cornell University Press, 1972.
Argues that the story is about the relationship between human illusions and the truth of life. Carden says that Babel pushes beyond that moment of freedom in

which the spirit seems to soar to the inevitable confrontation with necessity. Thus, the story ends with the narrator's confrontation with mortality as he reads of the tragic last days of Maupassant's life.

Ehre, Milton. *Isaac Babel*. Boston: Twayne, 1986.
Calling it one of Babel's best works, Ehre states that the story continues the satire of "In the Basement," which revolves around the comic conflict between the passion of art and the bourgeois passion of accumulation. What saves the story from sentimentalism, says Ehre, is the comic style of the language.

"How It Was Done in Odessa"
Falen, James E. *Isaac Babel: Russian Master of the Short Story*. Knoxville: University of Tennessee Press, 1974.
This detailed discussion of the story's rhetorical devices points out that the story stands apart from the others in the Odessa cycle in being the only one that has a special narrator and thus the only one that achieves the effect of speech. Oral devices dominate the structural organization, according to Falen, and style dominates the story.

"In the Basement"
Carden, Patricia. *The Art of Isaac Babel*. Ithaca, N.Y.: Cornell University Press, 1972.
Carden notes that this story deals with the theme of the relationship between truth and fiction more than any other Babel story. She supports her argument with several examples of the failure in the work to distinguish truth from fiction. For Babel, argues Carden, the imagination should not disguise the truth, but rather reveal the essential truth beneath the everyday disguise.

Ehre, Milton. *Isaac Babel*. Boston: Twayne, 1986.
Focusing on the satiric elements of this comic tale, Ehre classified the story as a comedy of manners of domestic disorder. Ehre finds the story less imaginative than the other stories in Babel's initiation cycle about young men achieving a mature vision.

"My First Goose"
Andrew, J. M. "Structure and Style in the Short Story: Babel's 'My First Goose.' " *The Modern Language Review* 70 (April, 1975): 366-379.
A reading of the story based on the theories of the Russian Formalists. This is a detailed formal analysis of the narrative structure that leads Andrew to interpret the killing of the goose on four major levels: in psychological terms as a sexual initiation, in religious terms as an initiation into the mysteries of life, in human terms as an outsider joining a group, and in political terms as an intellectual joining the people.

Falen, James E. *Isaac Babel: Russian Master of the Short Story*. Knoxville: University of Tennessee Press, 1974.

Discussion of the story's presentation of an initiatory ritual of blood sacrifice which is ironically undercut because the sacrifice is that of a harmless goose. Notes that the narrator's efforts to be one with his barbaric Cossack companions is a mockery that leaves him cursed with the consciousness of his act.

"The Story of My Dovecot"

Carden, Patricia. *The Art of Isaac Babel*. Ithaca, N.Y.: Cornell University Press, 1972.

A long, detailed discussion of how the story shows the pressures of history and social circumstances. Notes how the typical developmental pattern of the tale is that of a biographical fact followed by the drawing in of the surrounding historical, social, and family contexts. Shows also how the story presents a pattern of the escape from reality into the world of imagination, even though in its conclusion the boy experiences the redeeming power of recognizing necessity.

Ehre, Milton. *Isaac Babel*. Boston: Twayne, 1986.

A detailed discussion which argues that at the moment of the boy's crisis the story breaks away from its mimetic form to center on an intense poetic concentration. As typical of Babel's work, the story achieves a symbolic form, even though its surface is realistic.

SAMUEL BECKETT
(1906-   )
Ireland and France

General Biographical and Critical Studies

Abbott, H. Porter. *The Fiction of Samuel Beckett: Form and Effect*. Berkeley: University of California Press, 1973.
An analysis of Beckett's fiction between 1940 and 1959 in terms of his crafts-manship and his experiments with form. The approach is both formalist and affective; Abbott is concerned with examining the impact of the imitative form of Beckett's fiction on the reader.

Barge, Laura. *God, the Quest, the Hero: Thematic Structures in Beckett's Fiction*. Chapel Hill: North Carolina Studies in the Romance Languages and Litera-tures, 1988.
A book-length study of the ideas of God and the Quest in several of Beckett's works of fiction, including his first story "Assumption" and the collection *More Pricks than Kicks*. Discusses the works in terms of various levels of the Quest theme.

Ben-Zvi, Linda. *Samuel Beckett*. Boston: Twayne, 1986.
An introduction to Beckett's works which attempts to include at least brief comments on all of his plays, criticism, and fictional works.

Brienza, Susan D. *Samuel Beckett's New Worlds: Style in Metafiction*. Norman: University of Oklahoma Press, 1987.
A stylistic study of Beckett's later fiction. Brienza argues that Beckett creates a new style that is so fragmented it almost seems to be a new language. Each Beckett work creates its own metafictional closed system of language. The short fiction works she discusses are *Stories and Texts for Nothing* and *Fizzles*.

Bruns, Gerald L. "The Storyteller and the Problem of Language in Samuel Beck-ett's Fiction." *Modern Language Quarterly* 30 (June, 1969): 265-281.
Although this essay focuses primarily on the novels, it is helpful in posing a unity in Beckett's fiction determined by the way Beckett displays the ground of his art. Shows how Beckett's fictions are self-reflexive, embodying and laying bare their own narrative devices. His storytellers are extensions of Beckett himself.

Coe, Richard N. *Samuel Beckett*. New York: Grove Press, 1964.
An introduction to the major novels. Coe's concern is Beckett's quasi-mystical ideal of art and reality. According to Coe, Beckett's works attempt to do the

impossible—create and define what ceases to be when it is created and defined. Only passing remarks on the short fiction, but notes that the main themes of *Stories and Texts for Nothing* is the need to witness and be witnessed.

Culotta-Andonian, Cathleen. "Conceptions of Inner Landscapes: The Beckettian Narrator of the Sixties and Seventies." In *Critical Essays on Samuel Beckett*, edited by Patrick A. McCarthy. Boston: G. K. Hall, 1986.
A discussion of Beckett's fictions after the publication of the Trilogy, primarily in terms of the scheme for classification of the narrators developed by critic Tzvetan Todorov. Argues that this approach illustrates the evolution of Beckett's works from omniscient narrators who seem to comprehend their situations to anonymous voices uttering meaningless words.

Doherty, Francis. *Samuel Beckett*. London: Hutchinson University Library, 1971.
This introduction to Beckett's works includes a chapter on the short fiction. Briefly discusses three stories published in *Stories and Texts for Nothing*. Argues that the stories in this collection are attempts by the narrator to find a way to come alive. Also discusses the extremely short compressed fiction Beckett has written since *How It Is*.

Federman, Raymond. "Beckettian Paradox: Who Is Telling the Truth?" In *Samuel Beckett Now*, edited by Melvin J. Friedman. Chicago: University of Chicago Press, 1970.
Discussion of Beckett's fiction as a reflection of its own defective substance, that is, language itself. Beckett's fiction is a denunciation of the illusions of fiction, for fiction is not reality, but rather language that tells its own story.

_____ . *Journey to Chaos: Samuel Beckett's Early Fiction*. Berkeley: University of California Press, 1965.
Attempts to show how disintegration of form and content is gradually perfected into an aesthetic system in the Trilogy. Says that Beckett's early English fiction is often sardonic Swiftian satire. The early French work features ambiguous characters suspended between the real world and the world of fiction.

Gluck, Barbara Reich. *Beckett and Joyce*. Lewisburg, W. Va.: Bucknell University Press, 1979.
Discusses the personal friendship of Beckett and James Joyce, the intellectual milieu surrounding them, and how Beckett's fiction reflects Joyce's mature style both by imitation and by allusion.

Gontarski, S. E. "The Intent of Undoing in Samuel Beckett's Art." *Modern Fiction Studies* 29 (Spring, 1983): 5-23.

Notes that Beckett has always been preoccupied with form, but that there is no single or consistent formal pattern in the structure of his fictions. Points out that from the beginning Beckett has been antimimetic and that his fundamental subject matter is the absence of logic and causality. Argues that he is searching for a form that grows from the writing process.

Graver, Lawrence, and Raymond Federman, eds. *Samuel Beckett: The Critical Heritage*. London: Routledge & Kegan Paul, 1979.
An anthology of reviews and review-essays on Beckett's works, including such collections of stories as *More Pricks than Kicks* and *Stories and Texts for Nothing*. This valuable collection also contains two interviews with Beckett, a chronology of his life, and an extensive introduction that discusses Beckett's overall critical reputation.   .

Hamilton, Alice, and Kenneth Hamilton. *Condemned to Life: The World of Samuel Beckett*. Grand Rapids, Mich.: Wm. B. Eerdmans, 1976.
Argues that the misery of the human condition is not only the most obvious theme in Beckett's fiction, but that it is also the best clue to understanding his work. Each of Beckett's literary works is part of an effort to clarify his vision of man.

Journal of Modern Literature 6 (February, 1977).
A special issue of the journal with essays on Beckett's fiction and drama. Although there are no essays on the short stories, the discussion of Beckett as *Homo Ludens* (that is, man at play) and the essay on the text "Ping" are the most helpful for understanding the short fiction.

Kenner, Hugh. *Samuel Beckett: A Critical Study*. 2d ed. Berkeley: University of California Press, 1968.
A critical analysis of Beckett's fiction and drama based to some extent on Kenner's conversations with Beckett. Although most of the discussion of the fiction is on the novels, this readable and nontechnical analysis is helpful for understanding Beckett's fiction in general.

Knowlson, James, and John Pilling. *Frescoes of the Skull: The Later Prose and Drama of Samuel Beckett.* New York: Grove Press, 1980.
Provides analyses of Beckett's later work, with individual chapters on such collections as *Stories and Texts for Nothing* and *Fizzles*. No real unity in this jointly written book.

Levy, Eric P. *Beckett and the Voice of Species*. New York: Barnes & Noble Books, 1980.
States that the central idea in Beckett's fiction is that all that human experience

can know is the inability to interpret its own structure. Levy discusses Belacqua in *More Pricks than Kicks* as a forerunner of Beckett's protagonists and comments on *Stories and Texts for Nothing* as Beckett's most difficult and elusive work of fiction.

McMillan, Dougald. "Samuel Beckett and the Visual Arts: The Embarrassment of Allegory." In *Beckett: A Collection of Criticism*, edited by Ruby Cohn. New York: McGraw-Hill, 1975.
Discusses Beckett's references to the visual arts in his works, beginning with *More Pricks than Kicks*, his commentary on the visual arts, and how they have influenced his fiction.

Mercier, Vivian. *Beckett/Beckett*. New York: Oxford University Press, 1977.
A study of the various configurations of dialectical tension in Beckett's works—Ireland/the World, Artist/Philosopher, Eye/Ear, Gentleman/Tramp, Painting/Music. Argues that *More Pricks than Kicks*, with the exception of "Dante and the Lobster," "Ding Dong," and "Yellow," is more like a novel than a collection of stories.

Modern Fiction Studies 29 (Spring, 1983).
This special issue on Beckett, focuses solely on his fiction, with essays on the Trilogy, *Watt*, *The Lost Ones*, and other works, as well as general essays on his verbal slapstick and his later works. Also contains a bibliography of new works by Beckett published between 1976 and 1982.

Pilling, John. *Samuel Beckett*. London: Routledge & Kegan Paul, 1976.
A straightforward discussion of Beckett's life and work from the point of view of his own aesthetic thinking. The chapter on the prose fiction focuses primarily on the novels. A more valuable section for understanding the short fiction is the chapter on Beckett's literary sources and background.

Rabinovitz, Rubin. *The Development of Samuel Beckett's Fiction*. Urbana: University of Illinois Press, 1984.
A study of the innovations in fictional technique developed by Beckett. Although most of the book is devoted to a discussion of *Murphy* and *Watt*, There are helpful discussions of some of the short fictions as well.

_____ . "Style and Obscurity in Samuel Beckett's Early Fiction." *Modern Fiction Studies* 20 (Autumn, 1974): 399-406.
Discusses Beckett's devaluing of conventional characterization in such novels as *Watt* and such short story collections as *More Pricks than Kicks*. When Beckett weakens character, the reader is able to directly experience events,

according to Rabinovitz. Thus, the reader is forced to duplicate the struggles of the characters.

Scott, Nathan A. *Samuel Beckett*. London: Bowes & Bowes, 1965.
A brief introduction to Beckett's works with passing comments on the short fiction. Places Beckett in the French literary tradition from nineteenth century realism to the twentieth century New Novel. Also discusses him within the context of the phenomenology of Martin Heidegger.

Smith, Frederick N. "Beckett's Verbal Slapstick." *Modern Fiction Studies* 29 (Spring, 1983): 43-55.
Argues that humor in Beckett's fiction is not situational but linguistic. Discusses his shift from one sort of diction to another, his feel for specific words, and his intermixing of different lexical fields. Notes that whereas James Joyce exploited the etymological depth of the English language, Beckett has exploited its breadth.

Szanto, George H. *Narrative Consciousness*. Austin: University of Texas Press, 1972.
Argues that in Beckett's fiction the limits of narrative consciousness become increasingly generalized and the vision becomes more introspective. Claims that the reader's mind must coincide with the narrator's in order to comprehend and create the form and pattern of the work. However, in Beckett the characters affirm no truth; they simply exist.

Takahashi, Yasunari. "Fool's Progress." In *Samuel Beckett: A Collection of Criticism*, edited by Ruby Cohn. New York: McGraw-Hill, 1975.
A survey of Beckett's use of the fool character from its appearance in his first story, "Assumption," to its appearance in some of his major fiction. Discusses the basic characteristics of Beckett's fool, the literary tradition to which the character belongs, and the changes the character has undergone in Beckett's fiction.

Webb, Eugene. *Samuel Beckett: A Study of His Novels*. Seattle: University of Washington Press, 1973.
A general study of Beckett's themes rather than his technique in his fiction. Argues that Beckett's basic subject from the beginning of his career has been the difficulty of twentieth century man's efforts to understand his place in the universe.

Zurbrugg, Nicholas. *Beckett and Proust*. New York: Barnes & Noble Books, 1988.
Discusses Marcel Proust and Beckett as key figures in the two phases of twentieth century literature, modernism and postmodernism. Argues against

the critical studies that exaggerate the superficial similarity between Proust and Beckett. Discusses Beckett's idiosyncratic interpretation of Proust in his essay on him and reevaluates Beckett's vision by showing how he reverses Proustian values through his major fictional works.

Selected Titles

More Pricks than Kicks

Abbott, H. Porter. *The Fiction of Samuel Beckett: Form and Effect.* Berkeley: University of California Press, 1973.

Argues that the true subject of the collection is its composition—the wide range of expressive forms that it attacks. Discusses the literary self-consciousness of the stories and their parody of other fictional forms.

Barge, Laura. *God, the Quest, the Hero: Thematic Structures in Beckett's Fiction.* Chapel Hill: North Carolina Studies in the Romance Languages and Literatures, 1988.

States that the collection is a satire on literature and that the character Belacqua is a satire on the poet. Barge argues that Belacqua's quest is capsulated in his affinity for pseudosexual encounters with women who offer him artistic and mystical fulfillment.

Ben-Zvi, Linda. *Samuel Beckett.* Boston: Twayne, 1986.

A brief discussion of the stories in the collection, noting that "Dante and the Lobster" and "Yellow" are the most sustained in the group. Most of the comments are plot summaries and focus on theme rather than technique, but this book is a helpful introduction to the stories.

Federman, Raymond. *Journey to Chaos: Samuel Beckett's Early Fiction.* Berkeley: University of California Press, 1965.

Focuses on the central figure in the stories, Belacqua Shuah, and how he differs from other Beckett heroes. Argues that Belacqua's desire to return to the womb reflects a conscious but feeble revolt against the physical world; all of his actions and reflections negate what others consider to be rational.

Gluck, Barbara Reich. *Beckett and Joyce.* Lewisburg, W.Va.: Bucknell University Press, 1979.

Compares the collection with James Joyce's collection of stories *Dubliners.* Focuses particularly on Joyce's story "The Dead" and Beckett's story "Dante and the Lobster." Argues that Beckett's story coordinates the motifs of moon, murder, and mercy in a Joycean way. Notes the Joycean influence in the rest of the stories in the collection.

Hamilton, Alice, and Kenneth Hamilton. *Condemned to Life: The World of Samuel Beckett.* Grand Rapids, Mich.: Wm. B. Eerdmans, 1976.
Argues that Belacqua is a mouthpiece for Beckett's depressing estimate of human existence. Discusses Belacqua's involvement with women in the stories as the thread that holds the stories together. Also discusses the sexual puns as well as the allusions to Dante and to Jesus Christ.

Rabinovitz, Rubin. *The Development of Samuel Beckett's Fiction.* Urbana: University of Illinois Press, 1984.
Discusses patterns of repetition in the collection and the recurrent themes of love, sexuality, and death. Notes that Beckett's method is to introduce recurring details, which call attention to subjects that the narrator tries to avoid. According to Rabinovitz, the narrator's commentary corresponds to Belacqua's conscious thoughts and the recurring details to his unconscious thoughts.

Robinson, Michael. "Belacqua." In *Critical Essays on Samuel Beckett*, edited by Patrick A. McCarthy. Boston: G. K. Hall, 1986.
Argues that the collection suggests the majority of Beckett's later preoccupations. Says that the character of Belacqua is the initial guise of the Beckett hero who appears in the novels. Traces the source of the character in Dante and discusses his reincarnation in later Beckett works.

Stevenson, Kay Gilliland. "Belacqua in the Moon: Beckett's Revision of 'Dante and the Lobster.' " In *Critical Essays on Samuel Beckett*, edited by Patrick A. McCarthy. Boston: G. K. Hall, 1986.
Discusses the changes Beckett made in the story "Dante and the Lobster" from its first magazine publication to its publication in *More Pricks than Kicks.* Says that the changes primarily increase the ambiguity of Belacqua's character and presentation.

Tindall, William York. *Samuel Beckett.* New York: Columbia University Press, 1964.
An essay-length monograph which surveys Beckett's work chronologically. Calls *More Pricks than Kicks* a "precious and discouraging sequence" of stories. Argues that it is not ideas but particulars that concern Beckett. A readable introduction to Beckett's themes and techniques.

Webb, Eugene. *Samuel Beckett: A Study of His Novels.* Seattle: University of Washington Press, 1973.
Argues that, although two of the stories in the collection have been published separately, it reads more like a novel. Discusses the characteristics that the main character shares with Beckett's later characters. Suggests that in part the work is a commentary on Dante's *Purgatory.*

Zurbrugg, Nicholas. *Beckett and Proust*. New York: Barnes & Noble Books, 1988.
A brief discussion of the collection in terms of the themes of the fiasco of physical existence and the survival of the torments of the mind after the death of the body. Discusses the allusions to Proustian values in the stories, as well as Belacqua's similarity to other Beckett heroes.

Stories and Texts for Nothing

Abbott, H. Porter. *The Fiction of Samuel Beckett: Form and Effect*. Berkeley: University of California Press, 1973.
Argues that the greatest formal achievement of the collection is its effort to imitate in form the speaker's experience. Without people, things, space, or time, the book becomes its own words and syntax. The work is fiction as sheer text.

Ben-Zvi, Linda. *Samuel Beckett*. Boston: Twayne, 1986.
Notes that the stories repeat the familiar Cartesian split in previous Beckett fictions, but adds to it by creating a narrator who is dual. Notes how the stories allude to other characters and events in Beckett's fiction. Discusses the father/son image in the collection and how it introduces the process of storytelling.

Brienza, Susan D. *Samuel Beckett's New Worlds: Style in Metafiction*. Norman: University of Oklahoma Press, 1987.
Argues that in this collection more than in his previous works, the process takes precedence over the end product. A detailed discussion of the stories, primarily in terms of their self-reflexive nature. The linguistic devices used in the collection make style and content reflect each other as in a fun-house mirror.

Knowlson, James, and John Pilling. *Frescoes of the Skull: The Later Prose and Drama of Samuel Beckett*. New York: Grove Press, 1980.
Says that the stories in the collection are the first occurrence of Beckett's impulse toward shorter fiction that dominates his later work. The chapter includes a brief analytical commentary on each of the stories in the collection. Discussion of the short stories often focuses on how they contain motifs that appear in the longer works.

Krieger, Elliot. "Samuel Beckett's *Texts for Nothing*: Explication and Exposition." *Modern Language Notes* 92 (December, 1977): 987-1000.
Notes that the "I" which speaks in the stories is not a person, but the text itself. Discusses the basic tension between process and stasis which runs throughout the texts. Concludes that the collection makes the reader so aware of black words on a white page that it is impossible to use the words to imagine a human environment inhabited by the texts.

Rose, Marilyn Gaddis. "The Lyrical Structure of Beckett's *Texts for Nothing.*" *Novel: A Forum on Fiction* 4 (Spring, 1971): 223-230.

Argues that when one looks for literary likenesses to Beckett's fiction, one finds it in poems rather than in novels. Discusses how the stories in the collection incorporate aspects of lyrical prose poetry. Notes that the texts are disoriented within space and dissociated from time.

Stevens, Irma Ned. "Beckett's *Texts for Nothing*: An Inversion of Young's *Night Thoughts.*" *Studies in Short Fiction* 11 (Spring, 1974): 131-139.

Notes the allusion to Edward Young's *Night Thoughts* in the collection and discusses the similarities between the two works, such as images of darkness, death, and hell. Also notes the difference between the two texts based on the difference in philosophy of the two authors—for example, Beckett's focus on the self versus Young's focus on God.

HEINRICH BÖLL
(1917-1985)
Germany

General Biographical and Critical Studies

Conrad, Robert C. *Heinrich Böll*. Boston: Twayne, 1981.
An introduction to Böll's life and art up to 1978, focusing on the major novels and short stories. The short stories are discussed in three major groups depending on when they were published. This book contains the most extensive discussions of Böll's stories available.

MacPherson, Enid. *A Student's Guide to Böll*. London: Heinemann Educational Books, 1972.
A brief introduction intended for the student of German literature. In addition to devoting chapters to the novels and the short stories, MacPherson also discusses Böll's critical writings and lectures for the light they throw on his narrative practice. The stories are placed in two basic categories: stories concerned with war and its aftermath and satiric stories commenting on postwar society. The chapter on Böll as a writer of short stories, a form he wanted to become the main vehicle of his work, is divided mainly into short sections on Böll's major themes and character types.

Reid, James Henderson. *Heinrich Böll: Withdrawal and Re-Emergence*. London: Oswald Wolff, 1973.
A small booklet in the Modern German Authors series, this study first establishes Böll's political outlook and his attack on bureaucracy, then discusses his early postwar stories, the so-called family novels of the 1950's, and the artist novels of the 1960's, before devoting one short chapter to *Group Portrait with Lady*. The chapter on the stories is sketchy and general; Reid argues that Böll's war stories are utterly pessimistic.

_____ . "Time in the Works of Heinrich Böll." *The Modern Language Review* 62 (1967): 476-485.
Points out that a recurrent feature in Böll's works is the appearance of a sudden revelation into a higher reality, what James Joyce once called an epiphany. Reid notes the various types of these epiphanies in Böll's novels and stories, concluding that Böll attempts to subvert the temporal nature of the novel by the use of leitmotifs. Because Böll attempts to abolish time in his fiction, it makes sense that he felt most drawn to the short story form, which most often deals with a single encounter with life, an epiphany.

Schwarz, Wilhelm Johannes. *Heinrich Böll, Teller of Tales*. Translated by Alexander
Henderson and Elizabeth Henderson. New York: Frederick Ungar, 1967.
Schwarz says that the short story is Böll's appropriate literary form. His stories
are marked by precise descriptions, narrative movement toward a well-defined
solution, and dialogue that is stripped of all but the essential. Although this
brief introduction to Böll's work necessarily emphasizes the themes of his
major novels, it does not slight the short stories. Many of the major stories are
commented on briefly in an attempt to synthesize Böll's major themes and
clarify his place in German literature.

Ziolkowski, Theodore. "Albert Camus and Heinrich Böll." *Modern Language Notes*
77 (May 1962): 282-291.
Explores the spiritual affinity between the two writers in terms of their moral
stance and their craftsmanship. Whereas in Albert Camus' works the little man
is usually a secondary figure, in such Böll stories as "The Man with the
Knives" and "Murke's Collected Silences," he is central. Both Camus and
Böll are critics of their society, and both are characterized by a lucid style and
ironic tone derived from their conscious exploitation of the techniques of
Ernest Hemingway.

Selected Titles

"The Balek Scales"
Conrad, Robert C. *Heinrich Böll*. Boston: Twayne, 1981.
Argues that the story is an attempt to treat the traditional theme of man's
obsession with justice and injustice. Compares it briefly to Heinrich von
Kleist's *Michael Kohlhaas*. Through his manipulation of the traditional symbol
of the scales, Böll puts bourgeois legality in doubt by showing that those who
make the laws are the same ones who benefit from them. Conrad says that the
story is important in Böll's career because it is the first time he condemns the
economic conditions of society.

Fetzer, John. "The Scales of Injustice: Comments on Heinrich Böll's *Die Waage
Der Baleks*." *The German Quarterly* 45 (1972): 472-479.
An analysis that seeks to show that the story is not a mere propaganda piece.
The essay examines four phases of the story: the actions of the Baleks (the so-
called exploiters) the reactions of the "exploited" villagers, extenuating circumstances of the Baleks' "treachery," and the symbolic function of the scale
itself. Guilt in the story is attributed not to the Baleks, says Fetzer, but rather to
the community for its precipitous attempt to balance the scales of justice, and
to the world at large for its tolerance of injustice.

"The Man with the Knives"
Conrad, Robert C. *Heinrich Böll*. Boston: Twayne, 1981.

Argues that the story emulates Ernest Hemingway's technique of expressing inner reality through description of external objects. The story deals with a man who incorporates fear into his work and learns to live with danger because that danger has a purpose.

"Murke's Collected Silences"
Conrad, Robert C. *Heinrich Böll*. Boston: Twayne, 1981.

Says that the object of satire in the story is religion in postwar Germany as well as German cultural industry, for the decline of religion and the decline of art are closely interrelated. This is an extended discussion of the ironic complexity of Murke's protest against the absurd world of technology which itself depends on technology.

"The Seventh Trunk"
Conrad, Robert C. *Heinrich Böll*. Boston: Twayne, 1981.

Says that the story can be read as a model of Böll's artistic theory, which assumes that every work of art contains some element that defies explanation or analysis. An understanding of the symbolic meaning of names in the story suggests that for Böll art must have the fantasy and invention of Hermes (the god of imagination), as well as the craftsmanship of Böll's literary ancestors, Johann Peter Hebel and Heinrich von Kleist.

"Stranger, Bear Word to the Spartans We . . ."
Conrad, Robert C. *Heinrich Böll*. Boston: Twayne, 1981.

Points out that the story derives from an elegiac poem by Friedrich von Schiller. However, Conrad suggests that the story is a mock ironic version of the Schiller poem in many ways. Böll's intention in the story, however, is not to ridicule, but rather to reveal that the idealism of the past is inappropriate in an age that follows Hitler's death camps.

BERTOLT BRECHT
(1898-1956)
Germany

General Biographical and Critical Studies

Brooker, Peter. *Bertolt Brecht: Dialectics, Poetry, Politics*. London: Croom Helm, 1988.
Unlike other studies, which deal primarily with Brecht's drama, this book focuses on his poetry and criticism of poetry. Concerned with his use of dialectical materialism in poetry and theater, as well as the new forms and techniques that resulted from this theory. Indirectly helpful for the study of Brecht's fiction by providing an analysis of his theoretical framework.

Cook, Bruce. *Brecht in Exile*. New York: Holt, Rinehart and Winston, 1982.
A series of essays that covers Brecht's life in exile in America from 1933 to 1956. Briefly mentions that although Brecht had become quite skilled in the short story he never mastered the novel. Cites the story "The Augsburg Chalk Circle" as the source for the play *The Caucasian Chalk Circle*, suggesting that Brecht's reason for changing the setting from his native city during the Thirty Years' War to the Georgian Republic of the Soviet Union at the end of World War II was probably propagandistic.

Dickson, Keith A. *Towards Utopia: A Study of Brecht*. Oxford, England: Clarendon Press, 1978.
This book on Brecht's satire and utopianism is one of the few studies to discuss his fiction. Although most of the chapters are on Brecht's experiments with the novel form, a few pages are devoted to the short stories, which Dickson says are more impressive than his longer fiction. Briefly discusses the collection *Tales from the Calendar* and the story "Caesar and His Legionnaire" to show Brecht's ingenuity in using what Dickson calls a reactionary form for his own revolutionary purpose.

Esslin, Martin. *Bertolt Brecht*. New York: Columbia University Press, 1969.
A brief introduction to Brecht by a well-known scholar and critic of modern drama. Summarizes his career, noting that the polarities of Emotion/Reason, Selfishness/Discipline, and Chaos/Order sum up the dialectic of his life and work. Discusses his dramatic theory and his dramatic style. Only passing references to his fiction, but a good first essay on Brecht.

——————— . *Brecht: The Man and His Work*. New York: Doubleday, 1960, rev. ed. 1971.

A valuable introduction to the life and art of Brecht. Includes sections on his life, his dramatic theory and practice, his political commitment, and the general characteristics of his worldview. Also includes a descriptive list of his works, including the short fiction, briefly summarizing their plots and commenting on their publishing history.

Ewen, Frederic. *Bertolt Brecht: His Life, His Art and His Times.* Secaucus, N.J.: Citadel Press, 1967.
This critical biography briefly mentions the stories in *Calendar Tales*. According to Ewen, Brecht did his best work in the narrative form using the short apologue, the tale, and the anecdote. Notes that the character Herr Keuner is Brecht's alter ego. Mentions that the stories are the sources of many of his later plays.

Gray, Ronald. *Bertolt Brecht.* New York: Grove Press, 1961.
A brief and readable introduction to Brecht's life and art, dividing the discussion between early and later plays. Also includes a chapter on Brecht's theories and their implications. Only passing mention of the fiction, but a good overview of Brecht's importance.

Haas, Willy. *Bert Brecht.* Translated by Max Knight and Joseph Fabry. New York: Frederick Ungar, 1970.
A brief monograph surveying Brecht's life and achievements. Helpful in establishing Brecht's place in contemporary drama. No analysis of the fiction, but the first two chapters are valuable for the discussion of Brecht's background and early efforts.

Hayman, Ronald. *Brecht: A Biography.* London: Weidenfeld & Nicolson, 1983.
A full-length biography with many helpful reference items, such as a chronology of Brecht's life, a list of performances of his plays, and a helpful bibliography. Brief mention of the *Gesichten von Herrn Keuner* as well as the story "The Augsburg Chalk Circle." Notes its source in the biblical story of King Solomon and on a thirteenth century play by Li Hsing-dao. Says that the story demonstrates that justice has little to do with the law.

Hill, Claude. *Bertolt Brecht.* Boston: Twayne, 1975.
An overall introduction to Brecht's life and work. The only reference to the short fiction is a brief mention of the Keuner stories and the story "The Augsburg Chalk Circle" as the source for *The Caucasian Chalk Circle.* However, this is a good introduction to Brecht's work, written for the general reader.

Needle, Jan, and Peter Thomson. *Brecht.* Chicago: University of Chicago Press, 1981.

A chronological survey of Brecht's plays in the light of his political and dramatic theories. Although the book contains no discussion of the fiction, the first chapter is a valuable introduction to the impact and influence of Brecht; other chapters are very readable discussions of his politics and his theory of theater.

Morley, Michael. *Brecht: A Study.* London: Heinemann, 1977.
A straightforward introduction to Brecht, briefly summarizing his life and discussing his plays in terms of their major focus—for example, social involvement or the exceptional individual—and their genre—that is, comedy, farce, or satire. Also includes brief chapters on his theory and his poetry. Provides a helpful framework for Brecht's work.

Volker, Klaus. *Brecht: A Biography.* New York: Seabury Press, 1978.
A full-scale biography based on the facts gathered and published in *Brecht Chronicle*. Only brief mention of the stories, primarily noting that in the Keuner stories Brecht laid down certain rules of behavior later followed by characters in his novels. Contains a number of photographs.

_____ . *Brecht Chronicle.* Translated by Fred Wieck. New York: Seabury Press, 1975.
A daily notebook of facts about Brecht's life in chronological order. Helpful in establishing what little factual information is available about the writing and publishing of the short stories. A good resource about Brecht's life. Provides much information without interpretation.

Weideli, Walter. *The Art of Bertolt Brecht.* Translated by Daniel Russell. New York: New York University Press, 1963.
One of the few studies of Brecht to discuss his short stories. Suggests that the stories in *Calendar Tales* are a kind of popular almanac containing Brecht's rules of conduct. Says that Brecht reduces various heroes of history to the common denominator in his stories.

IVAN BUNIN
(1870-1953)
Russia

General Biographical and Critical Studies

Connolly, Julian W. *Ivan Bunin*. Boston: Twayne, 1982.
An introduction to Bunin's art for the general reader, focusing on his ideological positions and charting his evolution as an artist. The study includes a brief biographical sketch, but is primarily organized around thematic discussions of Bunin's major prose works in chronological order.

Kryzytski, Serge. *The Works of Ivan Bunin*. The Hague, Netherlands: Mouton, 1971.
A straightforward thematic analysis of Bunin's major prose works in chronological order. The study begins with a brief biographical sketch, delineates Bunin's use of the so-called peasant theme, and discusses the love theme in many of his stories, as well as the themes of crime and death.

Poggioli, Renato. *The Phoenix and the Spider*. Cambridge: Harvard University Press, 1957.
A general critical analysis of several of Bunin's most important works within the tradition of Russian classical realism, as represented primarily by Ivan Turgenev, Nikolai Gogol, and Leo Tolstoy. Notes that although "The Gentleman from San Francisco" is somewhat similar to Tolstoy's "The Death of Ivan Ilyich," it is different in that whereas Tolstoy's story ends in revelation and redemption, in Bunin's story there is only the triumph of nothingness.

Woodward, James B. *Ivan Bunin: A Study of His Fiction*. Chapel Hill: University of North Carolina Press, 1980.
The major focus of this study is Bunin's response to social changes in Russia in the late nineteenth and early twentieth centuries. The last chapters deal with Bunin's love stories.

Selected Titles

"Brethren"/"The Brothers"
Connolly, Julian W. *Ivan Bunin*. Boston: Twayne, 1982.
Connolly suggests that the story deals with the vanity of human desires and the suffering that results from attachment to things of the world. Notes that the elemental desires of the rickshaw driver and the more abstract striving of the

Englishman in the two parts of the story can only end in frustration and pain;
thus, they are brothers, not ironically, but in the sense of a deep and meaningful kinship.

Gross, Seymour. "Nature, Man, and God in Bunin's 'The Gentleman from San
Francisco.' " *Modern Fiction Studies* 6 (Summer, 1960): 153-163.
    Argues that "The Brothers" sheds light on "The Gentleman from San Fran-
    cisco" because the disease of the world, which is handled so distantly in the
    latter story, is handled more directly and personally in "The Brothers." Says
    that in both stories modern man has lost the capacity to respond to the
    supernatural awesomeness of life and the final mystery of death.

Kryzytski, Serge. *The Works of Ivan Bunin*. The Hague, Netherlands: Mouton, 1971.
    A brief summary analysis of the story, which takes the traditional view that the
    title is ironic. Kryzytski primarily discuses the story as an example of Bunin's
    use of exotic settings; what few critical remarks he makes about the story are
    drawn from D. S. Mirsky and other critics.

Woodward, James B. *Ivan Bunin: A Study of His Fiction*. Chapel Hill: University of
North Carolina Press, 1980.
    Notes that the story is the first of several which reflect Bunin's interest in
    Buddhism; the first part of the story is a parable of two of the noble truths of
    Buddha—the truth of the cause of pain and the truth of the cessation of pain.
    The second part of the story, says Woodward, parallels the life and death of the
    individual with the rise and fall of civilizations.

"The Gentleman from San Francisco"
Connolly, Julian W. *Ivan Bunin*. Boston: Twayne, 1982.
    Says that it is the most successful of Bunin's stories which expose the vanity of
    self-assertion. Offers a detailed interpretation of the story both in terms of its
    theme and style, pointing out that rather than using explicit statements from
    the Buddha or depending on moralizing reflections, the story's message is
    carried by its structure and imagery. Throughout the story, Bunin exposes
    modern society's preoccupation with the self and its indifference to nature and
    to God.

Gardner, John, and Lennis Dunlap, eds. *The Forms of Fiction*. New York: Random
House, 1962.
    A detailed interpretation of the story's symbolic and allegorical structure. The
    gentleman is representative of a caste supported on the backs of the poor,
    suggest Gardner and Dunlap, and the community on the ship is like a com-
    munity of believers in the fat idol, who is the captain, or the hotel, which is
    like a temple. They also point out the many allusions to the biblical book of
    Revelations in the story.

Gross, Seymour. "Nature, Man, and God in Bunin's 'The Gentleman from San Francisco.' " *Modern Fiction Studies* 6 (Summer, 1960): 153-163.

Gross argues that when the life of the gentleman is seen against the vision of Christian grace, all the details in the story become significant. He analyzes the story in terms of the gentleman's isolation from nature and the rest of humanity as a result of modern man having lost the religious sense of awe.

Jacobs, Willis D. "Bunin's 'Gentleman from San Francisco.' " *Explicator* 7 (March, 1949): 42.

Argues against a Socialist interpretation of the story; points out that it was conceived before the Communist Revolution and that Bunin himself was a violent anti-Communist. Argues instead that the story is a parable of the spiritual rot that Bunin saw infecting the whole world; its central focus is thus not the Communist Revolution but rather the universal condition of man.

Kryzytski, Serge. *The Works of Ivan Bunin*. The Hague, Netherlands: Mouton, 1971.

Disagrees with the Marxist reading of the story as an indictment of the capitalist world. Says that the theme is a common one in Bunin's works—man's vulnerability in the face of the forces of nature and death. He suggests that in the story Bunin's verbal mastery reaches its zenith, for in it he accomplishes, through purely descriptive effects, a rhythmic roll of passages.

Mirsky, D. S. *A History of Russian Literature*. New York: Alfred A. Knopf, 1949.

Mirsky says that the story is not a work of analysis, for Bunin is neither an analyst nor a psychologist; rather the story is a solid object, a thing of beauty, with the consistency and hardness of a steel bar. It is a masterpiece of Doric economy, says Mirsky.

Woodward, James B. *Ivan Bunin: A Study of His Fiction*. Chapel Hill: University of North Carolina Press, 1980.

Says that the story is an ironic dramatization of the conclusions reached by the colonel in part 2 of "The Brothers." Argues that the gentleman and the other inhabitants of the ship *Atlantis* have created a pagan, artificial reality cut off from all aspects of life that cannot be rationally controlled. The death of the gentleman, like that of the rickshaw boy in "The Brothers," symbolically reunites him with the cosmic unity of life.

DINO BUZZATI
(1906-1972)
Italy

General Biographical and Critical Studies

Venuti, Lawrence. "Dino Buzzati's Fantastic Journalism." *Modern Fiction Studies* 28 (Spring, 1982): 79-91.
Discusses Buzzati's work in terms of the concept of "adaption," a narrative technique in which the author attempts to make the reader believe that the most fantastic actions can occur in his own world. Argues that Buzzati often exploits journalistic genres to give his fantasy an air of verisimilitude. Discusses several Buzzati stories that use this technique.

——————— . Introduction to *Restless Nights: Selected Stories of Dino Buzzati*, by Dino Buzzati. San Francisco: North Point Press, 1983.
Venuti, who translated this volume and a subsequent collection, *The Siren: A Selection from Dino Buzzati*, published in 1984, provides a concise overview of Buzzati's life and work. Noting that Buzzati is a virtual unknown in the United States despite high standing in Europe, Venuti suggests that Buzzati's fantastic fictions reveal a sensitivity to the undercurrents of modern life (the dark side, for example, of science and technology)— that should recommend him to American readers.

ITALO CALVINO
(1923-1985)
Italy

General Biographical and Critical Studies

Adler, Sara Maria. *Calvino: The Writer as Fablemaker*. Madrid: José Porrúa
Turanzas, 1979.
One of the first full-length studies of Calvino, originally written as the author's
dissertation at Harvard University. Adler focuses on Calvino as a creator of
fantasy and argues that his central theme is the tension between a character
and the environment, which challenges him in some way; chapters on point of
view and imagery indicate how Calvino embodies this theme. A final chapter
summarizes and analyzes the various perspectives on Calvino of his Italian
critics.

Carter, Albert Howard, III. *Italo Calvino: Metamorphoses of Fantasy*. Ann Arbor,
Mich.: UMI Research Press, 1987.
A straightforward analysis of Calvino's major works in chronological order.
The focus is on the rhetorical means by which Calvino establishes fantasies for
the reader to follow. Carter attempts to show how Calvino moves steadily away
from plot and event toward exploring the mental processes of his characters.
Separate chapters are devoted to *Cosmicomics*, *Invisible Cities*, *Mr. Palomar*,
and others. An extensive checklist of criticism is appended.

Hume, Kathryn. "Italo Calvino's Cosmic Comedy: Mythography for the Scientific
Age." *Papers on Language and Literature* 20 (Winter, 1984): 80-95.
A discussion of the mythic nature of *Cosmicomics* and *t zero*. Focuses on a few
stories to show Calvino's metaphoric techniques for relating man to the external world. According to Hume, Calvino's cosmicomic stories should be read as
a set of privately devised myths depicting attraction and repulsion, transcendence and love, creation and survival.

Lucente, Gregory L. *Beautiful Fables: Self-Consciousness in Italian Narrative from
Manzoni to Calvino*. Baltimore: Johns Hopkins University Press, 1986.
The chapter on Calvino focuses on his developing use of self-reflexive fiction,
culminating in *If on a Winter's Night a Traveler*, which Lucente calls his most
programmatically self-conscious fiction. According to Lucente, Calvino's most
successful use of self-reflexivity in short fiction is in the collection entitled
Cosmicomics, published about midway through his career.

Olken, I. T. *With Pleated Eye and Garnet Wing: Symmetries of Italo Calvino*. Ann
Arbor: University of Michigan Press, 1984.

An analysis of Calvino's concern with the nature of patterns and with symmetry and correspondences. According to Olken, Calvino's poetics derive from the tension between the subjective and the objective, the universal and the specific. For Calvino, everything must be projected through its unique form. Olken develops this thesis in chapters that deal with structure and theme and with the relationships between nature and formal symmetry.

Selected Titles

"The Adventure of a Reader"
Adler, Sara Maria. *Calvino: The Writer as Fablemaker*. Madrid: José Porrúa Turanzas, 1979.
   Examines how the perspective of the protagonist in the story is conditioned by his constant reading; for example, he analyzes the girl in the story much as a literary critic would analyze a book. Points out how the imagery in the story creates an ideal backdrop for the mood of the protagonist.

"The Argentine Ant"
Adler, Sara Maria. *Calvino: The Writer as Fablemaker*. Madrid: José Porrúa Turanzas, 1979.
   A discussion of the story in terms of Calvino's use of the geometric patterning of images. The descriptions of the protagonist's neighbors are established in ordered, balanced patterns, with one set of neighbors set up, imagistically, directly antithetical to the other.

Carter, Albert Howard, III. *Italo Calvino: Metamorphoses of Fantasy*. Ann Arbor, Mich.: UMI Research Press, 1987.
   A discussion of how the story deals with the interrelation between fantasies and everyday life. The basic dilemma of the narrator in the story is between freedom through fantasy and the oppression of his everyday responsibilities. One of Calvino's most amusing tales, although not one of his most fantastic, it is, according to Carter, a pastoral gone wrong.

Olken, I. T. *With Pleated Eye and Garnet Wing: Symmetries of Italo Calvino*. Ann Arbor: University of Michigan Press, 1984.
   Discusses the story as an example of how Calvino focuses on the minute patterns in nature. The narrator's preoccupation with the ants, which he observes at close range, show how Calvino can reveal beauty in the singular nature of even the smallest organism.

"Last Comes the Crow"
Carter, Albert Howard, III. *Italo Calvino: Metamorphoses of Fantasy*. Ann Arbor, Mich.: UMI Research Press, 1987.

A close reading of the story showing the interrelationship of the fantastic and the realistic elements. The story's power derives largely from its presentation of death as the ultimate coincidence of a person and an inexorable force; it affirms our ignorance about, and fear of, death as an inevitable part of a natural system, which can be brutal in allowing its victims to aid in their own destruction.

Olken, I. T. *With Pleated Eye and Garnet Wing: Symmetries of Italo Calvino*. Ann Arbor: University of Michigan Press, 1984.
Points out that the boy in the story is less important as an individual than he is as a function. Moreover, in the story the German soldier is little more than the eagle sewn on his tunic. Both the title and the resolution of the story are ambiguous and ironic, for in the story the rules of the game change and the game ends with the death of the soldier.

"The Nights of the Unpa"
Adler, Sara Maria. *Calvino: The Writer as Fablemaker*. Madrid: José Porrúa Turanzas, 1979.
Discusses how the story exemplifies a young man's revelation of the cruelty of war. Adler pays particular attention to the active role which setting and the secondary characters play in the story. Points out differences between this story and the other two stories in the Entering the War trilogy.

ALBERT CAMUS
(1913-1960)
France

General Biographical and Critical Studies

Brée, Germaine. *Camus*. New York: Harcourt, Brace & World, 1959, rev. ed. 1961.
A critical biography, with more emphasis on literary criticism than on the life of Camus. Although most of the book deals with Camus' novels and plays, Brée makes some helpful suggestions about *Exile and the Kingdom*, arguing that with the collection Camus was moving toward his projection of a clearly defined art of living with dignity and self-honesty. He notes that the plots of the stories are conventional, each building to a revelatory climax, and suggests that in the short story Camus was seeking a form of "aesthetic equilibrium."

Carruth, Hayden. *After the Stranger: Imaginary Dialogues with Camus*. New York: Macmillan, 1965.
A speculative study of Camus' thought, especially in *The Stranger*, cast as a series of conversations between an American painter named Aspen, suffering from his own existential sense of anxiety and dread, and Camus himself. The fantasy is extended when Camus and Aspen go to the south of France and meet two characters from Camus' fiction, Dora Brilliant from *The Just Assassins* and d'Arrast from "The Growing Stone."

Cordes, Alfred. *The Descent of the Doves: Camus's Journey to the Spirit*. Lanham, Md.: University Press of America, 1980.
A routine study of Camus' development toward a final optimistic affirmation in the two stories "The Renegade" and "The Growing Stone." "The Renegade" is compared to *The Fall* and to Antoine de Saint-Exupéry's *The Little Prince*; "The Growing Stone" shows the way to spiritual salvation. Much of the discussion is little more than plot summary and is dominated by a Christian point of view that often does violence to the two stories.

Cryle, Peter. "Diversity and Symbol in *Exile and the Kingdom*." In *Essays on Camus's Exile and the Kingdom*, edited by Judith D. Suther. University, Miss.: Romance Monographs, Inc., 1980.
Argues that the collection expresses better than any of Camus' other works the tension between the desire for unity and the diversity that naturally exists in the world. Whereas previous works by Camus were dominated by the desire for unification, his short stories paint a more complete picture of the human condition and thus constitute art that is midway between reality and its stylization.

Erickson, John. "Albert Camus and North America: A Discourse of Exteriority." In *Critical Essays on Albert Camus*, edited by Bettina L. Knapp. Boston: G. K. Hall, 1988.

Focuses on those stories in *Exile and the Kingdom* that are located in North Africa, such as "The Adulterous Woman" and "The Guest," in which Camus depicts the Arab as first an idealized nomad and second as a representative of the inseparability of the fates of the French and the Arabs. The depiction of the Arab in Camus' later fiction suggests the possibility of individuals transcending their cultural differences.

Festa-McCormick, Diana. "Existential Exile and a Glimpse of the Kingdom." In *Critical Essays on Albert Camus*, edited by Bettina L. Knapp. Boston: G. K. Hall, 1988.

According to Festa-McCormick, the stories present man caught in a fragmented society in which he cannot recover harmony through intellectual ideas. Morality is revealed in the stories as a loose blend of personal experiences which allow resolutions to be reached out of uncertainty rather than by intellectual choices.

Fitch, Brian T. *The Narcissistic Text: A Reading of Camus' Fiction*. Toronto: University of Toronto Press, 1982.

A study which focuses on how the language of Camus' fiction moves from transparency to a high degree of stylization or self-preoccupation. Fitch claims that Camus is thus a precursor of the French New Novel. The most extensive example of Camus' use of self-referentiality in his short fiction, argues Fitch, is "The Artist at Work."

Hanna, Thomas. *The Thought and Art of Albert Camus*. Chicago: Henry Regnery, 1958.

An early English-language study of both the philosophic and the literary work of Camus, with most of the emphasis on how the philosophy affects the fiction. Half of the study focuses on Camus' concept of the absurd developed in *The Myth of Sisyphus* and how it informs such works as *The Stranger* and *Caligula*; the second half deals with Camus' idea of revolt and how it informs such works as *The Plague* and *The Fall*. Although this study was written before the publication of Camus' book of short stories, it is a valuable introduction to his work.

King, Adele. *Camus*. New York: Capricorn Books, 1964.

A brief monograph with short introductory chapters on Camus' life, his thought, and his three most important novels: *The Stranger*, *The Plague*, and *The Fall*. Only a few pages, mainly plot summaries with a few general interpretative comments, are devoted to the short stories. A bibliography of secondary criticism is included.

Knapp, Bettina L., ed. *Critical Essays on Albert Camus*. Boston: G. K. Hall, 1988.
A valuable collection of critical essays, some reprinted from other sources, by Jean-Paul Sartre, Serge Doubrovsky, and Maurice Blanchot; others were commissioned especially for this volume. Particularly interesting are those essays which apply contemporary concepts of intertextuality and deconstruction to Camus' work. Also valuable is a long article by Henri Peyre which reviews the major criticism published about Camus.

Lazere, Donald. *The Unique Creation of Albert Camus*. New Haven, Conn.: Yale University Press, 1973.
Lazere's chapter on the short stories in this academic study of Camus' artistic technique is primarily based on the approach of the American formalists. Because of his New Critical approach, Lazere finds the style of the interior monologue in "The Renegade" the most impressive technical feat in the collection and "The Growing Stone" the weakest piece of writing because of its mixing of a realistic and a symbolic style. In fact, says Lazere, "The Growing Stone" emphasizes the overall impression from the whole collection that Camus has not mastered the short-story form.

McCarthy, Patrick. *Camus*. New York: Random House, 1982.
Primarily a biography of Camus, but with critical commentary on his philosophy and his art. McCarthy calls Camus a bad philosopher and the author of wooden plays; however, he greatly admires Camus' novels. Much of McCarthy's efforts are spent in debunking Camus' claims to fame, admitting at the outset that it is the unsaintly and curiously indifferent Camus who is the subject of this book. Only passing remarks on the short stories.

Maquet, Albert. *Albert Camus: The Invincible Summer*. Translated by Herma Briffault. New York: George Braziller, Inc., 1958.
A routine general study of Camus' life and work. The chapter on the stories is made up of impressionistic plot summaries and simplistic interpretative descriptions. Maquet sees "The Growing Stone" as the most important story in the collection, the one in which Camus' resources as a prose writer are most obvious.

Modern Fiction Studies 10 (Autumn, 1964).
This special issue contains eight articles on Camus' novels and a selected checklist of criticism in English. Although there is nothing here on the short stories, the discussions of Camus' narrative technique and fictional themes are helpful in understanding the stories.

Noyer-Weidner, Alfred. "Albert Camus in His Short Story Phase." In *Essays on Camus's Exile and the Kingdom*, edited by Judith D. Suther. University, Miss.: Romance Monographs, Inc., 1980.
Suggests that the obscurity of the characters' feelings in the stories is intentionally reflected in the obscurity and mystery of the stories themselves. Noyer-Weidner discusses this aspect of Camus' stories both within the context of short-story theory since the twentieth century in America, Germany, and France, and within the context of Camus' thought since *The Myth of Sisyphus*.

Picon, Gaetan. "*Exile and the Kingdom*." In *Camus: A Collection of Critical Essays*, edited by Germaine Brée. Englewood Cliffs, N.J.; Prentice-Hall, 1962.
Claims that Camus' stories are not as powerful as his novels because they do not carry a line of thought through to its conclusion as the novels do; the stories are more concerned with concrete reality than the novels are. The success of the book is due to the fact that the concepts of "exile" and "kingdom" are not contradictory, but rather complementary, for it is only within exile that one finds the free and untrammeled existence of the kingdom.

Quilliot, Roger. "An Ambiguous World." In *Camus: A Collection of Critical Essays*, edited by Germaine Brée. Englewood Cliffs, N.J.; Prentice-Hall, 1962.
Although most of this essay discusses *The Fall*, Quilliot also briefly discusses Camus' stories. He suggests that Camus purposely introduced the idea of "kingdom" in these stories of exile, for they reveal his coming back full circle to images of Algerian barrenness in narrative movements of lyricism and irony. In the stories characters are condemned to live in both love and despair.

_____ . *The Sea and Prisons: A Commentary on the Life and Thought of Albert Camus*. Translated by Emmett Parker. Tuscaloosa: University of Alabama Press, 1970.
This often-cited study of Camus, which originally appeared in France in 1956, has been updated by Quilliot to include a discussion of *Exile and the Kingdom*.

Rhein, Phillip. *Albert Camus*. Boston: Twayne, 1969.
Rhein calls *Exile and the Kingdom* Camus' most perfectly finished work of art; in it characters search for an inner kingdom in order to forget their spiritual exile. Argues that Camus' theory of art developed in *The Rebel* (that it is necessary to construct a world of order and value in spite of the realization of exile) is essential not only to the narrative art of the stories but also to character motivation.

Suther, Judith D., ed. *Essays on Camus's Exile and the Kingdom*. University, Miss.: Romance Monographs, 1980.
A collection of sixteen essays, previously unavailable in English, on the stories

in *Exile and the Kingdom*. Originally published in the 1960's and early 1970's, the essays deal with psychological, structural, aesthetic, stylistic, philosophical, and sociological aspects of Camus' short-story collection.

Tarrow, Susan. *Exile from the Kingdom: A Political Rereading of Albert Camus*. Tuscaloosa: University of Alabama Press, 1985.
A study of the political aspects of Camus' fiction. The chapter on *Exile and the Kingdom* focuses on how the stories indicate a return to the early Camus theme of estrangement and misunderstanding. According to Tarrow, the stories reveal how Camus was caught between his identity as a Frenchman and his liberty-seeking roots in his childhood in Algeria.

Theis, Raimund. "Albert Camus's Return to Sisyphus." In *Essays on Camus's Exile and the Kingdom*, edited by Judith D. Suther. University, Miss.: Romance Monographs, 1980.
A discussion of how the stories reflect a shift in Camus' art from the presentation of characters as the embodiment of abstractions to the development of characters as empirically and historically actualized. Theis argues that Camus' ideas in the collection are more cynical and less complete than in previous works, for he had nothing more to say about humankind after the publication of *The Myth of Sisyphus* in 1942.

Thody, Philip. *Albert Camus: A Study of His Work*. New York: Grove Press, 1957.
In this general discussion of Camus' works, Thody says that the importance of the stories lie in their value as works of art rather than in any political or philosophical statement hidden within them. Concludes that in these stories Camus was entering a new phase of his creative activity, one in which he was more concerned with presenting actual human beings caught in moral dilemmas than with expressing moral values in a philosophic way.

Selected Titles

"The Adulterous Woman"
Onimus, Jean. "Camus, 'The Adulterous Woman,' and the Starry Sky." In *Essays on Camus's Exile and the Kingdom*, edited by Judith D. Suther. University, Miss.: Romance Monographs, 1980.
A brief summary analysis of the story, emphasizing its humor. Discusses the development of the narrative as based on the structure of its heroine's transition from her ordinariness and malaise to her mystic ecstasy. Argues that she resembles Gustave Flaubert's Emma Bovary in that the story shows what happens when consciousness intrudes into a previously dazed life.

Pelz, Manfred. "Camus's Two Styles in 'The Adulterous Woman.' " In *Essays on Camus's Exile and the Kingdom*, edited by Judith D. Suther. University, Miss.: Romance Monographs, 1980.

By stylistically analyzing key passages in the story, Pelz argues that the ambiguity of the story is reflected in its language, for language is what characterizes the people in it. The two basic styles in the work are the telegram style made up of short, choppy sentences, which reflect Janine's malaise, and the more poetic and symbolic style, which reflects her ecstasy.

"The Artist at Work"

Fitch, Brian T. *The Narcissistic Text: A Reading of Camus's Fiction*. Toronto: University of Toronto Press, 1982.

An extensive discussion of the story as a "self-generating" or "auto-referential" text, in which the final play on words "solitary/solidarity" is the end for which the rest of the story is a "pretext." The story fits what French critic Roland Barthes calls a "writerly" text, in which the process of writing is more important than the work's referentiality to the external world.

Tarrow, Susan. *Exile from the Kingdom: A Political Rereading of Albert Camus*. Tuscaloosa: University of Alabama Press, 1985.

Claims that this satire compares the tyranny of art to the tyranny of the Old Testament God. Jonas, like his namesake Jonah of the Bible, ignores the dictates of his "star" (God) and allows himself to be overcome by outside influences. The optimistic ending suggests that Camus knows that the artist must maintain a balance between the world of men and his need for the solitary life.

Thody, Philip. *Albert Camus: A Study of His Work*. New York: Grove Press, 1957.

Argues that the story's basic idea is that the artist is most at one with his time when he is solitary, that the artist cannot be made to come in contact with "real life"; the true artist will make such contact through the process of artistic creation. Thody says that the story is an ironic commentary drawn from Camus' own life.

"The Growing Stone"

Claire, Thomas. "Landscape and Religious Imagery in Camus's 'La Pierre Qui Pousse.' " *Studies in Short Fiction* 13 (Summer, 1976): 321-329.

An analysis of the development of d'Arrast in terms of the landscape and religious imagery. Points out how d'Arrast mediates between humankind and the forces that surround him to make possible a new human-oriented order; in this way d'Arrast is a religious savior.

Goodhand, Robert H. "The Omphalos and the Phoenix: Symbolism of the Center in Camus's 'La Pierre Qui Pousse.' " *Studies in Short Fiction* 21 (Spring, 1984): 117-126.

Argues that the fact that the stone is half buried in ashes and earth does not vitiate the otherwise positive implications of the work, for the reference is to the Greek center of the Earth (*omphalos*) and to the Greek legend of the resurrected phoenix. Goodhand points out the numerous allusions to these two myths throughout the story.

Rhein, Phillip. *Albert Camus*. Boston: Twayne, 1969.

Claims that the story presents a solution to many of the problems that run throughout Camus' works by suggesting a kind of victory over the absurdity of man's existence. In asserting his brotherhood with all men who labor, d'Arrast finds a place where he belongs. Rhein suggests that the story is the most compelling one in the collection.

Segovia, Jaime Castro. "Reflections of the Afro-Brazilian World in 'The Growing Stone.' " In *Essays on Camus's Exile and the Kingdom*, edited by Judith D. Suther. University, Miss.: Romance Monographs, 1980.

Attempts to define Camus' approach to Brazilian culture and society in the story. Although the essay briefly mentions Camus' use of Brazilian geography, the major focus is on the story's synthesis of the racial segregation of the country, as well as the religious rituals and beliefs of the Afro-Brazilian.

Tarrow, Susan. *Exile from the Kingdom: A Political Rereading of Albert Camus*. Tuscaloosa: University of Alabama Press, 1985.

Argues that, despite the similarity between d'Arrast and the figure of Christ, he is not a personification of Christ; he is, however, the only heroic figure in the collection of stories. Acting according to his individual human compassion rather than some abstract ideological system, d'Arrast shows the people the way to independence, both symbolically (by carrying the rock) and practically (by providing them work).

Thody, Philip. *Albert Camus: A Study of His Work*. New York: Grove Press, 1957.

Suggests that d'Arrast's problem is Camus'—the problem of coming into contact "with others without losing one's own individuality. The engineer's willingness to carry the stone suggests Camus' belief that one must assume tasks that on the surface seem meaningless and absurd, but that are in fact significant.

"The Guest"

Grobe, Edwin P. "The Psychological Structure of Camus's 'L'Hôte.' " *French Review* 40 (December, 1966): 357-367.

Argues that Daru and the Arab are spiritual doubles, victimized by the desert and cut off from society. Analyzes the story in terms of the psychological exile of both characters. Suggests that the sense of exile is the result of Camus' theory of the inadequacy of language.

Guers-Villate, Yvonne. "Rieux and Daru or the Deliberate Refusal to Influence Others." In *Essays on Camus's Exile and the Kingdom*, edited by Judith D. Suther. University, Miss.: Romance Monographs, Inc., 1980.
Compares the refusal of Rieux (the doctor in Camus' *The Plague*) to intervene with the similar refusal of Daru in "The Guest"; both decline to act not out of indifference or moral cowardice but rather out of personal convictions that all individuals are condemned to a solitude they must sometimes choose if they wish to attain a measure of dignity.

Rooke, Constance. "Camus' 'The Guest': The Message on the Blackboard." *Studies in Short Fiction* 14 (Winter, 1977): 78-81.
Argues that the Arab tribesmen who pose a threat to Daru at the end of the story do not exist; rather it is Daru himself who writes, "You handed over our brother. You will pay for this," as an expression of his own conscience for passing on the decision about the Arab to someone else.

Tarrow, Susan. *Exile from the Kingdom: A Political Rereading of Albert Camus*. Tuscaloosa: University of Alabama Press, 1985.
Focuses on how Daru has isolated himself from his fellow Europeans but is unable to identify with the colonized Algerians. Because of Daru's failure to understand the political reality behind the world of the policeman and the world of the prisoner, he alienates himself from both; by refusing to commit himself to either side, he loses everything.

Thody, Philip. *Albert Camus: A Study of His Work*. New York: Grove Press, 1957.
Says that the story is an appeal to understanding and tolerance; Daru, the protagonist, symbolizes the civilizing aspects of French administration in Algiers; his dilemma is that of many French residents, who are exiles in a country which once was their own.

"The Renegade"
Bartfeld, Fernande. "Two Exiles of Camus: Clamence and 'The Renegade.' " In *Essays on Camus's Exile and the Kingdom*, edited by Judith D. Suther. University, Miss.: Romance Monographs, Inc., 1980.
Compares the protagonist of "The Renegade" with the protagonist of *The Fall*. In a passage-by-passage comparison, Bartfeld shows that the 1957 version of the short story differs from its earlier version by emphasizing more clearly its sources in *The Fall*.

Fortier, Paul A. "The Creation and Function of Atmosphere in 'The Renegade.'"
    In *Essays on Camus's Exile and the Kingdom*, edited by Judith D. Suther.
    University, Miss.: Romance Monographs, 1980.
    A close analysis of several passages from the story, which supports Fortier's
    theory about the role of description in Camus' fictional works. Description
    must create a specific atmosphere that reflects meaning; thus, an overall inter-
    pretation of a work can be based on an analysis of just those passages in a
    story which define atmosphere.

Hutcheon, Linda. " 'The Renegade' as Nouveau Récit." In *Essays on Camus's Exile
    and the Kingdom*, edited by Judith D. Suther. University, Miss.: Romance
    Monographs, 1980.
    Rather than a simple interior monologue in a naturalistic manner, the story,
    according to Hutcheon, is a sophisticated and self-conscious linguistic organi-
    zation of images. In many ways it is an allegory of writing in which the
    renegade stands for the writer who renounces his identity in favor of styliza-
    tion; thus the renegade is a self-mocking Camus who realizes that by extreme
    stylization he renounces his humanistic and aesthetic ideals.

Joiner, Lawrence D. " 'Camus' 'Le Renegat': Identity Denied." *Studies in Short
    Fiction* 13 (Winter, 1976): 37-41.
    Joiner argues that the key to understanding the story lies in the renegade's
    desire to objectify his identity in the eyes of others. Yet at the end of the story
    he is refused identity and alienated even from himself; he cannot find himself
    because he does not know what it is that he desires.

Lekehal, Ali. "Aspects of the Algerian Landscape: The Fantastic in 'The Re-
    negade.'" In *Essays on Camus's Exile and the Kingdom*, edited by Judith D.
    Suther. University, Miss.: Romance Monographs, Inc., 1980.
    Discusses the Algerian setting of the story in terms of its symbolic echoes of
    the Christian hell. The explosion of the fantastic landscape in the story corre-
    sponds to the shattering of the mind of the hero, says Lekehal, for the Algerian
    landscape reflects a world where one cannot move for fear of making every-
    thing collapse.

Pelz, Manfred. "The Function of Interior Monologue in 'The Renegade.'" In
    Essays on Camus's Exile and the Kingdom, edited by Judith D. Suther. Univer-
    sity, Miss.: Romance Monographs 1980.
    Pelz claims that although an interior monologue forming the overall structure
    of a short story often is nonsense, Camus transformed the interior monologue
    in a closely controlled way to suit his own purposes. This essay is a close
    analysis of the style of presentation of the story, a style which Pelz says mirrors
    the entrapment of the narrator who must speak in spite of himself.

Rhein, Phillip. *Albert Camus*. Boston: Twayne, 1969.
Suggests that Camus experiments here with the stream-of-consciousness technique he so admired in the works of William Faulkner. The young missionary in the story mistakes his will to power for charity but ironically becomes converted himself. As a result of making two equally wrong commitments, he becomes an exile from the kingdom of man.

Tarrow, Susan. *Exile from the Kingdom: A Political Rereading of Albert Camus*. Tuscaloosa: University of Alabama Press, 1985.
Interprets the renegade as an example of a modern intellectual in search of ideological absolutes; the missionary's ostensible purpose to convert a fierce people to Christianity is only a disguise for his search for power. The major theme of the story is that violence, no matter how praiseworthy its aim, becomes a way of life.

Thody, Philip. *Albert Camus: A Study of His Work*. New York: Grove Press, 1957.
Thody suggests that the story illustrates one of the ideas from *The Rebel*—that whoever rebels completely will be most easily tempted by conformity to a new set of rules—and that it may be an allegory of the Christian intellectual who gives up Christianity for communism because of his worship of power. Yet the real impact of the story lies in its psychological depiction of intolerance.

"The Silent Men"
Rhein, Phillip. *Albert Camus*. Boston: Twayne, 1969.
Like many of the other stories in the collection, this one, says Rhein, is about misunderstanding and lack of communication. It is also a story of lost youth and lost physical happiness. Suggests that the men in the story suffer from being excluded from a fraternal universe and that they long for a realm of love and understanding.

Rothmund, Alfons. "Albert Camus: 'The Silent Men.' " In *Essays on Camus's Exile and the Kingdom*, edited by Judith D. Suther. University, Miss.: Romance Monographs, 1980.
A detailed academic analysis of the story based on its appearance in a textbook for use in German schools. Focuses primarily on the theme of silence due to broken relationships, but also notes other motifs common in Camus' work and comments briefly on the controlled and expressive style of the story.

KAREL ČAPEK
(1890-1938)
Czechoslovakia

General Biographical and Critical Studies

Harkins, William. *Karel Čapek*. New York: Columbia University Press, 1962.
The first English-language study of Čapek's works. Includes a biographical chapter and chapters on the major works, including *Zářivé hlubiny* (luminous depths), the collection he wrote with his brother, Josef; *Boží muka* (wayside crosses), his metaphysical tales; *Money and Other Stories*, his most pessimistic collection; and *Tales from Two Pockets*, his detective or police tales. Briefly comments on his relativist position in the story "The Last Judgment."

Matuska, Alexander. *Karel Čapek: An Essay*. Prague: Artia, 1964.
A highly fragmented study of Čapek, with chapters on the tradition to which he belongs, the sources of his art, the themes of his fiction, his stature as an artist, and his image of man. Brief discussions of the short story collections, but no detailed analyses of particular stories. Not an easy book to read because of its idiosyncratic style.

COLETTE
Sidonie-Gabrielle Colette
(1873-1954)
France

General Biographical and Critical Studies

Cottrell, Robert D. *Colette*. New York: Frederick Ungar, 1974.
A brief critical introduction to Colette's works. Devotes one chapter to the five Claudine novels, one to her novels about the music hall world, and one on the novels of her maturity, such as *Chéri*. No discussion of the short fiction, with the exception of the collection *Gigi*, in which, Cottrell says, Colette returns to the world of elegant corruption and achieves a triumph of style.

Crosland, Margaret. *Colette: A Provincial in Paris*. New York: British Book Center, 1954.
A popular biography with a readable introduction to the events that affected Colette's life. Provides helpful background to her fiction, details her reputation, discusses the publishing history of her work, and situates her within the culture of her time. A good first book to read on Colette, but not sufficient for understanding the complexity of her experience.

——————— . *Colette: The Difficulty of Loving*. London: Peter Owen, 1973.
More analytical than in her first book on Colette, Crosland not only recounts the major events of the French writer's life and literary career in this follow-up, but she also comments on Colette's prose style and on themes in several of her works. Only passing comments on the short fiction.

Dehon, Claire. "Colette and Art Nouveau." In *Colette: The Woman, the Writer*, edited by Erica Mendelson Eisinger and Mari Ward McCarty. University Park: Pennsylvania State University Press, 1981.
A discussion of the influence of Art Nouveau on Colette's fiction. Analyzes elements such as the interplay of art and reality, the idealization of the female character, and the circuitous approach to reality. Passing comments on Art Nouveau elements in the short fiction.

Eisinger, Erica Mendelson, and Mari Ward McCarty. Introduction to *Colette: The Woman, the Writer*, edited by Eisinger and McCarty. University Park: Pennsylvania State University Press, 1981.
A brief but stimulating discussion of Colette from the perspective of contemporary feminist criticism. Argues that Colette discovered that women's writing

is both a generation of self and a projection of self. Points out that her favored narrative forms are the traditional reflexive women's forms, such as letters, journals, and self-portraits. Claims that Colette's characters reveal the sexual power of women.

Jouve, Nicole Ward. *Colette*. Bloomington: Indiana University Press, 1987.
This study, based on new feminist criticism, describes itself as a personal "engagement" or "dialogue" with Colette. Although the work makes use of modern semiotic and psychoanalytic theory, it is highly subjective and intuitive rather than critically analytical. Focusing on Colette's relationship with her parents and her first husband, Jouve discusses the novels from a Freudian perspective, but makes only passing mention of the short fiction.

Ketchum, Anne Duhamel. "Colette and the Enterprise of Writing: A Reappraisal." In *Colette: The Woman, the Writer*, edited by Erica Mendelson Eisinger and Mari Ward McCarty. University Park: Pennsylvania State University Press, 1981.
Discussion of several Colette narratives as ideological acts and fictional efforts to solve oppressive contradictions in her life and in her society, particularly the conflict between man as the force of repression and woman as the preservation of life and desire.

Makward, Christiane. "Colette and Signs: A Partial Reading of a Writer 'Born Not to Write.' " In *Colette: The Woman, the Writer*, edited by Erica Mendelson Eisinger and Mari Ward McCarty. University Park: Pennsylvania State University Press, 1981.
Claims that in Colette's short work *Journal à rebours* one finds the most serious statement on art in all of her writings. Argues that the image Colette presents places the personal self in the shadows while focusing on the self as a writer who did not want to write.

Mallet-Joris, Françoise. "A Womanly Vocation." Translated by Eleanor Reid Gibbard. In *Colette: The Woman, the Writer*, edited by Erica Mendelson Eisinger and Mari Ward McCarty. University Park: Pennsylvania State University Press, 1981.
Discusses Colette's conviction that a woman's vocation is to give daily life its symbolic meaning, as well as Colette's admiration for those who struggle and cling to life. For Colette woman fulfills herself more by enduring than by acting.

Marks, Elaine. *Colette*. New Brunswick, N.J.: Rutgers University Press, 1960.
A critical study by a perceptive critic. Marks argues that Colette's works are

based on the moral imperative to look, to feel, to wonder, to accept, and to live. Describing Colette's life as a fight for personal freedom, Marks focuses on the game of love in the novels. In one short chapter on the short fiction, she argues that the short stories are less subjective than the novels and offer the reader an excellent means to study Colette's compositional techniques.

Massie, Allan. *Colette*. New York: Penguin Books, 1986.
One of a series of short biographies of women who have influenced modern thought. A fairly routine recounting of Colette's life, including chapters on her childhood, her relationship with her first husband, the birth of the Claudine novels, and her lesbian relationship. Although the discussion of Colette's fiction is very general, this book is an adequate introduction and orientation to the major stages of Colette's life and literary career.

Mitchell, Yvonne. *Colette: A Taste for Life*. New York: Harcourt Brace Jovanovich, 1975.
An annotated scrapbook of Colette's life. Because of Colette's background as a model and an actress, it is helpful to see her in her various roles to understand the personality behind the fiction. A fascinating portfolio, with ample text to accompany the photographs and summarize Colette's life.

Resch, Yannick. "Writing, Language, and the Body." In *Colette: The Woman, the Writer*, edited by Erica Mendelson Eisinger and Mari Ward McCarty. University Park: Pennsylvania State University Press, 1981.
Discussion of images of the body and the relationship between eating and sex in Colette's works. Argues that the relationship of the self to the body in the fiction is based on Colette's identification with her mother and her mother's influence. Relatively demanding reading in comparison with most of the generalized criticism of Colette's work.

Richardson, Joanna. *Colette*. New York: Methuen, 1983.
One of the first biographies of Colette written originally in English. Richardson uses some of Colette's unpublished papers. Arguing that Colette's work is primarily a study of feminine psychology, Richardson illuminates her life by generously quoting from her writings as well as from the writings of those who knew her. Only a passing reference to Colette's 1924 collection of short stories *La Femme cachée*, characterizing them as being inspired by small events with an unforeseeable effect, and calling the collection a brilliant anthology of miniature dramas.

Sarde, Michèle. *Colette: Free and Fettered*. Translated by Richard Miller. New York: William Morrow, 1980.

The most complete and comprehensive biography of Colette, it is most often accepted by feminist critics because of its basic feminist approach. In this fascinating and detailed study, which intermingles passages from Colette's letters and novels with discussions of her life, Sarde emphasizes her conviction that the writer's own text is the most important source of information about her life, for the fictional texts conceal the truth. An engrossing study of the relationship between fiction and life.

Stewart, Joan Hinde. *Colette*. Boston: Twayne, 1983.
A most helpful study, for it is one of the few that refuse to discuss Colette's fiction only in terms of biography. It is also the only study to devote a fully developed chapter to the short stories. The short stories illustrate a special effect which Stewart calls "autography"—though they purport to be drawn from life, they make use of fanciful and invented characters and plots. Essential reading for anyone interested in Colette's themes and techniques rather than simply the details of her life.

Stockinger, Jacob. "The Test of Love and Nature: Colette and Lesbians." In *Colette: The Woman, the Writer*, edited by Erica Mendelson Eisinger and Mari Ward McCarty. University Park: Pennsylvania State University Press, 1981.
Discussion of lesbianism in Colette's life and her fiction. Argues that lesbianism constitutes a significant part of her work and claims that it is a further reason for viewing Colette as an early pioneer of modernism. Notes the theme in some of the short stories as well as in her novels.

Wescott, Glenway. "An Introduction to Colette." In his *Images of Truth*. New York: Harper & Row, 1962.
In this appreciative essay, which originally appeared as the introduction to a collection of Colette's short novels, Wescott briefly summarizes Colette's life and comments on her fiction. There is no real discussion of the short stories, but Wescott is a sensitive reader of Colette's novels, and this informal and personal essay is a pleasant introduction to Colette's narrative techniques and themes by a writer who admires her work.

Whatley, Janet. "Colette and the Art of Survival." In *Colette: The Woman, the Writer*, edited by Erica Mendelson Eisinger and Mari Ward McCarty. University Park: Pennsylvania State University Press, 1981.
Discussion of Colette's literary apprenticeship in terms of the images and language of survival in her works. Analyzes the theme of characters living without happiness in her fiction. Overall focus is on the relationship between autobiography and fiction.

Selected Titles

"Chance Acquaintances"
Stewart, Joan Hinde. *Colette*. Boston: Twayne, 1983.
  A discussion of the narrator's role in the story, both as an intermediary and as one who elevates to the story level events that otherwise would not be seen as such. The story crystallizes obscure tensions, especially the tension between the narrator's stated boredom and her desire to distance herself from involvement in the story that she creates.

"The Kepi"
Stewart, Joan Hinde. *Colette*. Boston: Twayne, 1983.
  Stewart argues that few of Colette's narratives differentiate masculine and feminine so starkly. A symbolic story, "The Kepi" presents its protagonist, a ghostwriter, as a double for Colette herself, even though Colette also functions in the story as the narrator. Stewart sees the story as a complex work about the transformation of oral discourse into written discourse and thus as reflective of a typical Colette fictional technique. One of the few discussions of Colette's technique.

"The Rainy Moon"
Stewart, Joan Hinde. *Colette*. Boston: Twayne, 1983.
  A fable about the dangerous seductions of the past, this story, Stewart argues, brings the narrator face to face with her former self and interweaves her present state with her problematic past as well as with someone else's drama. Calls it a lyrical description of the attraction of the past, reflecting the double movement of rejection and nostalgia, which characterizes Colette's work.

Norrell, Donna. "The Relationship Between Meaning and Structure in Colette's 'Rain-Moon.' " In *Colette: The Woman, the Writer*, edited by Erica Mendelson Eisinger and Mari Ward McCarty. University Park: Pennsylvania State University Press, 1981.
  A discussion of the story in terms of its dual narrative structure and its digressive passages, both of which support the tension in the narrator's mind between accepting or rejecting the idea of black magic. Focuses on how the story involves the reader.

"The Tender Shoot"
Stewart, Joan Hinde. *Colette*. Boston: Twayne, 1983.
  Points out that here, for once, the common Colette theme about the effect of aging and bodily limits focuses on a man; Stewart says that "The Tender Shoot" deals with two kinds of knowledge—sexual and intellectual. Argues that in addition to a pervasive color symbolism, the key symbols in the story are eyes, light, and the gaze.

58

ISAK DINESEN
Baroness Karen Blixen-Finecke
(1884-1962)
Denmark

General Biographical and Critical Studies

Gossman, Ann. "Sacramental Imagery in Two Stories by Isak Dinesen." In *Isak Dinesen, Storyteller*, edited by Aage Jorgensen. Aarhus, Denmark: Akademisk Boghandel, 1972.
An academic analysis of "Babette's Feast" and "Echoes," which reveals the imagery of the Christian Communion service. Primary focus is on the imagery of the sacrament in the two stories; both stories focus on an artist who, in trying to assert the self, struggles against adverse destiny.

Green, Howard. "Isak Dinesen." In *Isak Dinesen, Storyteller*, edited by Aage Jorgensen. Aarhus, Denmark: Akademisk Boghandel, 1972.
A general appreciation of Dinesen's art, which argues that her stories create a singular world whose unfamiliar atmosphere appeals to the most primitive human need for a story. Yet, beneath the mask of timelessness, Green says, lies the modern combination of irony and deliberate obscurity. He concludes that Dinesen's appeal is based on her narrative inventiveness and that the unique fascination of her work lies in the subtle mockery of her attitudes and the shimmering pattern that she creates.

Hannah, Donald. *'Isak Dinesen' and Karen Blixen: The Mask and the Reality*. New York: Putnam, 1971.
Summarizes the life of Dinesen in three phases: her youth, her sojourn in Africa, and her professional life as a writer. The biographical sections are particularly valuable in charting the development of Dinesen's aesthetic, especially Dinesen's emphasis on the nature of story, her masklike impersonality, and the nature of her characters. The second half of the book, devoted to Dinesen's art, focuses on her process of writing and the general characteristics of her stories.

Henriksen, Aage. "The Empty Space Between Art and Church." In *Out of Denmark*, edited by Bodil Warmberg. Copenhagen: Danish Cultural Institute, 1985.
Henriksen says that the underlying principle of all Dinesen's tales is the discovery that reality is transformed into a dream. Says that Dinesen's stories are based on the complicated nature of human love.

Johannesson, Eric O. *The World of Isak Dinesen*. Seattle: University of Washington Press, 1961.

An extended analysis of Dinesen's art rather than of her life, focusing on the pervasive theme of the art of storytelling. Johannesson illustrates Dinesen's treatment of characters as marionettes, her focus on epiphanies, her use of the oral tradition, her metaphoric style, and her theatricality and humor. Individual chapters focus on stories that reflect Dinesen's concern with the gothic, the mask, the marionette theater, and the code of the aristocracy.

Langbaum, Robert. *The Gayety of Vision: A Study of Isak Dinesen's Art*. New York: Random House, 1964.
The most thorough and profound study of Dinesen's imaginative vision. Langbaum places Dinesen in the context of modern fiction and shows how her fiction deals with a psychology deeper than that of the novel, a psychology on the level of myth.

Migel, Parmenia. *Titania: The Biography of Isak Dinesen*. New York: Random House, 1967.
Although this is the biography that Isak Dinesen herself commissioned, and although it is based on many hours of conversation with Dinesen, reviewers have criticized it for its exaggeration of Dinesen's aristocratic snobbishness. More recent biographers have argued that instead of the real Dinesen the book reflects the sort of self-caricature that Dinesen communicated to the adoring Migel.

Thurman, Judith. *Isak Dinesen: The Life of a Storyteller*. New York: St. Martin's Press, 1982.
The most detailed and factual biography of Dinesen, it is the first to make use of many letters and unpublished documents in Dinesen's archives. Although the book is biographical and not critical, it does contain helpful comments on the compositional history of many of the tales as well as many of their inspirational sources. Particularly helpful are the chapters on *Seven Gothic Tales* and *Winter's Tales*.

Walter, Eugene. "Isak Dinesen." In *Isak Dinesen, Storyteller*, edited by Aage Jorgensen. Aarhus, Denmark: Akademisk Boghandel, 1972.
An interview originally published in *The Paris Review*, in which Dinesen recounts how she began writing; she tells of her joy in humor, and startles her interviewer by saying she is three thousand years old and has dined with Socrates.

Wescott, Glenway. "Isak Dinesen, the Storyteller." In *Isak Dinesen, Storyteller*, edited by Aage Jorgensen. Aarhus, Denmark: Akademisk Boghandel, 1972.
An appreciation of Dinesen's work, particularly of *Out of Africa*, this essay also comments on Dinesen as a storyteller in the primitive mode. Wescott finds

that, unlike many modern writers, Dinesen silences her own personal misfortunes and depressed states of mind in her work.

Whissen, Thomas R. *Isak Dinesen's Aesthetics*. Port Washington, N.Y.: Kennikat Press, 1973.
A discussion of Dinesen's aesthetic theory drawn from analyses of her stories. The book is ordered according to the process of artistic creation: from inspiration, to embodiment, to reception. Drawing largely on such stories as "The Cardinal's First Tale," "Sorrow-Acre," and "The Poet," Whissen discusses the importance to Dinesen's aesthetic of the notions of masquerade, pride, and loneliness, and of the use of romance, tragedy, and comedy.

Selected Titles

"The Blank Page"
Whissen, Thomas R. *Isak Dinesen's Aesthetics*. Port Washington, N.Y.: Kennikat Press, 1973.
An explication of the story in terms of the importance of the audience to the tale. Whissen argues that the blank page suggests both all stains and no stains at once. Mythos or story can only reflect the infinite possibilities of reality by calling attention to something beyond itself, which is the purpose of the blank page in the story.

"The Deluge At Norderney"
Hannah, Donald. *'Isak Dinesen' and Karen Blixen: The Mask and the Reality*. New York: Putnam, 1971.
Discusses the story in terms of the theme of the relationship between a character's consciousness and the mask or role he or she plays, as well as the theme of characters acting within the Christlike spirit. Hannah also focuses on the inset story in the tale of "The Wine of the Tetrarch" as a reflection of Kasparson's taking his redemption into his own hands and becoming the master of his own destiny.

Johannesson, Eric O. *The World of Isak Dinesen*. Seattle: University of Washington Press, 1961.
Analyzes the story in terms of the theme of masks and role playing. Notes that often in Dinesen's work the mask is not always a deception; instead it reveals something of the spirit of the wearer. The philosophy of the mask in the story is both aristocratic and Romantic, says Johannesson, for it asserts that reality is a creation of the imagination and that one is judged by one's mask.

Langbaum, Robert. *The Gayety of Vision: A Study of Isak Dinesen's Art*. New York: Random House, 1964.

Langbaum calls this story Dinesen's supreme achievement in tragicomedy, combining the greatest number of her characteristic themes. In a long and detailed analysis of the story, Langbaum discusses the significance of the inset stories and explains how Kasparson and Miss Malin make an artwork of the night and are thus able to meet their deaths with fulfillment and self realization. Both the young couple and the old couple symbolize at the end of the story the whole progress of the imagination in the Romantic version of the myth of the fall.

"The Monkey"

Johannesson, Eric O. *The World of Isak Dinesen*. Seattle: University of Washington Press, 1961.

Johannesson says that this is Dinesen's finest gothic tale, complete with the various stylistic characteristics and thematic concerns of the gothic story. Notes that the central motif of the tale is the traditional gothic device of the double. As is typical of Dinesen's gothic tales, "The Monkey" deals with an individual who is trapped. Johannesson supports his thesis by noting the many images of imprisonment and escape in the story.

Langbaum, Robert. *The Gayety of Vision: A Study of Isak Dinesen's Art*. New York: Random House, 1964.

Considers this story to be as ambitious in scope as any of Dinesen's stories. Langbaum analyzes it primarily in terms of the prioress' double nature, suggested by the two stories—one Apollonian the other Dionysian—that she tells. The story ends, says Langbaum, with the prioress urging her auditors to obey both Apollo and Dionysus.

Phillips, Robert S. "Dinesen's 'Monkey' and McCullers' 'Ballad.' " In *Isak Dinesen, Storyteller*, edited by Aage Jorgensen. Aarhus, Denmark: Akademisk Boghandel, 1972.

Suggests that Dinesen's story "The Monkey" served as inspiration for Carson McCullers' novella *The Ballad of the Sad Café*. The essay presents a point-by-point comparison of the two works in terms of their atmosphere, their character configuration, their setting, and their thematic motifs. Both stories are derived from ancient fairy tales in which the supernatural world of giants is juxtaposed against the natural world of men.

"Roads Around Pisa"

Hannah, Donald. *'Isak Dinesen' and Karen Blixen: The Mask and the Reality*. New York: Putnam, 1971.

Focuses on the story-within-a-story, or Chinese-boxes structure of the tale, and its relationship to Dinesen's interest in the motif of the marionette theater. The main character, Augustus, is analyzed as one whose life is rooted in the real world for which he has no role. Unable to create his own identity, he finds it mirrored only in the minds of others.

Langbaum, Robert. *The Gayety of Vision: A Study of Isak Dinesen's Art*. New York: Random House, 1964.
  Discusses the "modern" theme of Augustus' search for identity, as well as the common Dinesen theme that life is to be understood through the analogy of art. The story reflects Dinesen's view that the artist is like God, who does not share in the flesh-and-blood life He creates. Langbaum sees the story as central to understanding Dinesen's art, especially her insistence that one does not get at truth except by artifice and tradition, that is, by assimilating a particular event to a recurring pattern or archetype.

"Sorrow-Acre"

Hannah, Donald. *'Isak Dinesen' and Karen Blixen: The Mask and the Reality*. New York: Putnam, 1971.
  Hannah points out that the source of the story is a Danish folktale, then notes the significant differences between the original and Dinesen's version, particularly the introduction of Adam as the new main character and the shift of the time from 1634 to 1775. Hannah argues that these changes were made in order to focus on the shift from the semifeudal eighteenth century to a new era; Adam serves as the new voice of criticism of the ways of the old lord of the manor.

Johannesson, Eric O. *The World of Isak Dinesen*. Seattle: University of Washington Press, 1961.
  Suggests that the story is Dinesen's most dramatic illustration of the aristocratic code that civilized individuals preserve the beauty and grace of life by making life into an elegant game. The story attempts to answer such related questions as, Why is life so precious and pitiless? and Is there a God who can temper necessity with mercy? Much of the analysis focuses on the conversations in the story, which, Johannesson argues, illustrate the difference between the aristocratic eighteenth century and the romantic nineteenth century.

Langbaum, Robert. *The Gayety of Vision: A Study of Isak Dinesen's Art*. New York: Random House, 1964.
  Says that the story is perhaps Dinesen's cruelest because she does not sentimentalize the reality that she wants to justify. Because the lord's cruelty transcends ordinary human compassion, it is an emblem of a truth beyond the human, a truth signified by adherence to ceremony. At the end of the story, Anne-Marie fulfills her role as a tragic victim of necessity.

MAXIM GORKY
(1868-1936)
Alexey Maximovich Peshkov
Russia

General Biographical and Critical Studies

Borras, F. M. *Maxim Gorky the Writer*. Oxford, England: Clarendon Press, 1967.
An interpretation of Gorky's work, with references to his life and his cultural framework. The chapter on his short fiction provides general readings of several stories, focusing primarily on the nature of the characters and the general theme of the disintegration of the human personality in his fiction.

Bowen, Elizabeth. "Bowen on Gorky." In *Storytellers and Their Art*, edited by Georgianne Trask and Charles Burkhart. Garden City, N.Y.: Doubleday, 1963.
Claims that even in the short story of the greatest integrity there has to be a sort of concealed trick—a fact of which Gorky was well aware. Argues that Gorky's aim in the short story was philosophic portraiture, to which he made action subordinate. Whatever limitations he has, they are the limitations of a master who has learned a technique too well.

Clowes, Edith W. *Maksim Gorky: A Reference Guide*. Boston: G. K. Hall, 1987.
A book-length annotated bibliography. The introduction is valuable for sketching out the basic problems in the study of Gorky. The primary bibliography includes all the publication data for both Russian and English editions of Gorky's works. The secondary bibliography, which encompasses most of the volume, provides a year-by-year checklist of commentary and criticism on Gorky.

Donchin, Georgette. "Gorky." In *Russian Literary Attitudes from Pushkin to Solzhenitsyn*, edited by Richard Freeborn. New York: Barnes & Noble Books, 1976.
An essay on Gorky, which attempts to place him within his biographical and historicosocial framework. Includes brief comments on the short stories, particularly in terms of his romanticism, his instinctivism, and his characters' search for an ideal.

Habermann, Gerhard. *Maksim Gorki*. Translated by Ernestine Schlant. New York: Frederick Ungar, 1971.
A monograph-length introduction to Gorky, mostly biographical in its focus, but with passing critical comments on the stories, primarily in terms of their publishing record and their biographical sources. A readable but sketchy overview with no extended interpretative discussions of the fiction.

Hare, Richard. *Maxim Gorky: Romantic Realist and Conservative Revolutionary*. London: Oxford University Press, 1962.
A short biography with brief summary critical remarks on Gorky's stories. Illustrates the various Russian character types featured in his stories, discusses his debt to folk legend, and outlines his role in the Russian Revolution as well as his later role as an emissary of Soviet culture. Very superficial discussions of the fiction.

Holtsman, Filia. *The Young Maxim Gorky: 1868-1902*. New York: Columbia University Press, 1948.
A biographical and critical study of Gorky's early life and literary career. Provides general thematic comments on the short stories and anecdotes about their sources. Discusses Gorky's debt to folklore tradition and genres as well as his social humanism and his literary relation to Chekhov and Tolstoy. Cursory comments on a number of short stories.

Kaun, Alexander. *Maxim Gorky and His Russia*. London: Jonathan Cape, 1931.
An early biography integrating Gorky's fiction and his reminiscences. Focuses on his participation in and reflection of his cultural milieu. A dramatic portrait of Gorky in the transition from the rule of the czars to the rule of the Bolsheviks. Places the stories within the context of Gorky's experience.

Lavrin, Janko. *From Pushkin to Mayakovsky: A Study in the Evolution of a Literature*. London: Sylvan Press, 1948.
In the chapter on Gorky in this study of nineteenth and early twentieth century Russian literature, Lavrin provides a brief critical summary of Gorky's fiction. Claims that nowhere else in all of Gorky's works is his faith in the latent value of the social outcast more emphatic than in the short story "Twenty-six Men and a Girl." Discusses Gorky generally as the people's author.

Levin, Dan. *Stormy Petrel: The Life and Work of Maxim Gorky*. New York: Appleton-Century-Crofts, 1965.
A popular biography. No real criticism of the stories, but contains brief general comments on such stories as "Chelkash" and "Twenty-six Men and a Girl" as a reflection of some of Gorky's social concerns early in his career. Discusses how the stories brought him fame. A readable first book on Gorky's life.

Lukács, Georg. *Studies in European Realism*. New York: Grosset & Dunlap, 1964.
Says that the main theme in Gorky's work is that men can no longer live as they have in the past. Gorky's humanism manifests itself in a fierce hatred of apathy and indifference. However, what is most valuable about Lukács' discussion is his analysis of those generic characteristics of the short story, which Gorky struggled to master. Argues that the short story offers Gorky the pos-

sibility of presenting the dialectic of social necessity by means of extreme cases.

Nabokov, Vladimir. "Maxim Gorky." In *Lectures on Russian Literature*, edited by Fredson Bowers. New York: Harcourt Brace Jovanovich, 1981.
A lecture on Gorky which summarizes his life and literary career. Claims that as a creative artist he is of little importance. Argues that because of the poverty of his art he always went after the striking and sensational subject. Asserts that "Twenty-six Men and a Girl" is an utterly false and sentimental story, "all pink candy with just that amount of soot clinging to it to make it attractive."

Olgin, Moissaye Joseph. *Maxim Gorky: Writer and Revolutionist*. New York: International, 1933.
A general, appreciative essay marking forty years of Gorky's literary career. Focuses on his socialism and his realism. Hails him as the father of Russian proletarian literature and the friend and guide of young proletarian writers. Not so much a work of literary criticism as it is a tribute to Gorky for his services to the working classes of the Soviet Union.

Ovcharenko, Alexander. *Maxim Gorky and the Literary Quests of the Twentieth Century*. Translated by Joy Jennings. Moscow: Raduga, 1978.
Although most of this study focuses on Gorky's epic controversial work *The Life of Klim Samgin*, it also contains a long chapter on the short stories and tales written between 1922 and 1925. Argues that Gorky's strength lies in the fact that his stories and parables never break away from reality, that they proceed more often from character than from plot.

Scherr, Barry. *Maxim Gorky*. Boston: Twayne, 1988.
An introduction to Gorky's life and art with chapters on the short story, the novels, the plays, and the memoirs. Provides brief critical discussions of several stories from early in Gorky's career, as well as a short chapter on the later collection, *Stories of 1922-1924*. A good introduction, which focuses on Gorky's artistic technique as well as his themes.

Weill, Irwin. *Gorky: His Literary Development and Influence on Soviet Intellectual Life*. New York: Random House, 1966.
Traces Gorky's literary career and analyzes his impact on Soviet culture. Discussions of the short stories focus on the development of his tramp figures early in his career. Brief comments on such stories as "Chelkash" and "Twenty-six Men and a Girl." Says that the style of the latter turns an otherwise crude story into a delicate impression.

Yarmolinksy, Avrahm. *The Russian Literary Imagination*. New York: Funk & Wagnalls, 1969.

A discussion of Gorky as the Soviet laureate, as a socialist and a democrat. Claims that he has serious faults as a short-story writer—for example, a weak narrative sense, a tendency to fall into bathos and fanciful imagery, a failure to refrain from sophomoric commentary, and the frequent need for heroic utterance. Primarily discusses his long fiction as representative of a voice from old Russia.

Selected Titles

"Chelkash"
Proffer, Carl R. "Chelkash." In *From Karamzin to Bunin*, edited by Proffer. Bloomington: Indiana University Press, 1969.
   Says that Gorky's favorite theme is the struggle between pride and pity and his favorite characters are strong, independent representatives of the lower classes. Argues that in "Chelkash" the dialogue is realistic whereas the narrative passages are romantic. Suggests that although this story succeeds, many of Gorky's other works fail when the romantic-realistic tendency develops into social realism.

Scherr, Barry. *Maxim Gorky*. Boston: Twayne, 1988.
   Argues that the story is Gorky's first extensive treatment of the vagabond hero, typifying Gorky's early stories in its presentation of the oppressiveness of daily life. Discusses Gorky's attempts to rework the story and thus correct his tendency to overwrite. Notes also the biographical element in the story.

"Makar Chudra"
Scherr, Barry. *Maxim Gorky*. Boston: Twayne, 1988.
   Discusses this early Gorky story in terms of its debt to folk legends. Argues that the metaphors and turns of phrases used by the characters in the story derive also from folklore. Says that the story is typical of Gorky's early style of narration in that the narrator is effaced from the story soon after he begins the tale.

"Twenty-six Men and a Girl"
Bartkovich, Jeffrey. "Maxim Gorky's 'Twenty-six Men and a Girl': The Destruction of an Illusion." *Studies in Short Fiction* 10 (Summer, 1973): 287-288.
   Argues that the story illustrates that Gorky is basically a nihilistic rather than a humanistic writer. Claims that just as the men tried to escape an understanding of their own condition in terms of their own humanity, they sought to explain their condition in a fantasized relation to an imaginative idol. The exploit of the soldier with Tanya forces them to confront the reality they have been trying to evade.

Gutsche, George. "The Role of the 'One' in Gorky's 'Twenty-six and One.' " In *Studies in Honor of Xenia Gasiorowska*, edited by Lauren G. Leighton. Columbus, Ohio: Slavica, 1983.
Focuses on the girl Tanya in terms of her moral and psychological relationship with the twenty-six men. Sees the girl as the dominant figure in the story — one of Gorky's types who challenge conventional morality. Says that it is an existential story insofar as it presents human beings in situations in which their actions lead to being authentically alive.

O'Toole, L. Michael. *Structure, Style and Interpretation in the Russian Short Story*. New Haven, Conn.: Yale University Press, 1982.
Discusses plot similarity between Gorky's story and Pushkin's "The Shot." Argues that Gorky's greatest achievement in the story is the control of the interplay between group and individual psychology, although the story is a brilliant revelation of the death in life of the collective consciousness and the reassertion of the life force in the individual.

Scherr, Barry. *Maxim Gorky*. Boston: Twayne, 1988.
Calls this Gorky's early masterpiece. Notes that its effectiveness is due to its tight structure, its evocative imagery, its sparse details, and its careful use of setting. Argues that the theme combines a statement on human nature with an insight into the relationship between the group and the individual.

Turner, C. J. G. " 'Iconoclasm' as a Structural Device in Three of Gorky's Stories." *The Modern Language Review* 67 (January, 1972): 141-150.
Discusses how the story sets up a religious image of the girl in the minds of the twenty-six men and the reader and then shatters that image. Shows how the narrator keeps the reader at a distance from the collective hero of the story.

HERMANN HESSE
(1877-1962)
Germany

General Biographical and Critical Studies

Boulby, Mark. *Hermann Hesse: His Mind and His Art*. Ithaca, N.Y.: Cornell University Press, 1967.
A detailed and extensive analysis of the major novels in terms of their symbolic patterns and Hesse's search for insight. Occasional comments on the short stories indicate the relationship of their themes to the themes of the novels. Boulby's discussion of the stories of the so-called Gaienhofen period focus on Hesse's debt to Gottfried Keller; notes the penetrating poetic and psychological style of the stories.

Field, George Wallis. *Hermann Hesse*. Boston: Twayne, 1970.
A general introduction, focusing on the major works. No discussion of the short stories, except some brief mention of the novellas and the fairy tales. A readable overview of Hesse's themes and techniques written for the lay person. Includes a chronology of Hesse's life and a bibliography.

Freedman, Ralph. *Hermann Hesse: Pilgrim of Crisis.* New York: Pantheon Books, 1978.
A full-length scholarly biography with many scattered comments on the short stories, particularly the background to the Gaienhofen period when many of them were written. Not a critical study, but it does provide plot sources of some of the stories and brief comments on their publishing history and reception.

_____ . *The Lyrical Novel*. Princeton, N.J.: Princeton University Press, 1963.
Although the focus here is on Hesse's novels rather than on his short stories, Freedman's discussion of the lyrical nature of Hesse's prose is helpful in understanding the basic narrative style and techniques of his work. A valuable genre study, for the lyricism of Hesse's fiction is even more obviously seen in his short fiction than in his novels.

Mileck, Joseph. *Hermann Hesse: Life and Art*. Berkeley: University of California Press, 1978.
A critical biography, complete with analyses of the major novels and a chronological account of Hesse's literary career. Only passing comments on the short stories, mainly noting their publishing record or their biographical sources.

However, this is a valuable book for clarifying the major Hesse themes as well as summarizing his critical reputation.

_____ . *Hermann Hesse and His Critics*. New York: AMS Press, Inc., 1966.
A helpful reference work on Hesse that includes a brief biographical sketch, a summary of books and articles appearing on Hesse through 1955, and a bibliography of works by and about Hesse. The section on Hesse's critics is particularly helpful, for it summarizes many books and articles that have not been translated from the German. The discussions of the criticism are organized around basic themes such as youth, nature, music, religion, and the cultural climate of Hesse's milieu.

Norton, Roger C. *Hermann Hesse's Futuristic Idealism*. Frankfurt: Peter Long, 1973.
In this study of Hesse's futurism, primarily in *The Glass Bead Game*, Norton notes that in two of Hesse's stories, "An Evening with Dr. Faust" and "A Man by the Name of Ziegler," he satirizes humankind's worship of technology, for he sees that such worship will result in a return to a speechless, primitive state, destroying human individuality and expression.

Rose, Ernst. *Faith from the Abyss: Hermann Hesse's Way from Romanticism to Modernity*. New York: New York University Press, 1965.
This study of the major novels focuses on the development of Hesse's narrative art from the Romanticism of the nineteenth century to the modernism of the twentieth century. Although the brief discussion of the short fiction focuses mainly on how they reflect the themes and techniques of the novels, this study is useful for understanding Hesse's artistic development. Rose calls attention to the Romantic and impressionistic style of the early lyrical stories.

Sorell, Walter. *Hermann Hesse: The Man Who Sought and Found Himself*. London: Oswald Wolff, 1974.
A brief monograph, half devoted to biography and half to criticism. Largely a discussion of Hesse's most common themes, the study stresses the relationship between his poetic awareness and his prose fiction. No discussion of the short fiction here, but contains chapters on how Hesse's interest in music, nature, and painting is reflected in his fiction.

Stelzig, Eugene L. *Hermann Hesse's Fictions of the Self*. Princeton, N.J.: Princeton University Press, 1988.
Focuses on the confessional nature of Hesse's fiction and Hesse as an autobiographical writer. After an introductory chapter on the generic nature of autobiography and confessional fiction, the book centers on parallels between events in Hesse's past and events described in his novels. Although the major

emphasis here is on the novels, a brief section on the Gaienhofen stories deal with their concern with family and community pressures.

Ziolkowski, Theodore. *Hermann Hesse*. New York: Columbia University Press, 1966.
A short monograph or essay by one of the best-known and most respected critics of Hesse's work. Although it does not discuss any of the novels in detail and hardly mentions the short stories at all, it is a good first book to read in order to become oriented to Hesse's most typical thematic concerns and fictional techniques.

_____ . Introduction to *Stories of Five Decades* by Hermann Hesse. New York: Farrar, Straus & Giroux, 1972.
A discussion of Hesse's search for a prose style. Notes that with such stories as "A Man by the Name of Ziegler" and "An Evening with Dr. Faust" one has a foretaste of the surreal style of the major novels of the 1920's and 1930's. Discusses the biographical and literary sources of his stories.

_____ . *The Novels of Hermann Hesse: A Study in Theme and Structure*. Princeton, N.J.: Princeton University Press, 1965.
Primarily a discussion of Hesse's craftsmanship, with structural analyses of the major novels. Notes the development of Hesse's work as he attempted to formulate the vision of an ideal; also discusses the major Hesse themes. Although there is no discussion of the short stories, this study is valuable for understanding Hesse's fictional techniques.

Selected Titles

"The Poet"

Howard, Patricia J. "Hermann Hesse's 'Der Dichter': The Artist/Sage as Vessel Dissolving Paradox." *Comparative Literature Studies* 22 (Spring, 1985): 110-119.
Points out that the story deserves further attention because it foreshadows many of Hesse's later themes, especially the idea of the artist performing a special and magical role in apprehending the unity of nature and spirit, art and science. Analyzes the circular structure of the story.

"Walter Kompff"

Stelzig, Eugene L. *Hermann Hesse's Fictions of the Self*. Princeton, N.J.: Princeton University Press, 1988.
Describing this story as a bleak satire on the stifling of individuality by a callous society, Stelzig calls the protagonist's dilemma in the story a grotesquely simplified mirror image of Hesse's own situation at Gaienhofen, for he could not be true to himself because of his attachment to middle-class life.

FRANZ KAFKA
(1883-1924)
Czechoslovakia

General Biographical and Critical Studies

Asher, J. A. "Turning-Points in Kafka's Stories." *The Modern Language Review* 57 (1962): 47-52.
Describes the basic structure of Kafka's stories as a three-part pattern: normal beginning, turning point, dreamlike ending. Briefly discusses "In the Penal Colony," "The Judgment," "A Country Doctor," and others to illustrate the typical pattern of Kafka's stories. Also notes the relationship between Kafka's stories and dreams, using citations from Kafka's diaries for support.

Auden, W. H. "The I Without a Self." In his *The Dyer's Hand*. New York: Random House, 1962.
States that his finest works can be found in the collection of stories *The Great Wall of China*. Argues that in a typical Kafka story the goal is peculiar to the hero and that the Kafka hero differs from the traditional hero in that he must always ask, "What must I do?" Briefly discusses the narrator hero of "The Burrow."

Brod, Max. *Franz Kafka*. New York: Schocken Books, 1947.
An early biography written by Kafka's friend and thus based on conversations with Kafka and personal observations of his activities; also contains a number of letters. The most frequently cited study of Kafka's life, this book is essential for anyone wishing to understand the relationship between Kafka's life and his work. However, Brod's interpretation of Kafka's psychic life has been a frequent subject of contention by critics.

Corngold, Stanley. "Kafka's Other Metamorphosis." In *Kafka and the Contemporary Critical Performance*, edited by Alan Udoff. Bloomington: Indiana University Press, 1987.
Discussion of Kafka's use of metaphor to expose the way metaphors work. Analyzes several stories briefly to illustrate his point. Makes use of the theories of Paul de Man to show how Kafka deconstructs metaphor.

Foulkes, A. P. *The Reluctant Pessimist: A Study of Franz Kafka*. The Hague, Netherlands: Mouton, 1967.
Argues that Kafka's works cannot be understood without some understanding of the pessimistic spirit in which they were written. Briefly discusses several of the major stories from the point of view of two different spheres of reality.

Kafka's position between the two realities makes him despair on the one hand because of the truth he has unveiled, and distressed on the other hand by the forces determined to conceal this truth.

Gooden, Christian. "Points of Departure." In *The Kafka Debate*, edited by Angel Flores. New York: Gordian Press, 1977.
Argues that Kafka's characters are not characterized by negativity and despair, but rather by an "apparent" negativity, which conceals a temporary, frustrated optimism. Gooden briefly discusses "The Burrow," "Josephine the Singer: Or, The Mouse Folk," and other stories to support his argument.

Goodman, Paul. *Kafka's Prayer*. New York: Vanguard Press, 1947.
An idiosyncratic early study of Kafka, written at the very beginning of the so-called Kafka vogue. No extended analyses of any of the major stories; instead Goodman provides a philosophical and personal encounter with Kafka, beginning with his aphorisms and running through *The Castle*. An exploration of the truth in the thought of Kafka from the point of view of writing as prayer.

Gordon, Caroline. "Notes on Hemingway and Kafka." In *Kafka: A Collection of Critical Essays*, edited by Ronald Gray. Englewood-Cliffs, N.J.: Prentice-Hall, 1962.
Compares briefly some of Ernest Hemingway's stories with the stories of Kafka; claims that both authors are masters of naturalism. Discusses "The Hunter Gracchus" in particular and notes how Kafka uses devices in the story that were also used by Hemingway

Grandin, John M. "Defenestrations." In *The Kafka Debate*, edited by Angel Flores. New York: Gordian Press, 1977.
Discussion of windows as a significant recurring motif in Kafka's works, referring to the role of windows in "The Judgment" and "The Metamorphosis": Both Georg and Gregor rely on windows as an access to life.

Gray, Ronald. *Franz Kafka*. Cambridge, England: Cambridge University Press, 1973.
An introduction to Kafka's life and art with discussions of the major works, including the biographical sources and publishing histories of the stories. Detailed analyses of half a dozen major stories as well as brief discussions of the minor stories. Concludes with a discussion of Kafka's religious ideas.

Greenberg, Martin. *The Terror of Art: Kafka and Modern Literature*. New York: Basic Books, 1968.
An attempt to trace the evolution of what Greenberg calls Kafka's dream narrative form from its beginnings to *The Castle*. Discusses the relationship

between art and dreams and establishes Kafka's imagination as a psychoanalytic one because he intuitively was aware of the split in the self. Discusses three of the major stories and makes passing references to many minor ones.

Hall, Calvin S., and Richard E. Lind. *A Study of Franz Kafka*. Chapel Hill: University of North Carolina Press, 1970.
Not a book of literary criticism, but rather a study of the relationship between Kafka's dreams, as recorded in his diaries, and his life. The dreams are not analyzed in terms of Freudian or Jungian content analysis, but rather in terms of quantitative methods devised by Hall. The book also contains a chapter focusing on a content analysis of the novels, using the same methods as the dream analysis.

Hayman, Ronald. *Kafka: A Biography*. New York: Oxford University Press, 1982.
A detailed interpretative biography. Numerous references to the short stories, both in terms of their biographical context and in terms of their reflection of Kafka's psyche. A very readable biography. Contains several photographs. Hayman argues that for Kafka writing was not so much an alternative to life as it was a terminal cure for it.

Heller, Erich. *Franz Kafka*. New York: Viking Press, 1974.
A short monograph on Kafka's works with chapters on the major novels and a brief discussion of some of the short stories. Focuses on the effect of Kafka's relationship with Felice Bauer on his work. One chapter, for example, is on Kafka's love letters to her.

Hughes, Kenneth, ed. and trans. *Franz Kafka: A Collection of Marxist Criticism*. Hanover, N.H.: University Press of New England, 1981.
An anthology of previously published, but not previously translated, essays on Kafka by Soviet and German Marxist critics from the late 1950's to the early 1980's. None of the essays focuses on the short stories and few mention them at all. Most of the discussions are general analyses of Kafka and modern art, Kafka and the socialist world. Hughes says that no other writer has so divided Marxist critics as Kafka has.

Kuna, Franz. *Franz Kafka: Literature as Corrective Punishment*. Bloomington: Indiana University Press, 1974.
An analysis of the philosophic assumptions on which Kafka's writings are based. Primary focus is on the novels, emphasizing the biographical elements in *The Trial* and the metaphysical elements in *The Castle*. Includes chapters on Kafka's masochistic disposition, his literary and cultural background, and "The Metamorphosis."

Lawson, Richard. *Franz Kafka*. New York: Frederick Ungar, 1987.
A general introduction to Kafka's works, with brief discussions of a large number of the short stories. A good initial book to read on Kafka, for the interpretations are general enough not to be forbidding, yet the study provides an orientation to Kafka's work that should make a later study of his themes and techniques easier.

McElroy, Bernard. "The Art of Projective Thinking: Franz Kafka and the Paranoid Vision." *Modern Fiction Studies* 32 (Summer, 1985): 217-232.
Discusses projective thinking, an essential element of paranoia, as the basis of Kafka's literary technique. The paranoiac experiences inner fears and guilt as coming from the outside world. Briefly discusses "The Judgment" and "The Metamorphosis" from this point of view. Also notes other categories of projective thinking, such as the paranoid's sense of centrality, grandiosity, and the fear of loss of autonomy.

Magny, Claude-Edmonde. "The Objective Depiction of Absurdity." In *The Kafka Problem*, edited by Angel Flores. New York: New Directions, 1946.
States that it is the union of realism and mysticism that gives Kafka's work its exceptional value. According to Magny, Kafka perceives in the most trivial things a profound significance.

Modern Fiction Studies 8 (Spring, 1962).
A special issue on Kafka, with essays on individual stories and novels, as well as general essays on his thought, his language, his obscurity, and his characters. Also includes a checklist of criticism.

Neider, Charles. *The Frozen Sea: A Study of Franz Kafka*. New York: Oxford University Press, 1948.
In the brief chapter on Kafka's short fiction, Neider comments on most of the major stories, but claims that they lack emotional and spiritual complexity. Argues that Kafka's novellas are highly imaginative but that they approach to allegory at the expense of symbolism. Focus is on the motif of the irrational and the influence of Freud.

Parry, Indris. "Kafka, Gogol and Nathanael West." In *Kafka: A Collection of Critical Essays*, edited by Ronald Gray. Englewood Cliffs, N.J.: Prentice-Hall, 1962.
Compares Nikolai Gogol and Kafka with regard to their use of precise detail. Focuses particularly on the central images in Gogol's "The Nose" and Kafka's "The Metamorphosis." Also notes the hands of Homer Simpson in West's *The Day of the Locust*. A discussion of how physical objects in the work of the three writers assume an independent existence of their own.

Pascal, Roy. *Kafka's Narrators: A Study of His Stories and Sketches*. New York: Cambridge University Press, 1982.
The most thorough single study of Kafka's short fiction. The focus is on Kafka's narrative voice, with a general introduction to the structure and meaning of Kafka's short fiction and individual chapters on several of the major stories.

——————— . "Kafka's Parables: Ways Out of the Dead End." In *The World of Franz Kafka*, edited by J. P. Stern. New York: Holt, Rinehart and Winston, 1980.
Cites three brief Kafka parables and argues that although they set up an expectation of a coherent and meaningful ending, the ending is actually never reached. Discusses several humorous sketches and argues that they provide a different slant on evading despair than the stories.

Pasley, Malcolm. "Semi-Private Games." In *The Kafka Debate*, edited by Angel Flores. New York: Gordian Press, 1977.
Discussion of Kafka's covert jokes and puns and his literary allusions, both to his own texts and to the texts of others. Discusses several stories, especially those in the *A Country Doctor* collection, to illustrate Kafka's "semi-private games."

Pawel, Ernst. *The Nightmare of Reason: A Life of Franz Kafka*. New York: Farrar, Straus & Giroux, 1984.
Focuses on Kafka's Jewishness, his relationship with his parents, his relationship with women, and his friends. Although this book is not a critical biography and does not analyze the stories, it is nevertheless a valuable resource since so many of Kafka's stories are based on his life. A highly praised biography filled with details as well as the author's interpretations of the events and motivations of Kafka's life.

Politzer, Heinz. "Frank Kafka's Language." *Modern Fiction Studies* 8 (Spring, 1962): 16-22.
Argues that Kafka's language is oriented more toward questions than toward statements. Notes that Kafka often uses the device of exposing language itself as an instrument of deceit. Shows how Kafka attempts to conquer the treacherous nature of language through paradox and wordplay.

——————— . *Parable and Paradox*. Ithaca, N.Y.: Cornell University Press, 1962, rev. ed. 1966.
A study of Kafka's style, focusing particularly on his imagery. The paradox of Kafka's parables is that instead of bridging the gap between the empirical and the mysterious they reveal and perpetuate this gap in an insoluble enigma.

Argues that Kafka's genius lies in his ability to present the opaque content of each parable in narrative structures as clear as crystal.

Rahv, Philip. "An Introduction to Kafka." In his *Image and Idea*. New York: New Directions, 1957.
This essay, which originally appeared as the introduction to the Modern Library edition of *Selected Stories of Franz Kafka*, discusses Kafka's combination of the subjective and the objective, the real and the unreal, the factual world and the dream world. Briefly discusses Kafka's themes in several of the major short stories.

Robertson, Ritchie. *Kafka: Judaism, Politics, and Literature*. New York: Oxford University Press, 1985.
A detailed study of Kafka's exploration of Judaism, his use of Jewish images and allusions in his works, his concern with the Zionist movement, and the sources of his thought and art. The one long chapter on the shorter fiction is not so much a discussion of the major stories as it is a running commentary on Jewish allusions in many of the minor stories.

Rolleston, James. *Kafka's Narrative Theater*. University Park: Pennsylvania State University Press, 1974.
A small book focusing on several of Kafka's individual works, mostly from the point of view of the metaphor of theater. Discusses Kafka's heroes in terms of their existence within a closed structure, in which they are cast unwillingly in the central role of a drama beyond their control.

_____ . "Kafka's Time Machines." In *Franz Kafka (1883-1983): His Craft and Thought*, edited by Roman Struc and J. C. Yardley. Waterloo, Ontario, Canada: Wilfred Laurier University Press, 1986.
Notes Kafka's debt to Gustave Flaubert; argues that a radical difference between the two authors is that whereas Flaubert's work is conditioned by nineteenth century realistic style, Kafka's is conditioned by the impossibility of that style. Discusses Kafka as a direct exponent of Romantic poetics with its assumption that fantasy invents the world.

Roth, Philip. " 'I Always Wanted You to Admire My Fasting'; or, Looking at Kafka." In his *Reading Myself and Others*. New York: Farrar, Straus & Giroux, 1975.
A personal account of an imaginative, intellectual encounter with Kafka by a modern novelist and admirer of his works. The first half of the essay is a conventional biographical and critical treatment; the second half is a fictional account of a nine-year-old boy's fantasies about his Hebrew teacher, whose name is Franz Kafka.

Schwartz, Egon. "Kafka's Animal Tales and the Tradition of the European Fable." In *Franz Kafka (1883-1983): His Craft and Thought*, edited by Roman Struc and J. C. Yardley. Waterloo, Ontario, Canada: Wilfred Laurier University Press, 1986.
A discussion of the animal fable genre and the extent to which it sheds light on a number of Kafka texts. Discusses various fable motifs in Kafka's stories. Notes that Kafka reformed the fable form by making them into uninterpretable riddles. Claims that Kafka's animal fables are indices of an antiutopian world.

Sharp, Daryl. *The Secret Raven: Conflict and Transformation in the Life of Franz Kafka*. Toronto: Inner City Books, 1980.
A Jungian interpretation of Kafka as a twentieth century man whose personal neurosis reflects the neurosis of the modern age. Not an analysis of his work, but rather an attempt to clarify some of the psychological factors of his conflicts, paying particular attention to Kafka's dreams.

Sokel, Walter H. "Freud and the Magic of Kafka's Writing." In *The World of Franz Kafka*, edited by J. P. Stern. New York: Holt, Rinehart and Winston, 1980.
Notes that Kafka shared Sigmund Freud's view on the importance of childhood experiences. Discusses the relationship between the fantastic in Kafka's works and the Freudian notion of repression and projection. Uses "The Metamorphosis" as his primary example of the connection. Argues that the convergences of Kafka's and Freud's views are numerous and profound.

Spahr, Blake Lee. "Frank Kafka: The Bridge and the Abyss." *Modern Fiction Studies* 8 (Spring, 1962): 3-15.
Uses the metaphor of the bridge, derived from one of Kafka's short sketches, to represent the various tensions in his works. Man is poised like a bridge in a state of tension over the abyss of destruction, possessing the knowledge to act but lacking the strength to act.

Spann, Meno. *Franz Kafka*. Boston: Twayne, 1976.
A general introduction to Kafka, with chapters on the teachers who influenced him, his adult life, his literary style, and the major stories and novels. Much of the book is a summary of previous criticism rather than original interpretations. Also includes a checklist of criticisms and a chronology of Kafka's life.

Sparks, Kimberly. "Radicalization of Space in Kafka's Stories." In *On Kafka: Semi-Centenary Perspectives*, edited by Franz Kuna. New York: Barnes & Noble Books, 1976.
A discussion of the development of the concept of spatialized time in modern literature, followed by an analysis of Kafka's stories, particularly "The Judgment," in terms of the spatialization of time. Argues that even his most

conscious and apparently sophisticated characters experience space and time in primitive ways.

Spilka, Mark. *Dickens and Kafka: A Mutual Interpretation*. Gloucester, Mass.: Peter Smith, 1969.
Roughly half of this book compares Charles Dickens' *David Copperfield* and *Bleak House* with Kafka's *Amerika* and *The Trial*. The first half of the study, however, generally discusses the influence of Dickens on Kafka, especially Kafka's recognition that he had a psychological bond with Dickens. Also discusses the form of comedy that both authors develop out of their shared "arrested sensibility."

Sussman, Henry. *Franz Kafka: Geometrician of Metaphor*. Madison, Wis.: Coda Press, 1979.
A poststructuralist approach to Kafka, focusing on his experiments into the nature of the literary image, particularly the relations of language to logic. Provides a background to this approach by surveying previous Kafka criticism, especially the essay on Kafka by Walter Benjamin. Includes chapters on three major novels and the story "The Burrow."

Szanto, George H. *Narrative Consciousness*. Austin: University of Texas Press, 1972.
Discussion of Kafka's narrators and how the narrative never goes beyond what the main character sees in his immediate situation. Includes comments on this aspect of narrative consciousness on "The Judgment," "The Metamorphosis," and "Josephine the Singer."

Thorlby, Anthony. "Anti-Mimesis: Kafka and Wittgenstein." In *On Kafka: Semi-Centenary Perspectives*, edited by Franz Kuna. New York: Barnes and Noble Books, 1976.
A study of Kafka's writings in terms of how they relate to the writing itself. Argues that there is no conceivable structure of reality behind his texts that can be separated from the structure of their utterance. Kafka offers a view of the play of ordinary language around a basically incomprehensible reality. In Ludwig Wittgenstein's terms, language for Kafka is seen to be entirely a function of the circumstances in which it is used.

——————— . "Kafka and Language." In *The World of Franz Kafka*, edited by J. P. Stern. New York: Holt, Rinehart and Winston, 1980.
A discussion of Kafka's observations about language and writing, as well as his way of using language to tell a story. Uses "Josephine the Singer: Or, The Mouse Folk" and "The Burrow," both stories about Kafka's own art, to make his points. Argues that Kafka's fiction is often concerned with its own processes.

White, J. J. "Endings and Non-endings in Kafka's Fiction." In *On Kafka: Semi-Centenary Perspectives*, edited by Franz Kuna. New York: Barnes & Noble Books, 1976.

A discussion of the problem of endings in Kafka's fiction, especially the short stories. Discusses those stories that seem to have resolved endings and those that remain as fragments without endings. Notes that it is not always easy to distinguish between the tales that Kafka completed and those that he did not, for it has been argued that Kafka never forcefully brought any of his works to a close.

Selected Titles

"The Burrow"

Coetzee, J. M. "Time, Tense and Aspect in Kafka's' The Burrow.' " *Modern Language Notes* 96 (April, 1981): 556-579.

An analysis of the relationship between the linguistic style of the story and its narrative structure. Points out the difficulty in laying out the events in a temporal order. Discusses previous critics who have dealt with this problem, and explains the time scheme of the story.

Pasley, Malcolm. "The Burrow." In *The Kafka Debate*, edited by Angel Flores. New York: Gordian Press, 1977.

Discusses the burrow in the story as both an image of Kafka's work and an image of his inner self. Also notes that the story radiates thematic images of the mother figure and the grave.

Politzer, Heinz. *Parable and Paradox*. Ithaca, N.Y.: Cornell University Press, 1962, rev. ed. 1966.

Says that in an almost allegorical way the story is a metaphor for the body of Kafka's work; the reader passes through Kafka's books when he follows the animal through the corridors of its cave. To the animal the burrow represents a work of creation, a solid element among the nightmarish uncertainties of life. Argues that the story crowns Kafka's late development by revealing the literary and personal roots of his metaphysical conflict.

Sussman, Henry. *Franz Kafka: Geometrician of Metaphor*. Madison, Wis.: Coda Press, 1979.

A deconstructive analysis of the problem of duplicity in the story—the uncontrollable opposites between appearance and reality, transparency and obscurity, mastery and subjection. Discusses the effect of the incorporation of the literal within the metaphoric on the structure of the work.

Weigand, Hermann J. "Franz Kafka's 'The Burrow' ('Der Bau'): An Analytical Essay." *PMLA* 87 (March, 1972): 152-166.
Avoids a symbolic interpretation of the story to analyze it in terms of its own data. Looks at the content of the story as well as its formal pattern as discourse. Focuses on the sexual anxieties suggested by the story, such as the animal's refusal to enter the maze and the fantasies he has that someone is staring at his sexual organs.

"The Country Doctor"

Brancato, John J. "Kafka's 'A Country Doctor': A Tale for Our Time." *Studies in Short Fiction* 15 (Spring, 1978): 173-176.
Discusses the story as a metaphor for the failure of scientific man to assuage the pain of dying. The dreamlike incidents objectify the doctor's sense of futility against the bitter truth that everyone must die and that science fares no better than religion in relieving the pain of this horrible knowledge.

Busacca, Basil. "A Country Doctor." In *Franz Kafka Today*, edited by Angel Flores and Homer Swander. Madison: University of Wisconsin Press, 1958.
In this story a doctor is shocked out of the rational, orderly world into a world in which order is but a limited and fallible human construct. Discusses several possible interpretations of the story: doctor as medical man who sacrifices everything for his patient; doctor as being roused by homosexual desires; the story as an ironic history of the Jews.

Church, Margaret. "Kafka's 'A Country Doctor.' " In *Literary Symbolism*, edited by Maurice Beebe. Belmont, Calif.: Wadsworth, 1960.
Discusses the quest theme in the story, focusing on the alienation and frustrations of man in seeking a goal. Argues that it is not possible to interpret the story in narrow religious terms or in narrow Freudian terms; the action of the story takes place in a more general arena.

Cooperman, Stanley. "Kafka's 'A Country Doctor': Microcosm of Symbolism." In *Literary Symbolism*, edited by Maurice Beebe. Belmont, Calif.: Wadsworth, 1960.
States that the reader must accept a simple dream narrative as the literal level of the story, since only a dream can provide any literal meaning at all. As a dream, the story can be interpreted psychoanalytically. Also argues that the story is a symbolic restatement of the classic existential situation of being isolated in a meaningless and hostile universe.

Gardner, John, and Lennis Dunlap, eds. *The Forms of Fiction*. New York: Random House, 1962.

Discusses the story as a nightmare flowing in a single chaotic stream, rendering a conventional paragraph structure impossible. Says that the doctor is the modern scientific man who is a failure as a man. He is judge, advisor, and agent, and he fails in each of these roles. Discusses a number of religious and psychological symbols in the story.

Gray, Ronald. *Franz Kafka*. Cambridge, England: Cambridge University Press, 1973.

Terms it the most dreamlike of all Kafka's stories, with a remarkable nightmarish quality. The general point of the story is that answering the call of charity as the doctor does is misguided and leads to disaster. However, the story offers no alternatives, says Gray, which may suggest that all alternatives are bad.

Lainoff, Seymour. "The Country Doctors of Kafka and Turgenev." *Symposium* 16 (1966): 130-135.

Compares the realism of Ivan Turgenev's story "The District Doctor" with the dream allegory of Kafka's story "A Country Doctor." Notes the difference in theme: Turgenev focuses on the failure of a love relationship, while Kafka deals with the disorder of the institutions of both family and religion. Discusses the comparative complexity of style and symbol in Kafka's story.

Marson, Eric, and Keith Leopold. "Kafka, Freud, and 'Ein Landarzt.' " *The German Quarterly* 37 (1964): 146-160.

Asserts that the story is an illustration of Kafka's attitude toward Freudian psychology. Traces Kafka's remarks about psychoanalysis in his correspondence and then analyzes the story to show that Kafka believed that psychological illness exists and that a psychoanalyst can reveal it. Also argues that the story is in the form of a dream, according to the laws of dream work in Sigmund Freud's *The Interpretation of Dreams*.

Spann, Meno. *Franz Kafka*. Boston: Twayne, 1976.

States that the meaning of the story lies in the metaphorical expression of gloom and despair at the end. The story offers a prime image of humanity's dehumanization. Rejects Christian allegorical readings of the story.

"A Fratricide"

Wolkenfield, Suzanne. "Psychological Disintegration in Kafka's 'A Fratricide' and 'An Old Manuscript.' " *Studies in Short Fiction* 13 (Winter, 1976): 25-29.

Discusses how the two works illuminate how Kafka's conviction of the inability to achieve psychological integration conditions his perception of the relationships between the individual and society and the individual and God.

The key to the mystery of the story is Kafka's characterization of each of the figures in it as an aspect of the human psyche.

"The Great Wall of China"

Gooden, Christian. "The Great Wall of China: The Elaboration of an Intellectual Dilemma." In *On Kafka: Semi-Centenary Perspectives*, edited by Franz Kuna. New York: Barnes & Noble Books, 1976.

A detailed analysis of the story, which argues that the building of the wall has some other objective than its completion, which hides an ulterior motive. The building of the wall serves as a collective escape from a disconcerting nothingness, giving the people a sense of purpose and a reason for being.

Greenberg, Clement. "At the Building of the Great Wall of China." In *Franz Kafka Today*, edited by Angel Flores and Homer Swander. Madison: University of Wisconsin Press, 1958.

Discusses the great wall as a symbol of Jewish law and China as an image of the Diaspora. Furthermore, the wall represents more than Jewish law, for it alludes to the entire human condition. Argues that the art of the story consists of the interweaving of motives that enter as ideas rather than acts or events.

"A Hunger Artist"

Mitchell, Breon. "Kafka and the Hunger Artists." In *Kafka and the Contemporary Critical Performance*, edited by Alan Udoff. Bloomington: Indiana University Press, 1987.

Shows how Kafka drew on newspapers and contemporary scientific studies of his day for the specific details and language of the story. Discusses several historical hunger artists to show the intertextual complexity of the narrative voice.

Moyer, Patricia. "Time and the Artist in Kafka and Hawthorne." *Modern Fiction Studies* 4 (Winter, 1958/1959): 295-306.

Compares the story to Nathaniel Hawthorne's "The Artist of the Beautiful" as reflections of the authors' views on the artist's position in the modern world. However, also notes that the basic differences in the stories reflect Hawthorne's dualism and Kafka's monism. Even though "A Hunger Artist" is unique among Kafka's works for its concept of actual time, it still suggests simultaneity.

Pascal, Roy. *Kafka's Narrators: A Study of His Stories and Sketches*. New York: Cambridge University Press, 1982.

A closely detailed analysis of the narrator's role in the story. Argues that the narrator is not the objective narrator of Kafka's earlier stories. Describes him as an echo of the impresario, a comic character. The personalization of the narrator suggests a profound reflection on the complexity of life and suffering, for it allows the reader to view the tragedy of the situation from more than one angle.

Politzer, Heinz. *Frank Kafka: Parable and Paradox*. Ithaca, N.Y.: Cornell University Press, 1962.

Notes the paradox of the artist's art as a negative act, a passive performance. The hunger artist shares with Kafka an insatiable need for spiritual security; yet in this story art is fatal, because it can be perfected only by the artist's death. The hunger artist's problem is a paradox that cannot be resolved.

Sheppard, Richard W. "Kafka's *Ein Hungerkünstler*: A Reconsideration." *The German Quarterly* 46 (1973): 219-233.

Discusses the role of the narrator of the story. Examines the narrator's diction and syntax to conclude that he is a bureaucrat who is incapable of dealing with the complex problems before him. Throughout the story his vision is distorted by false priorities, misplaced emphases, and a quirky perspective. Readers realize with shock that they have been fooled by identifying with an unreliable narrator.

Spann, Meno. *Franz Kafka*. Boston: Twayne, 1976.

Rejects religious interpretations of the story. Discusses the autobiographical aspects, arguing that Kafka realizes through the artist that uniqueness is not greatness.

Stallman, R. W. "A Hunger Artist." In *Franz Kafka Today*, edited by Angel Flores and Homer Swander. Madison: University of Wisconsin Press, 1958.

States that the story presents a critique of the philosophical problem that complete detachment from physical reality implies spiritual death. In Kafka's allegories, images have different meanings at different times.

Steinhauer, Harry. "Hungering Artist or Artist in Hungering: Kafka's 'A Hunger Artist.' " *Criticism: A Quarterly for Literature and the Arts* 4 (1962): 28-43.

Argues against the common interpretation that the story is an allegory of the artist's role in modern society. Instead, the story concerns the tragedy of hungering, that is, ascetic idealism. As such, the story is a phenomenology of religion. Discusses the work as an allegory of the history of organized religion.

"The Hunter Gracchus"

Steinberg, Erwin. "The Three Fragments of Kafka's 'The Hunter Gracchus.' " *Studies in Short Fiction* 15 (Summer, 1978): 307-317.

Discusses three fragments, or false starts, of the story in terms of the myths and archetypes Kafka used in them. Notes parallels in Vergil's the *Aeneid* as well as myths discussed by James Frazer in *The Golden Bough*. Concludes that the highly allusive fragments express the alienation of the artist in the twentieth century.

"In the Penal Colony"

Fickert, Kurt J. "A Literal Interpretation of 'In the Penal Colony.' " *Modern Fiction Studies* 17 (Spring, 1971): 31-36.

Analyzes the story in terms of the interrelationship among the three episodes and the many details that make the nightmarish event seem real. Argues that the story ends with a refutation of the premise with which it began—that God created the world as a penal colony.

Gray, Ronald. *Franz Kafka*. Cambridge, England: Cambridge University Press, 1973.

According to Gray, the story suggests that the world is ruled by a sadistic god. Notes the sources of the story in Arthur Schopenhauer, Friedrich Wilhelm Nietzsche, Soren Kierkegaard, Edgar Allan Poe, and even Albert Schweitzer. Acclaims the story's ability to grip the reader's imagination.

Greenberg, Martin. *The Terror of Art: Kafka and Modern Literature*. New York: Basic Books, 1968.

Argues that because the story leaves aside the question of truth, it is obscurantist and equivocal. The story fails to be subjective, says Greenberg. It is too allegorical to be dream narrative, for in Kafka's dream narrative there is no outside observer who must choose between rival historical conceptions as there is in "In the Penal Colony."

Heller, Erich. *Franz Kafka*. New York: Viking Press, 1974.

The story provides the starkest exposition of the incongruity between guilt and penalty. Notes that Kafka literalizes the idea of learning through experience.

Kramer, Dale. "The Aesthetics of Theme: Kafka's 'In the Penal Colony.' " *Studies in Short Fiction* 5 (Winter, 1967/1968): 362-367.

Argues that in the story Kafka makes a case for basic understanding and tolerance in matters of relative morality. The personality of the explorer implies a morality that survives the old system; yet he does not attack the old to placate the new commandant.

Mendelsohn, Leonard. "Kafka's 'In the Penal Colony' and the Paradox of Enforced Freedom." *Studies in Short Fiction* 8 (Spring, 1971): 309-316.

Argues that the explorer is in the reverse situation of the medieval hero caught on the Wheel of Fortune, for he must spin the wheel himself. The result of this ironic reversal is that the heroic endeavor is not philosophic resolve but the futile effort to conceal from the self one's own power and freedom. Claims that the story concludes with the hero's failure to remain uninvolved and the officer's realization of a freedom he had hoped did not exist.

Neider, Charles. *The Frozen Sea: A Study of Franz Kafka*. New York: Oxford University Press, 1948.

Argues that for the first time in his fiction Kafka transforms the conception of authority from the father figure to society as a father. Says that the story is a brilliant tour de force without emotional and spiritual complexity.

Pascal, Roy. *Kafka's Narrators: A Study of His Stories and Sketches*. New York: Cambridge University Press, 1982.

A long discussion of the narrative structure of the story, noting that although there is some difference between the narrator and the explorer, the two coalesce to a large degree. Argues against interpretations of the story as a religious allegory. Says that the explorer is not the hero; rather, he embodies the main theme. He is the modern, enlightened man, who has detached himself from action and material interests. Although he may be freed from partisanship, he is also incapable of acting.

Pasley, Malcolm. "In the Penal Colony." In *The Kafka Debate*, edited by Angel Flores. New York: Gordian Press, 1977.

Says that the story is an example of Kafka's favorite technique of taking the metaphoric literally. Also discusses Kafka's use of his own private life in the story and what it owes to his reading of Fyodor Dostoevsky in the story.

Politzer, Heinz. *Frank Kafka: Parable and Paradox*. Ithaca, N.Y.: Cornell University Press, 1962.

Notes that the machine so dominates the story that the human characters have minor roles. The mystery of the machine is the mystery of the law that exists beyond civilized justice or logic. Claims that the explorer is a caricature of twentieth century materialism, willing to pay lip service to liberal ideas but incapable of applying them.

Rolleston, James. *Kafka's Narrative Theater*. University Park: Pennsylvania State University Press, 1974.

Discusses the symmetrical form of the story, showing how Kafka infuses each element with its own negation. Sees the story as a closed form in which all the elements are combined into a single configuration as the stage set for the hero's struggle to exist.

Spann, Meno. *Franz Kafka*. Boston: Twayne, 1976.
>Summarizes and criticizes some of the previous interpretations of the story. Argues against allegorical readings—either religious or psychoanalytic. Provides no interpretation to counter the criticism that he rejects.

Thieberger, Richard. "The Botched Ending of 'In the Penal Colony.'" In *The Kafka Debate*, edited by Angel Flores. New York: Gordian Press, 1977.
>Notes that the narrative perspective of the story is split between the officer and the explorer—a setup that poses the questions what perspective the reader should adopt and what perspective the author holds.

Thiher, Allen. "Kafka's Legacy." *Modern Fiction Studies* 26 (Winter, 1980/1981): 543-561.
>Discussion of Kafka as a precursor of postmodernism in fiction. Brief analysis of "The Judgment," "The Metamorphosis," and "In the Penal Colony" in terms of metaphors of discourse and interpretation. Argues that because of Kafka, the modern fictional text has become de-centered and creates meaning out of the playful use of language.

Thomas, J. D. "The Dark at the End of the Tunnel: Kafka's 'In the Penal Colony.'" *Studies in Short Fiction* 4 (1966): 12-18.
>Discusses the machine as the apparatus of rabbinism; it is the almemar, or pulpit, which focused the ritual and, along with the Ark, was one of the two most important areas of a synagogue. Says that the old commandant is the tribal god of the Hebrews, the new commandant is his image passed through the prism of reform.

Warren, Austin. "Cosmos Kafka." In his *Rage for Order*. Chicago: University of Chicago Press, 1948.
>Argues that the Earth is a penal colony and that all men are under judgment for sin. The story is an allegory of the conflict between the two basic beliefs: There is a natural law that an individual might know and there is a religious law that can never be known. The machine is the elaborate machinery of the old law.

"Investigations of a Dog"
Heller, Erich. "Investigations of a Dog and Other Matters." In *The World of Franz Kafka*, edited by J. P. Stern. New York: Holt, Rinehart and Winston, 1980.
>A transcription—whether fictional or real is not clear—of a literary discussion group, providing perspectives and insights on the story from people of various academic backgrounds. Inconclusively determines that the story is a comic version of original sin.

Lawson, Richard. *Franz Kafka.* New York: Frederick Ungar, 1987.
A discussion of the story as whimsically ironic and more a meditation than a story. Suggests that the charm of the tale, with Kafka himself speaking in the persona of a dog, outweighs the drawbacks of the long stretches of tedium in the personal and philosophical reflections of the animal.

Pascal, Roy. *Kafka's Narrators: A Study of His Stories and Sketches.* New York: Cambridge University Press, 1982.
Discusses the story as a long meditation by the dog upon the peculiarity of his own character, in which he tries to understand and justify himself. Supports this interpretation by analyzing the diction and syntax of the narrator. Calls the character the Don Quixote of the dog world, for he seeks a reality behind actual appearances, a reality that is an illusion.

"Josephine the Singer: Or, The Mouse Folk"
Gross, Ruth. "Of Mice and Women: Reflections on a Discourse." In *Franz Kafka (1883-1983) His Craft and Thought*, edited by Roman Struc and J. C. Yardley. Waterloo, Ontario, Canada: Wilfred Laurier University Press, 1986.
Discussion of the story from a poststructuralist, feminist point of view. Argues that the story is about the discourse on women; thus, it is a discourse on discourse. The one constant of the story is that women are creatures of being and men are creatures of doing. Story is a demystification of the means by which discourse creates illusions that masquerade as reality.

Pascal, Roy. *Kafka's Narrators: A Study of His Stories and Sketches.* New York: Cambridge University Press, 1982.
Argues that the narrator's difficulty in trying to find the exact word and the precise judgment is the same problem that the protagonist Josephine has. At the end of the story, Josephine lives on in the folk memory after her death. Pascal disagrees with critics who say that Josephine, like the hunger artist, stands for the alienation and tragic fate of the modern artist.

Politzer, Heinz. *Frank Kafka: Parable and Paradox.* Ithaca, N.Y.: Cornell University Press, 1962, rev. ed. 1966.
Discusses the artist theme in the story. Notes the precarious coexistence of Josephine with the mouse folk. The paradox of the heroine's existence is that in order to save her self-respect she has to be accepted for what she obviously is not—a singer. The paradox is that of the performer who wants her personal appeal to last forever, knowing that it is the gift of the moment.

Rolleston, James. *Kafka's Narrative Theater.* University Park: Pennsylvania State University Press, 1974.

Discusses the drama of the story in three acts. Argues that the story presents
an extreme case of Kafka's method of combining contradictory principles,
for in it the creation and destruction of a myth proceed simultaneously.
Josephine's mythopoeic claims are negated by her dependence on a society
that would reject her if it could.

Woodring, Carl R. "Josephine the Singer, or the Mouse Folk." In *Franz Kafka
Today*, edited by Angel Flores and Homer Swander. Madison: University of
Wisconsin Press, 1958.
Calls the story a metaphorical character sketch, which rejects the traditional
techniques of immediacy and adopts a leisurely relaxed pace. The virtue of the
story is characterization; where other Kafka's heroes need to suffer, Josephine
opposes, in the name of art and with mild dignity, the firm authority of the
public.

"The Judgment"
Beicken, Peter U. " 'The Judgment' in the Critics' Judgment." In *The Problem of
the Judgment*, edited by Angel Flores. New York: Gordian Press, 1977.
A survey of the criticism of the story. Concludes that in the work Kafka
embodies the insight that empirical reality is undermined by laws of mythical
origin. Argues that the story is the expression of a radically estranged individuality, which has raised a personal experience to a universal law.

Bernheimer, Charles. "Letters to an Absent Friend: A Structural Reading." In *The
Problem of the Judgment*, edited by Angel Flores. New York: Gordian Press,
1977.
A psychoanalytic approach to the story, arguing that Georg's friend in Russia
is a purely abstract, relational concept linking father and son. Using concepts
of psychoanalyst Jacques Lacan, Bernheimer claims that the story illustrates
the psychotic consequences of the foreclosure of the father's metaphoric
function.

Binder, Harmut. "The Background." Translated by Elke H. Gordon. In *The Problem of the Judgment*, edited by Angel Flores. New York: Gordian Press, 1977.
Discusses the psychological, biographical, and literary backgrounds of the
story, as well as some of its structural sources in the popular theater of the
time. Binder cites numerous literary works that influenced Kafka's writing of
the story as well as diary entries and letters that he used in the story.

Corngold, Stanley. "The Hermeneutic of 'The Judgment.' " In *The Problem of the
Judgment*, edited by Angel Flores. New York: Gordian Press, 1977.
Argues that the story symbolizes the force with which it exacts meaning and

that it indirectly thematizes its refusal of meaning. Focuses on Georg Bendemann as a writer who writes to maintain his connection with the world. Describes him as a persona for Kafka the writer.

Ellis, John. "The Bizarre Texture of 'The Judgment.' " In *The Problem of the Judgment*, edited by Angel Flores. New York: Gordian Press, 1977.
Discusses the interrelationship between the realistic introduction to the story and the absurd and irrealistic central episode. It is only through technical achievement that Kafka can turn upside down the moral values of the protagonist in the story.

Flores, Kate. "The Judgment." In *Franz Kafka Today*, edited by Angel Flores and Homer Swander. Madison: University of Wisconsin Press, 1958.
Claims that Georg's soliloquy is also Kafka's, for it is an objectification of his inner debate and an analogy of his inner writing self. Indicates that the father's judgment is not what Kafka's father would have said, but what Kafka's self-tortured imagination would have him say. Furthermore, Georg's father's scorn for his scribbling notes to the friend in Russia reflects Kafka's contempt for his writing.

——————— . "The Pathos of Fatherhood." In *The Problem of the Judgment*, edited by Angel Flores. New York: Gordian Press, 1977.
Discussion of the story in terms of the fear of aloneness—one of the typically human traits distinguishing man from animals, which always fascinated Kafka. Also analyzes the story's focus on the human discovery of paternity, the shift to a patriarchal system, and thus Georg's conflict with his father.

Freedman, Ralph. "Kafka's Obscurity: The Illusion of Logic in Narrative." *Modern Fiction Studies* 8 (Spring, 1962): 61-74.
A discussion of narrative logic in Kafka's works. Suggests that within a framework of realism and deliberate distortion, Kafka's fiction evolves as a problem-solving activity. Notes examples of Kafka's stylistic manner of shifting physical, moral, and psychological perspectives in "The Metamorphosis," "In the Penal Colony," and "A Country Doctor."

Goldstein, Bluma. "Bachelors and Work: Social and Economic Conditions in 'The Judgment,' 'The Metamorphosis,' and *The Trial*." In *The Kafka Debate*, edited by Angel Flores. New York: Gordian Press, 1977.
A discussion of the interrelationship between economic factors and social behavior in the story. Notes that the crucial relationships in Georg's life are connected with his involvement with his job.

Gray, Ronald. *Franz Kafka*. Cambridge, England: Cambridge University Press, 1973.

Notes that although the story seems intelligible at first, on going back over it the reader finds it to be incomprehensible. Like a nightmare the story does not deal with the real world but is a cryptic account of gaining knowledge through a waking dream.

—————— . "Through Dream to Self-Awareness." In *The Problem of the Judgment*, edited by Angel Flores. New York: Gordian Press, 1977.
Discussion of the dream reality that dominates the story. Notes that only when the conscious mind goes back over the story does its dreamlike obscurity manifest itself. Argues that the story is a cryptic account of Kafka's attainment of self-knowledge.

Greenberg, Martin. *The Terror of Art: Kafka and Modern Literature*. New York: Basic Books, 1968.
Analyzes the story in terms of its atmosphere of surcharged significance. In the story's subjective depth there is nothing, not even the humblest object or gesture, that does not become charged with significance. It is a story that demands to be interpreted, for, like a dream, its surface hides shadowy depths of meaning.

Heller, Erich. *Franz Kafka*. New York: Viking Press, 1974.
Discussion of the autobiographical element in the story, including Kafka's relationship with Felice Bauer and with his father. Discusses the son's helplessness in face of the father's authority. Also notes Georg's conviction that the sex act is a corruption of love and an invasion of the father's territory.

Hobson, Irmgard. "The Kafka Problem Compounded: *Trial* and *Judgment* in English." *Modern Fiction Studies* 23 (Winter 1977/1978): 511-529.
Points out several translation errors in the standard Muir translation of the story. Some errors in the first part of "The Judgment" distort Georg's role as interpreter of his friend's existence. In the second part of the story, there are errors that can lead to misinterpretation about the struggle between the father and son.

Murrill, V., and W. S. Marks III. "Kafka's 'The Judgment' and *The Interpretation of Dreams*." *The Germanic Review* 48 (May, 1973): 212-228.
Argues that Kafka's story was inspired and influenced by his reading of Sigmund Freud's study of dreams. This is a fairly detailed analysis of the story from the Freudian perspective of dream interpretation. Argues that the story, both in its narrative technique and its plot detail, is profoundly indebted to the "allegories"—by which Murrill and Marks mean dramatic expositions—of Freud's dream book.

Neider, Charles. *The Frozen Sea: A Study of Franz Kafka*. New York: Oxford University Press, 1948.

Calls it the first work to reveal Kafka's major literary traits: the nightmarish atmosphere, the personal allusions, the father-son conflict, and the symbolism of darkness and illness. Argues that Kafka's portrayal of the father as ill indicates both his aggression and his guilt toward the father.

Pascal, Roy. *Kafka's Narrators: A Study of His Stories and Sketches*. New York: Cambridge University Press, 1982.

Argues that it is the absence of an authoritative voice in the story that has prompted so many interpretations. Attempts to disentangle stylistic evidence for the objective viewpoint of the narrator as distinct from the viewpoint of the character Georg. Discusses the meaning resulting from this dual perspective.

Politzer, Heinz. *Parable and Paradox*. Ithaca, New York: Cornell University Press, 1962, rev. ed. 1966.

Discusses Georg's offense as being his self-centeredness and argues that at the end, not only is the son forced to accept the judgment of the father, but the reader is compelled to approve it as well. Concludes that the story does not carry any discernible meaning beyond the warning against the loss of bachelor-hood. Discusses the dual nature of the story: the realistic and the surrealistic, the psychological and the metaphysical.

Pondrom, Cyrena N. "Coherence in Kafka's 'The Judgment': Georg's Perceptions of the World." *Studies in Short Fiction* 9 (Winter, 1972): 59-79.

A detailed explication of the story in terms of the status of Georg's reality and his perceptions of reality. Notes that the two essential components of Kafka's handling of the central character are his realization that even the smallest actions have significance and his telling of the story through Georg's eyes, in spite of the fact that it is told in third person.

Rolleston, James. *Kafka's Narrative Theater*. University Park: Pennsylvania State University Press, 1974.

Argues that the protagonist in the story is so self-absorbed that he denies the existence of any conflict. Says that Kafka so combines ordered thinking in the story with its antithesis that the reader cannot make a distinction between them.

——————. "Strategy and Language: Georg Bendemann's Theater of the Self." In *The Problem of the Judgment*, edited by Angel Flores. New York: Gordian Press, 1977.

Argues that although the conflict between father and son is the central one in the story, the focus is on the mechanism of Georg's responses. Georg sees life in static terms, like a chessboard in which every move takes place according to rules of its own making.

Sokel, Walter H. "Perspectives and Truth in 'The Judgment.' " In *The Problem of the Judgment*, edited by Angel Flores. New York: Gordian Press, 1977.
A long, detailed study of the story in terms of a duality of perspectives: Georg as representative of the rational, empiricist, rebellious, liberal outlook and the father as the embodiment of the irrational, archaic, still-powerful organization and structure. Argues that the ultimate statement of the story is that love and self-erasure are one.

Spann, Meno. *Franz Kafka*. Boston: Twayne, 1976.
A discussion of the lyrical, metaphorical nature of the story, as well as its allegorical nature by four influential German critics between 1958 and 1965. Also discusses psychoanalytic criticisms of the story.

Steinberg, Erwin R. "The Judgment in Kafka's 'The Judgment.' " *Modern Fiction Studies* 8 (Spring, 1962): 23-30.
Discusses the father in the story as being the image of the powerful patriarchal God of the Old Testament. Analyzes crucial passages in the story to illustrate Kafka's guilt feelings that motivated the work. Steinberg argues that other interpretations of the story's conflict complements his own symbolic interpretation.

Stern, J. P. "Guilt and the Feeling of Guilt." In *The Problem of the Judgment*, edited by Angel Flores. New York: Gordian Press, 1977.
Discussion of the story in terms of Kafka's fictionalization of autobiographical writings, particularly in terms of his preoccupation with guilt, punishment, and laws. Concludes that all Georg's acts are bound up with his exclusive self-preoccupation.

Szanto, George H. *Narrative Consciousness*. Austin: University of Texas Press, 1972.
Says that this story is the most typical of Kafka's works to employ narrative consciousness almost completely. To understand the protagonist the reader must identify with him, says Szanto. He analyzes the story in some detail from the thematic perspective of its being a story of individual failure.

White, John J. "Georg Bendemann's Friend in Russia: Symbolic Correspondences." In *The Problem of the Judgment*, edited by Angel Flores. New York: Gordian Press, 1977.
An extended discussion of the role of the problematic friend in Russia to whom Georg writes a letter. Notes the similarities between the friend and Georg's father. Concludes that the symbolic correspondence between Georg, the friend, and the father highlight Georg's egocentricity and make his betrayal of himself more vivid.

"Metamorphosis"

Cantrell, Carol Helmstetter. " 'The Metamorphosis': Kafka's Study of a Family." *Modern Fiction Studies* 23 (Winter 1977-1978): 578-586.

Argues that the story of Gregor's experience emerges as part of a coherent and destructive pattern of family life. Uses British psychiatrist R. D. Laing's approach to family dynamics to analyze the story. Says that the center of the story is a network of shared perceptions centering on fear of shame, the habit of secrecy, and the hope for power.

Fleissner, Robert F. "Is Gregor Samsa a Bed Bug? Kafka and Dickens Revisited." *Studies in Short Fiction* 22 (Spring, 1985): 225-228.

A humorous discussion of the literary genealogy of Gregor's status as an insect. Focuses primarily on Charles Dickens' use of animal and insect imagery, as that in turn is derived from William Shakespeare. Concludes that although Gregor can be classified as a "bed bug," he has no specific identity.

Goldstein, Bluma. "Bachelors and Work: Social and Economic Conditions in 'The Judgment,' 'The Metamorphosis,' and *The Trial*." In *The Kafka Debate*, edited by Angel Flores. New York: Gordian Press, 1977.

Discusses Gregor Samsa as alienated from social bonds and engaged in meaningless labor. Accounts for his insect condition being parallel to his way of life — imprisoned in his society and exploited by a capitalist system.

Gray, Ronald. *Franz Kafka*. Cambridge, England: Cambridge University Press, 1973.

Discusses the story as a reflection of Kafka's own situation. By excluding the interminable debate of later stories and projecting his conflict into the single act of transformation, Kafka is able to take in the feelings of other people. In the story, Kafka sees his own experiences as though from the outside.

Greenberg, Martin. *The Terror of Art: Kafka and Modern Literature*. New York: Basic Books, 1968.

A detailed analysis of the story. Says that the story does not unfold as an action, but as a metaphor, which is spelled out and brought to its ultimate conclusion. Consequently, there is no question of tension or drama; the story is like a vision. Like Fyodor Dostoevski's underground man or William Shakespeare's Hamlet, Gregor can neither live in the world nor find the world he craves.

Holland, Norman. "Realism and Unrealism: Kafka's 'Metamorphosis.' " *Modern Fiction Studies* 4 (Summer, 1958): 143-150.

Argues that Kafka's method in the story is quite straightforward, for he charges specific realistic elements with a specific nonrealistic or spiritual value. Discusses both the elements of realism and the elements of nonrealism that make up the story. Concludes that Gregor's transformation dramatizes the blindness of all human beings, trapped between a set of instinctive urges on the one hand and an obscure drive to serve "gods" on the other.

Kuna, Franz. *Franz Kafka: Literature as Corrective Punishment*. Bloomington: Indiana University Press, 1974.
Takes a sociological approach to the story, noting that it describes an existence hopelessly alienated from normality. Gregor is economic man debased to a functional role. Analyzes the story in terms of three orders of being: the transcendental, the natural, and the unnatural, the latter suggesting enslavement to an economic system.

Luke, F. D. "The Metamorphosis." In *Franz Kafka Today*, edited by Angel Flores and Homer Swander. Madison: University of Wisconsin Press, 1958.
A detailed discussion of the various comic, tragicomic, and dream effects in the story. A detailed discussion of the techniques in the story that explore the self-protective devices of the mind beneath the rational level. Concludes that humorous distance is an essential feature of Kafka's technique; it enables him to exploit the effects of understatement and report extreme cases with absolute detachment.

Moss, Leonard. "A Key to the Door Image in 'The Metamorphosis.' " *Modern Fiction Studies* 17 (Spring, 1971): 37-42.
Argues that the story is a series of approaches and withdrawals by Gregor, which Kafka makes concrete by the constant allusion to doors—the most important image in the story after the insect analogy. Notes the ironic conclusion that once Gregor is dead, all the doors and windows are thrown open in celebration.

Neider, Charles. *The Frozen Sea: A Study of Franz Kafka*. New York: Oxford University Press, 1948.
Calls it the most masochistic piece of Kafka's mature period. Argues that the transformation is symbolic of more real and more deadly transformations, which haunt man. Says that the story is filled with the neurotic horror of losing control.

Pascal, Roy. *Kafka's Narrators: A Study of His Stories and Sketches*. New York: Cambridge University Press, 1982.
Discusses the nonpersonal narrator of the story and his subordination to the main character. Explores the basic question of why the narrator, if his chief function is to communicate the view of Gregor to the reader, still has some

independent function in the story. Argues that the impersonal narrator confirms the character's situation differently than the character himself does.

Pfeiffer, Johannes. "The Metamorphosis." In *Kafka: A Collection of Critical Essays*, edited by Ronald Gray. Englewood Cliffs, N.J.: Prentice-Hall, 1962.
An analysis of the story in terms of its parabolic structure. Concludes that the work presents an image of radical estrangement from society and that a distantly sensed escape into the open remains blocked. The narrative presentation itself provides no guideposts; instead it gives the reader the feeling that there is a hidden background, which provides meaning to the whole. Kafka's artistry is not stimulated by the need for truth, but rather by an interest in the success of an experiment in portrayal.

Spann, Meno. *Franz Kafka*. Boston: Twayne, 1976.
Says that the story offers the worst example in Kafka criticism of disagreement about the moral qualities of his work. Argues that the real vermin in the story are the people who surround Gregor. Summarizes some of the previous criticism of the story.

Spilka, Mark. "Sources for 'The Metamorphosis.'" *Comparative Literature* 11 (1959): 289-307.
Discusses the origins of the story in such works as Nikolai Gogol's "The Nose," Fyodor Dostoevski's *The Double*, and Charles Dickens' *David Copperfield*. Argues that this tradition, especially in its focus on childhood as the last refuge of human worth, finds a brilliant synthetic performance in Kafka's story, for it contains the dreamlike contours, the realistic surface, the psychological depth, and the infantile perspective seen in the work of Dickens, Dostoevski, and Gogol.

Wolkenfield, Suzanne. "Christian Symbolism in Kafka's 'The Metamorphosis.'" *Studies in Short Fiction* 10 (Spring, 1973): 205-207.
Analyzes the story in terms of the Christian symbolism, which is an integral part of the ironic pathos of the story. Discusses the parallels between Gregor and Jesus Christ: his status as potential savior of the family, his crucifixion-like death, his metamorphosis. Ironically, his sufferings are not redemptive.

"A Report to an Academy"
Pascal, Roy. *Kafka's Narrators: A Study of His Stories and Sketches*. New York: Cambridge University Press, 1982.
Argues against those critics who take the ape as a symbol of conformism; by doing do, they judge the ape as if it were human. Discusses the various features of style, mood, and tone of the story. Notes the tone of playful fantasy in the story; instead of asserting any dogmatic truth, says Pascal, it only presents a playful hypothesis.

Rubinstein, William. "A Report to an Academy." In *Franz Kafka Today*, edited by
Angel Flores and Homer Swander. Madison: University of Wisconsin Press,
1958.
States that the key to the interpretation of the story is the symbolic significance
of the ape; he represents a Jew who allows himself to be converted to Christianity in order to escape persecution. Discusses the symbolism of the rest of
the story as consistent with this reading.

Stuart, Dabney. "Kafka's 'A Report to an Academy': An Exercise in Method."
Studies in Short Fiction 6 (Summer, 1969): 413-420.
Illustrates how the story fulfills its own symbolic suggestions. Argues that to
understand the story one must not look for familiar allegorical equivalents in
the world of ideas but must pay complete attention to the concrete details of
the story itself and the patterns that Kafka imposes on the details. Notes that
the ape in the story, for example, is not an allegorical representation of the idea
of evolution, but is a symbol of transformation from ape into human being.

Weinstein, Leo. "Kafka's Ape: Heel or Hero?" *Modern Fiction Studies* 8 (Spring,
1962): 75-79.
Discusses the story within the context of Kafka's usual themes. Argues that the
ape is a successful hero in the Kafkaesque sense and that he is the only Kafka
hero who succeeds in making progress.

PÄR LAGERKVIST
(1891-1974)
Sweden

General Biographical and Critical Studies

Ellestad, Everett. "Lagerkvist and Cubism: A Study of Theory and Practice." *Scandinavian Studies* 45 (Winter, 1973): 38-53.

Discussion of Lagerkvist's shift from the expressionist works of despair during World War I to the structural principles of cubism after the war for his fiction. Compares Lagerkvist's theories of language and style with cubist principles. Shows how he develops his notions of cubism from theory to practice in representative stories and novels.

Linnér, Sven. "Pär Lagerkvist's *The Eternal Smile* and *The Sibyl.*" *Scandinavian Studies* 37 (May, 1965): 160-167.

Compares the two works by Lagerkvist, one from 1920 and the other from 1956. But the main point of the article is to show a basic difference in the two works, and thus a development in Lagerkvist toward an integration of experience instead of suppression or escape. Thus the latter work marks a more mature attitude toward life than does the former.

Sjöberg, Leif. *Pär Lagerkvist.* New York: Columbia University Press, 1976.

A short monograph introduction with summary discussions of the major works. The scant three pages on *The Eternal Smile and Other Stories* notes that the stories downplay transcendental aspects in favor of life on earth, suggesting that the fear of death expressed in Lagerkvist's early works has been conquered.

Spector, Robert Donald. "Lagerkvist's Short Fiction." *American Scandinavian Review* 57 (Autumn, 1969): 260-265.

Discusses Lagerkvist's fables as the work of a moralist, but says that his short stories, especially "Father and I" and "The Basement," are examples of the modern short story. Both embody structures of revelation similar to those of James Joyce, and both depend on carefully organized contrasts for their effectiveness. Both stories end in an epiphany that masks the character of Lagerkvist's moral preaching.

_____ . *Pär Lagerkvist.* Boston: Twayne, 1973.

The opening chapter of this introduction to Lagerkvist deals with his short fiction, providing brief discussions of the fables (which focus on a moral issue), the short stories (which deal with a sudden insight or with the assessment of a character), and the novellas (which deal with a philosophic or social problem. This is a good study of Lagerkvist's variety of fictional technique in treating a limited range of subjects.

Vowles, Richard. Introduction to *The Eternal Smile and Other Stories*. New York: Random House, 1954.
   Brief comments on several of the more important stories. Calls the title story Lagerkvist's *divina commedia* and "Father and I" a revelation of the unknown. Claims that his real originality lies in what might be called choral fiction, and that his most common prose vehicle lies somewhere between the parable and the fable, for it lacks the moral tag of the former and the brevity of the latter. A good short introduction to Lagerkvist's central themes and techniques.

Weathers, Winston. *Pär Lagerkvist*. Grand Rapids, Mich.: Wm. B. Eerdmans, 1962.
   An introduction to Lagerkvist's work from a Christian perspective. The stories discussed, such as "The Basement" and "The Eternal Smile" emphasize Lagerkvist's religious concerns and the demand he sees for modern man to open his eyes to his spiritual need for transfiguration. Only passing references here to the short fiction.

White, Ray Lewis. *Par Lagerkvist in America*. Atlantic Highlands, N.J.: Humanities Press, 1979.
   Summarizes more than forty American reviews of *The Eternal Smile and Other Stories* in 1954. Although White provides no unifying connection between the reviews, he quotes the salient passages. A valuable source to determine the American reception of Lagerkvist's short stories.

Selected Title

"The Eternal Smile"
Spector, Robert Donald. *Pär Lagerkvist*. Boston: Twayne, 1973.
   Discusses the choral structure of revelation in the story. Argues that it demonstrates the variety of Lagerkvist's fictional achievement. The story suits Lagerkvist's needs as a moralist while he can also maintain his narrative technique as a fabulist.

TOMMASO LANDOLFI
1908-1979
Italy

General Biographical and Critical Study

Capek-Habekovic, Romana. *Tommaso Landolfi's Grotesque Images*. New York: Peter Lang, 1986.

Argues that in Landolfi's fictional world, his grotesques emerge as human, while logic and technology are truly grotesque. Includes a long chapter on grotesque images in his short stories, emphasizing how he was influenced by the German romantic tradition and by psychoanalysis. Discusses his parodies of Franz Kafka and Nikolai Gogol, both authors whom he admired.

Selected Titles

"Gogol's Wife"

Capek-Habekovic, Romana. *Tommaso Landolfi's Grotesque Images*. New York: Peter Lang, 1986.

Discusses the story's play with the fantastic. Compares it to E. T. A. Hoffmann's story "The Sandman" in its use of an automaton, but argues that it is really closer to the works of Kafka in its attempt to uncover the real in the absurd.

"Wedding Night"

Brew, Claude C. "The 'Caterpillar Nature' of Imaginative Experience: A Reading of Tommaso Landolfi's 'Wedding Night.' " *Modern Language Notes* 89 (1974): 110-115.

An explication of the story in terms of its theme—the power of the imagination. The bride's imagined experience of the wedding night, suggesting pain, revulsion, and fear deadens her possible joy. The theme is how our imagined anticipation of a future event can affect our emotional adjustments to that event.

STANISŁAW LEM
(1921-   )
Poland

General Biographical and Critical Studies

Barnouw, Dagman. "Science Fiction as a Model for Probabilistic Worlds: Stanisław
Lem's Fantastic Empiricism." *Science-Fiction Studies* 6 (July, 1979): 153-163.
Examines Lem's concept of science fiction as a cognitive aesthetic model
whereby he focuses on contemporary social and psychological behavior. Discusses briefly a number of stories by Lem, particularly in *The Cyberiad*.
Argues that Lem is concerned with the symbiosis between man and machine—
both in terms of the benefits and the dangers.

Jarzebski, Jerzy. "Stanisław Lem's 'Star Diaries.'" *Science-Fiction Studies* 13
(November, 1986): 361-371.
Discusses this story cycle as a collection of many different styles and objects of
parody. Offers brief interpretations of some of the stories and generalizes
about the basic themes of the stories. Also discusses Lem's critique of both
Hegelianism and positivism in the stories. Discusses the influence of Arthur
Schopenhauer's philosophy on Lem.

Kandel, Michale. "Stanisław Lem on Men and Robots." *Extrapolation* 14 (December, 1972): 13-24.
Notes that cybernetics lies at the heart of all Lem's work and thought. Discusses some of the ideas on this subject that have influenced Lem as well as
some of the moral implications of the subject for him. No real discussion of
the stories, but a valuable analysis of the issues that underlie the themes of the
stories.

Scholes, Robert, and Eric S. Rabkin. *Science Fiction: History, Science, Vision*. New
York: Oxford University Press, 1977.
A brief introduction to Lem's central concerns, particularly the interface between men and machines. No discussion of the short stories here, but because
the book places Lem within the broader context of science fiction generally, it
is helpful in understanding his place in this tradition.

Science-Fiction Studies 13 (November, 1986).
A special issue on Lem, with essays on almost all facets of his work and
discussions of his major novels and short-story collections. Also contains an
interview with Lem, a scathing review of Richard Ziegfield's book on Lem,
and a general introduction to criticism of Lem, including the essays in this
special issue.

Warrick, Patricia S. "Stanisław Lem's Robot Fables and Ironic Tales." In her *The Cybernetic Imagination in Science Fiction*. Cambridge, Mass.: MIT Press, 1980.
    Discusses Lem's use of irony to parody cybernetic fiction in both the utopian and dystopian modes. A brief discussion of the tone and content of the typical Lem short story. Notes how in his stories the weaknesses of the robots mirror the weaknesses of the men who made them.

Ziegfield, Richard. *Stanisław Lem*. New York: Frederick Ungar, 1985.
    The first full-length study of Lem in English. Ziegfield provides a good introductory summary of Lem's life, and his basic themes and techniques, as well as discussions of the individual works. Individual chapters focus on the stories in *The Star Diaries* and *Memoirs of a Space Traveler* and the fables in *Mortal Engines* and *The Cyberiad*. A concluding analytical chapter on Lem's achievement and a bibliography of criticism round out the book.

THOMAS MANN
(1875-1955)
Germany

General Biographical and Critical Studies

Apter, T. E. *Thomas Mann: The Devil's Advocate*. New York: New York University Press, 1979.

In this discussion of the tension between art and life in Mann's works, Apter deals primarily with the novels. The only short fictions examined in any detail are the two major novellas, "Death in Venice" and "Tonio Kröger." Apter argues that "Tonio Kröger" presents the isolation of the artist as an anguish to be enjoyed, whereas "Death in Venice" reveals Mann's mistrust of the impulses and emotions he finds in the works of Richard Wagner.

Berendsohn, Walter E. *Thomas Mann: Artist and Partisan in Troubled Times*. Translated by George C. Buck. Tuscaloosa: University of Alabama Press, 1973.

Although this study does deal with Mann's art, it also focuses on his role as an active citizen in the social and political world. The structural and stylistic analysis of the stories focuses primarily on the early narratives such as "Tonio Kröger" and "Death in Venice."

Brennan, Joseph G. *Thomas Mann's World*. New York: Columbia University Press, 1942, rev. ed. 1970.

Discusses Mann's basic views of art and the artist, as well as Mann's own artistic personality as revealed in his works. Deals with the relationships in Mann's works between disease and genius, morality and the artist, art and politics, and art and nature. Although most of the discussion centers on the novels, there are passing comments on these themes in the short stories.

Burgin, Hans, and Hans-Otto Mayer. *Thomas Mann: A Chronicle of His Life*. Translated by Eugene Dobson. Tuscaloosa: University of Alabama Press, 1965, 1969.

A day-by-day account (at least as far as can be determined) of Mann's life. Although not all Mann's notes were available for this chronicle, the letters provided enough information to create a highly detailed account, enlivened with quotations, of Mann's activities. Also included is a bibliography providing publication information about Mann's works.

Cleugh, James. *Thomas Mann: A Study*. London: Martin Secker & Warburg, 1933. Reprint. New York: Russell & Russell, 1968.

Although this study was published too early to cover all Mann's works, it does include some discussion of the early novellas as well as the major novellas, such as "Death in Venice" and "Tonio Kröger," the latter which Cleugh sees as prototypical of Mann's romantic-realistic idiom. Other early stories are discussed briefly.

Feurlicht, Ignace. *Thomas Mann*. Boston: Twayne, 1968.
A critical introduction to Mann, which analyzes the plots, characters, ideas, and styles of his stories and novels against the background of his life. Notes that most of his early stories focus on a marked man, one who is weak, sick, or odd, an outsider who cannot endure everyday life. Discusses Mann's classification of his individual stories under the generic title *Novellen*.

Hamburger, Michael. "Thomas Mann." In his *Contraries: Studies in German Literature.* New York: E. P. Dutton, 1970.
A general discussion of Mann's place among his German contemporaries. Notes how Mann's noncommitment differs from the great realists who preceded him; Mann realizes that his characters have no reality other than the one lent to them by the author's skill. Discusses previous critics, especially on Mann's irony Also discusses Mann's comic gifts. Passing mention of some of the short fictions.

Hatfield, Henry. *From the Magic Mountain: Mann's Later Masterpieces*. Ithaca, New York: Cornell University Press, 1979.
Although this work deals with Mann's works that appeared later than most of his short fiction, the first chapter notes how some of the short stories reflect Mann's awareness of the difficulty, even the impossibility, of writing well. Examines his development of the leitmotif in such early works as "Tristan," "Tonio Kröger," and "Death in Venice." The only other short fiction work discussed in any detail is the later story "Mario and the Magician," which Hatfield discusses briefly as a political fable.

——— . *Thomas Mann*. New York: New Directions, 1951.
This introduction to Mann deals with several basic themes and motifs that run throughout his fiction. The focus of the early stories is on the tension between the characters who represent life and are dull or brutal, and the protagonists who are isolated and psychologically maladjusted. "Tonio Kröger" and "Death in Venice" are discussed in terms of their use of the Narcissus theme and their use of the leitmotif as a structural and thematic device.

Heiney, Donald W. *Barron's Simplified Approach to Thomas Mann*. Woodbury, N.Y.: Barron's Educational Series, 1966.
A basic introduction to Mann's life and art for students, with chapters on each of the important novels. The chapter on the short stories and tales includes

brief discussions of each of the important stories in *Stories of Three Decades*. The discussions are primarily summaries rather than analyses, but the discussions of "Tonio Kröger" and "Death in Venice," although not original interpretations, provide some necessary orientation to these difficult but central works.

Heller, Erich. *The Ironic German: A Study of Thomas Mann*. Boston: Little, Brown, 1958.
A study of Man and his intellectual ancestry. Includes a discussion of the influence of Arthur Schopenhauer's philosophy on the novel *Buddenbrooks* and a dialogue about the novel *The Magic Mountain*. Also contains a chapter on "Mario and the Magician" and "Death in Venice." A stimulating and influential book about Mann.

Hirschbach, Frank Donald. *The Arrow and the Lyre: A Study of the Role of Love in the Works of Thomas Mann*. The Hague, Netherlands: Martinus Nijhoff, 1955.
Although the focus of this study is primarily on the novels, the first chapter is devoted to the theme of love in the stories, particularly "Little Herr Friedemann," "Tonio Kröger," and "Death in Venice."

Hollingdale, R. J. *Thomas Mann: A Critical Study*. Lewisburg, Pa.: Bucknell University Press, 1971.
Rather than an analysis of individual novels and stories, this study discusses the basic philosophic assumptions, especially the philosophy of Friedrich Nietzsche, in Mann's works. Hollingdale focuses on such themes as crime, sickness, decadence, irony, and myth. Such stories as "Gladius Dei," "Little Herr Friedemann," and "The Infant Prodigy" are cited by Hollingdale to illustrate his points.

Hughes, Kenneth, ed. *Thomas Mann in Context*. Worcester, Mass.: Clark University Press, 1978.
A collection of papers presented at a celebration of the one hundredth anniversary of Mann's birth. Two of the essays deal with the relationship between Mann and the thought of Sigmund Freud, one with the affinities between Mann and James Joyce, and one on Georg Lukács' fascination with, and advocacy of, Mann's works.

Jonas, Ilsedore B. *Thomas Mann and Italy*. Translated by Betty Crouse. Tuscaloosa: University of Alabama Press, 1969, 1979.
A study of the influence of Italian culture and people on Mann's work, as well as the reception of his work among Italian readers and his influence on Italian literature. Although some discussion is devoted to such early stories as "Tonio

Kröger" and "Gladius Dei," the most extensive discussions focus on "Death in Venice" and "Mario and the Magician."

Kahler, Erich. *The Orbit of Thomas Mann*. Princeton, N.J.: Princeton University Press, 1969.
A collection of five essays by Kahler. In addition to two papers on *Doctor Faustus*, one essay deals with Mann's focus on "things of the mind," and another (a memorial lecture) focuses on Mann as the most important representative of the radical shift from nineteenth century thought to modernism. Kahler argues that Mann's representation of the German spirit at the turn of the century was revolutionary in character and that this led to a revolution in literary forms and motifs as well.

Kaufmann, Fritz. *Thomas Mann: The World as Will and Representation*. Boston: Beacon Press, 1957.
The first part of this study focuses on Mann's philosophy, particularly in terms of its spiritual background and its derivation from the metaphysics of Arthur Schopenhauer. The second half focuses on the application of Mann's thought in his major novels. Although there is only passing mention of the short fiction, this helpful study discusses the development and application of Mann's thought.

McWilliams, James R. *Brother Artist: A Psychological Study of Thomas Mann's Fiction*. Lanham, Md.: University Press of America, 1983.
A discussion of guilt and its effect on the protagonists in Mann's fiction. The focus is on how guilt compels the Mann protagonist to work obsessively, to strive for precision in his art, and to impose suffering on the self. The ultimate results of guilt in Mann's works, says McWilliams, are the abhorrence of life exhibited by his characters and their death wish.

Marcus, Judith. *George Lukács and Thomas Mann: A Study in the Sociology of Literature*. Amherst: University of Massachusetts Press, 1987.
A study of the process of interaction between Mann and Lukács. Part 1 focuses on their spiritual and personal relationship; Part 2 deals with *The Magic Mountain* as a novel of its time. Marcus is particularly interested in this second part on Georg Lukács as the inspiration for the fictional character Leo Naphta in the novel. Most of the information in Part 1 is derived from previously undiscovered or untranslated material discovered in the Mann and Lukács archives.

Neider, Charles. "The Artist as Bourgeois." In *The Stature of Thomas Mann*, edited by Charles Neider. New York: New Directions, 1947.
Discussion of Mann's position in the artistic tradition. Distinguishes three periods of his development: a prewar literary period; the period of *The Magic*

Mountain when he made peace with his burgher-artist role; and the period of *Joseph and His Brothers* when he carried out the political implications of his role. Discusses several early stories briefly to illustrate their focus on the artist.

Nemerov, Howard. "Themes and Methods in the Early Stories of Thomas Mann." In his *Poetry and Fiction: Essays*. New Brunswick, N.J.: Rutgers University Press, 1963.
Discusses the types of characters in Mann's stories, for example, disappointed lovers of life, those whose love has turned to hatred and those whose love masquerades as indifference and superiority. Discusses briefly "Little Herr Friedemann," "Little Lizzy," "Gladius Dei," and others. Says that "The Infant Prodigy" is the first appearance in Mann of some sinister qualities belonging to the underside of the artist nature.

Reed, T. J. *Thomas Mann: The Uses of Tradition*. London: Oxford University Press, 1974.
A full-scale study of Mann's dialogue with his culture's literary tradition. Discussion of the early stories focuses on development of Mann's use of irony and the relative immaturity of his earliest works. Discusses the derivative nature of his narrative method, which employs detached exploitation of pathetic or pathological anecdotes.

Rey, W. H. "Tragic Aspects of the Artist in Thomas Mann's Work." *Modern Language Quarterly* 19 (1958): 195-203.
Argues that the ambiguity, irony, parody, and self-parody in Mann—what might seem to be nothing more than irresponsible artistic playfulness—is the expression of very serious personal convictions. Discusses artistic irony in "Tonio Kröger," "Death in Venice," and Mann's novels. Notes that Mann's view that the artist is a mediator between the sensual and the spiritual is based on artistic irony.

Thomas, R. Hinton. *Thomas Mann: The Mediation of Art*. Oxford, England: Clarendon Press, 1956.
A discussion of selected Mann works from the point of view of Mann's concern with art as a moral task of self-discipline. The short stories are discussed as Mann's apprenticeship, especially "Little Herr Friedemann," to the central theme of the yearning for art as an escape from practical life into infinity. Generally Mann's early stories exhibit an element of coldness, says Thomas, reflecting a bitterness with which the characters in the stories experience the harshness of their environment.

Wescott, Glenway. "Thomas Mann: Willpower and Fiction." In his *Images of Truth*. New York: Harper & Row, 1962.

A long essay focusing on Mann's resoluteness, particularly in *The Magic Mountain* and *Doctor Faustus*, with passing comments on "Death in Venice," which Wescott faults for not presenting a true picture of homosexuality. Focuses on Mann's Herculean work ethics but argues that this willpower had a regrettable effect on his later work.

Winston, Richard. *Thomas Mann: The Making of an Artist: 1875-1911*. New York: Alfred A. Knopf, 1981.
A readable biography of the early development of Mann's career, particularly helpful for the background of the short stories since most of them were published during Mann's early career. Particularly interesting is the final chapter on the biographical sources of "Death in Venice," such as Mann's giving Aschenbach many of his own personal habits, and his deriving the character of Tadzio from Count Władysław Moes, observed by Mann when the count was a young boy on holiday.

Selected Titles

"Death in Venice"
Apter, T. E. *Thomas Mann: The Devil's Advocate*. New York: New York University Press, 1979.
Argues that the story reveals Mann's recalcitrant mistrust of the impulses and emotions in Richard Wagner. Says that although the novella reveals the stagnation of Mann's own imagination, the revelation is so vivid that the story's excellence transcends its source. Argues that Aschenbach's problem is not that he is an artist, but that he is not a great artist and is therefore unable to mold life's horror creatively.

Baron, Frank. "Sensuality and Morality in Thomas Mann's *Tod in Venedig*." *The Germanic Review* 45 (March, 1970): 115-125.
Argues that a comprehensive view of the story is not possible without a detailed consideration of chapter 2, in which a strange transformation takes place in Aschenbach's view of art. Discusses the relationship between this changed view and the ideas about balance that Mann's discusses in his essay on Johann Wolfgang von Goethe. What is important to Mann is the work as a whole. Mann's view of morality and sensuality in the Goethe essay refers to tendencies in the characters and in Mann himself.

Beharriell, Frederick J. " 'Never Without Freud': Freud's Influence on Mann." In *Thomas Mann in Context*, edited by Kenneth Hughes. Worcester, Mass.: Clark University Press, 1978.

Builds on Beharriell's previous study on psychology in the early works of Mann. Attempts to justify Mann's statement that he would not have written "Death in Venice" had it not been for Sigmund Freud. Discusses Aschenbach's death wish, his repressed homosexuality, and his unsuspected sexual desires. Also notes the relationship to psychoanalysis in the so-called indecent psychology passage in the story, as well as in the treatment of dreams.

Berendsohn, Walter E. *Thomas Mann: Artist and Partisan in Troubled Times*. Tuscaloosa: University of Alabama Press, 1973.
Brief discussion of the story's style as a fusion of the personal with the factual. Argues that Aschenbach's love of the boy requires a style of language to connect it to the Grecian world.

Braverman, Albert, and Larry David Nachman. "The Dialectic of Decadence: An Analysis of Thomas Mann's " 'Death in Venice.' " *The Germanic Review* 45 (November, 1970): 288-298.
Argues that the work is the last place where Mann presented his primary dilemma as the dialectic of the decadence of culture in the context of bourgeois society. The tragedy of the story lies in its complete articulation of a problem for which there is no solution. Says that Apollonian and the Dionysian elements in the story are mutually exclusive.

Brennan, Joseph Gerard. *Thomas Mann's World*. New York: Columbia University Press, 1942, rev. ed. 1970.
Discusses the nature of disease embodied in the story as a result of artistic creation, which burns not only physical but also psychic energy. Disease is presented both as a hostile, dehumanizing force and as a highly dignified phenomenon, for it is the result of the consuming force of art.

Consigny, Scott. "Aschenbach's 'Page and a Half of Choicest Prose': Man's Rhetoric of Irony." *Studies in Short Fiction* 14 (Fall, 1977): 359-367.
Argues against the usual interpretation of Aschenbach's prose within the story. Suggests that we read the passage as ironic and see his page and a half of prose not as ideal but rather as a distorted and self-deceptive act. Makes use of Wayne C. Booth's book *A Rhetoric of Irony* and discusses the context of Socratic irony, which Mann establishes for the passage.

Feurlicht, Ignace. *Thomas Mann*. Boston: Twayne, 1968.
Discusses the relationships in the story that are confusing to many readers: the relationship between spirit and beauty, between love and life, and between the sea and death. Notes the mythology on which the story is based and its use of the Venice locale. Calls it one of the most accomplished German stories, written in a masterly style, full of ideas, meanings, and overtones.

Frank, Bruno. "Death in Venice." In *The Stature of Thomas Mann*, edited by Charles Neider. New York: New Directions, 1947.
A general discussion of the story's focus on the struggle the artist wages against himself. Aschenbach pays for a life based on spirit alone with an eruption of the repressed. Says that the story reflects Mann's knowledge that whoever is great today owes his greatness to an inspired naïveté.

Gronicka, André von. "Myth Plus Psychology: A Stylistic Analysis of 'Death in Venice.' " In *Thomas Mann: A Collection of Critical Essays*, edited by Henry Hatfield. Englewood Cliffs, N.J.: Prentice-Hall, 1964.
Argues that Mann's bifocal view of life as encompassing both the transcendent and the real reaches its highest level of perfection in "Death in Venice." A detailed analysis of the story employing this duality, showing how the various characters and actions are spectral, even though they do not strain our sense of the real.

Heller, Erich. *The Ironic German: A Study of Thomas Mann*. Boston: Little, Brown, 1958.
Discusses the story as Mann's self-parody. Argues that the story is alone among works of extreme psychological realism in achieving in all seriousness the parodistic semblance of mythic innocence. Also notes that the story is a paradox, for it is such a radical critique of art that it amounts to a moral rejection of art.

Hirschbach, Frank Donald. *The Arrow and the Lyre: A Study of the Role of Love in the Works of Thomas Mann*. The Hague, Netherlands: Martinus Nijhoff, 1955.
Says the story is meant to be read on both a naturalistic and a symbolic level. Briefly analyzes the story from both these points of view. Argues that the irony and tragedy of Aschenbach is that his iron will which carries him to such heights finally collapses of its own weight. Both love and the uncontrolled contemplation of beauty play their role in this story of the gradual disintegration of the will.

Jonas, Ilsedore B. *Thomas Mann and Italy*. Translated by Betty Crouse. Tuscaloosa: University of Alabama Press, 1979.
Discusses Mann's use of the seductive, exotic nature of Venice in the story as well as the theme of the longing of the northern individual for the south. Discusses the south as the embodiment of Aschenbach's discovery of his true self, free from restraint. Also discusses the hidden disease embodied in the city, which Mann uses to suggest its sinister and dangerous aspect.

Kirchberger, Lida. " 'Death in Venice' and the Eighteenth Century." *Monatshefte* 58 (Winter, 1966): 321-334.

Discusses the inspiration of eighteenth century German writers on the story, focusing on specific references to Frederick the Great and Friedrich von Schiller. Draws on several letters of Mann during the period he was writing the story to support the argument of the eighteenth century sources of the work.

Kohut, Heinz. " 'Death in Venice' by Thomas Mann: A Story About the Disintegration of Artistic Sublimation." *Psychoanalytic Quarterly* 26 (1957): 206-228.
Discusses the story as that of a man who is emotionally impelled by forces beyond his reason or control. Also analyzes the work as an attempt by Mann to communicate threatening personal conflicts. Concludes that the story depicts the return of unsublimated libido under the influence of aging, loneliness, and guilt over success.

Lehnert, Herbert. "Thomas Mann's Early Interest in Myth and Erwin Rohde's *Psyche.*" *PMLA* 79 (June, 1964): 297-304.
Discusses how Mann uses myth to complement naturalism in the story. Focuses on Aschenbach's dream of the strange god Dionysus and argues that the major source for the mythical world of the story is the book *Psyche* by Mann's friend Erwin Rohde. Refers to Mann's own pencil-marked copy of the book to support the argument.

Leppmann, Wolfgang. "Time and Place in 'Death in Venice.' " *The German Quarterly* 48 (January, 1975): 47-75.
A description of the actual city of Venice in 1911. Discusses the incidences of cholera that Mann uses in the story, the weather of the city, and other factual details about Venice. Leppmann's purpose is to show how Mann elevates to symbolic significance the commonplace.

Lewisohn, Ludwig. "Death in Venice." In *The Stature of Thomas Mann*, edited by Charles Neider. New York: New Directions, 1947.
A general discussion of the story, arguing that its basic theme is the dizziness that the artist feels when he walks on the edge of an abyss of art. Lewisohn says that the work achieves a perfect union of nature and spirit.

McNamara, Eugene. " 'Death in Venice': The Disguised Self." *College English* 24 (December, 1962): 233-234.
Explicates the story as a parable of the unexamined life. Claims that the story embodies the idea that no one can live a splintered existence; being both spirit and matter, an individual must reconcile these diverse natures. To live in one rather than in both is to invite destruction.

McWilliams, James R. *Brother Artist: A Psychological Study of Thomas Mann's Fiction*. Lanham, Md.: University Press of America, 1983.

Claims that the story stands at the end point of Mann's severe and chaste attitude toward himself and represents his failure to subdue his feelings by repression. Discusses the many signs and symbols of death in the story as well as its structure. Suggests that more than in any other major work, Mann focuses on the hero's psychic conflict rather than on the external story situation.

Reed, T. J. *Thomas Mann: The Uses of Tradition*. London: Oxford University Press, 1974.

A long, detailed discussion of the many complexities in the story. Argues that the story is an experiment for Mann in changing his literary ways, a decision to reject the values by which he had previously worked. Claims that Mann's ambivalent art is brought to maturity with the story and that he rescues the novel of ideas from the mechanical methods of allegory. In "Death in Venice" ambivalence is the central technique of Mann's art, suggesting layers of meaning which lie beneath the surface of immediate experience.

Seyppel, Joachim H. "Two Variations on a Theme: Dying in Venice." *Literature and Psychology* 7 (February, 1957): 8-12.

Discusses the theme of the mystical union between beauty and death and between sex and death in "Death in Venice" and Ernest Hemingway's *Across the River and into the Trees*. A point-by-point comparison of Hemingway's Richard Cantwell and Mann's Aschenbach in terms of their experiences in Venice. Concludes that both works show that dying in Venice is dying from within.

Thomas, R. Hinton. *Thomas Mann: The Mediation of Art*. Oxford, England: Clarendon Press, 1956.

Compares Aschenbach to Mann himself, who has come to see art as a highly questionable activity. Discusses parallels between the story and Johann Wolfgang von Goethe's *Elective Affinities*, but also explains how the comparison is misleading. A long, detailed analysis of how the story develops through a flow of interweaving and coalescing motifs. Argues that no other major work of Mann is more removed from social and ideological intentions.

Traschen, Isadore. "The Uses of Myth in 'Death in Venice.' " *Modern Fiction Studies* 11 (Summer, 1965): 165-179.

Discusses how the story uses both the Apollonian-Dionysian myth and the so-called monomyth discussed by Joseph Campbell in *The Hero with a Thousand Faces*. A detailed discussion of the elements of these myths in the story; Traschen concludes that the story reflects Mann's conviction of the necessity of myth, both psychologically and cognitively as a mode of knowledge.

Urdang, Constance. "Faust in Venice: The Artist and the Legend in 'Death in
Venice.' " *Accent* 18 (Autumn, 1958): 253-267.
Compares Aschenbach to the Faust figure in Johann Wolfgang von Goethe's
drama. Notes that with the exception of the *Walpurgisnacht* all the references
are implied. Argues generally that the artist's guilt is due to reaching beyond
the humanly knowable, which, Urdang notes, is a Romantic view of the artist
as creator; it is Faust's guilt. By choosing to be an artist Aschenbach sealed his
pact with the devil.

Venable, Vernon. "Death in Venice." In *The Stature of Thomas Mann*, edited by
Charles Neider. New York: New Directions, 1947.
Discusses the basic dualities of life and death, time and individuality, fertility
and decay, and flesh and spirit, which constitute his works. Venable gives a
long, detailed discussion of the pattern of symbolism in the work to reveal the
inherent complicated structural relations.

"The Dilettante"
Feurlicht, Ignace. *Thomas Mann*. Boston: Twayne, 1968.
Says that in the story Mann shows the effects of decadence; claims that it may
also express his early fear of artistic sterility and his conviction that the artist
is an outsider and a sort of clown whom the normal do not respect and who
does not even respect himself.

"Disorder and Early Sorrow"
Bolkosky, Sidney. "Thomas Mann's 'Disorder and Early Sorrow': The Writer as
Social Critic." *Contemporary Literature* 22 (Spring, 1981): 218-233.
Discusses the social theme of the story. Describes it as a realistic fiction with a
deeper significance, suggesting a more pointed analysis of the time than is
found in any of Mann's previous works. Claims that the story is a significant
turning point in Mann's career, for it bridges earlier and later work. In the
work, Mann declares that change is inescapable; he describes an impending
social catastrophe—the rise of Fascism.

Court, Franklin E. "Deception and the 'Parody of Externals' in Thomas Mann's
'Disorder and Early Sorrow.' " *Studies in Short Fiction* 12 (Spring, 1975):
186-189.
A brief discussion of how the leitmotif of deception in the story is reinforced
through a description of physical externals. Argues that in the story outer traits
complement inner peculiarities, for example, the bifocals of Dr. Cornelius
represent his divided personality, which adjusts its view according to circumstances.

Feurlicht, Ignace. *Thomas Mann*. Boston: Twayne, 1968.
Says that the character Dr. Cornelius is Mann himself and that the children in

the story are his own children. The basic elements of the story—the gulf between the generations, the bourgeois tradition, and parental love and worries—are all handled with humor and gentle irony, says Feurlicht. Calls it a professorial sketch free of ponderousness, bitterness, or sentimentality.

McWilliams, James R. *Brother Artist: A Psychological Study of Thomas Mann's Fiction*. Lanham, Md.: University Press of America, 1983.
Discusses the basic situation of the story and how Dr. Cornelius observes and then interprets the situation to the reader. Notes the similarity of the work, in its emphasis on a society in dissolution, to other Mann novels and stories.

"Gladius Dei"
Feurlicht, Ignace. *Thomas Mann*. Boston: Twayne, 1968.
Examines the contrast in the story between the easygoing, art-loving people and the deadly serious and fanatical man. In the story, art for its own sake or for the sake of mere enjoyment is rejected by Hieronymus, but art as a moral force and a means of redemption is upheld.

Hoffman, Ernst Fedor. "Thomas Mann's 'Gladius Dei.' " *PMLA* 83 (October, 1968): 1353-1361.
Argues that the story is largely an exercise in contemporary and local satire and a good example of Mann's technique of structuring. A detailed analysis of the formal devices of the story: Hoffman concludes that the devices here do not have the same philosophic purposes that they do in Mann's greater work, for here they are purely rhetorical.

"A Gleam"
McWilliams, James R. *Brother Artist: A Psychological Study of Thomas Mann's Fiction*. Lanham, Md.: University Press of America, 1983.
Discusses the figure of Baron Harry, as representative of life at its most commonplace, as the central figure in the story; notes that he is placed opposite to the hero, the artistic and sensitive Avantageur. Compares it to "Tonio Kröger," for both heroes passively view the mediocre qualities of life.

"The Infant Prodigy"
Feurlicht, Ignace. *Thomas Mann*. Boston: Twayne, 1968.
Calls the piece a "sketch" rather than a story; notes that in it Mann creates several satirical glimpses of such characters as the critic, the piano teacher, the princess, the impresario, and others. Notes that the sketch caricatures a successful artist and the public's reaction to him.

McWilliams, James R. *Brother Artist: A Psychological Study of Thomas Mann's Fiction*. Lanham, Md.: University Press of America, 1983.
Because the artist is a child here, his immaturity is not seen as pathological,

114 Twentieth Century European Short Story

according to McWilliams. Notes that by shifting the attention away from the
prodigy to the audience, Mann manages to put distance between himself and
his hero and finally to focus the attention on the nameless artist figure in the
story.

"Little Herr Friedemann"
Feurlicht, Ignace. *Thomas Mann*. Boston: Twayne, 1968.
Notes the irony of the word "mann" in the title, for the central character is not
much of a man. Suggests that the title is repeated so often throughout the story
that it becomes a leitmotif and that the theme of the story is similar to the
theme of "Death in Venice."

Garrison, Joseph M. " 'Little Herr Friedemann': Thomas Mann's First Critique of
Perfection." *Studies in Short Fiction* 11 (Summer, 1974): 277-282.
An explication of the story's theme and place in Mann's works. Argues that it
makes the same kind of distinctions that form the aesthetic foundations of
"Death in Venice." Concludes that the artistic flaws of the story reflect Mann's
inability at this early point in his career to resolve the problem of the artist's
isolation.

Hirschbach, Frank Donald. *The Arrow and the Lyre: A Study of the Role of Love in
the Works of Thomas Mann*. The Hague, Netherlands: Martinus Nijhoff, 1955.
Notes that Friedemann's two injuries are both from women and thus create his
deep hatred of those who live a more extroverted life than he, especially
women. Discusses the relationship between Friedemann and Gerda and
Friedemann's masochistic personality.

"Mario and the Magician"
Feurlicht, Ignace. *Thomas Mann*. Boston: Twayne, 1968.
Argues that Cipolla is a caricature of the artist, reminiscent of the marked men
of Mann's earlier stories. Also notes Cipolla's Fascism and says that the story is
one of Mann's earliest pronouncements against the deadly menace of political
mass hypnosis and overbearing nationalism.

Gray, Ronald. *The German Tradition in Literature: 1871-1945*. Cambridge, England:
Cambridge University Press, 1965.
Notes that the magician Cipolla has the ability to read the thoughts of others
because he shares the artist's sympathy with them; he projects himself into the
situation of the audience. Argues that the narrator of the story, like Cipolla
himself, uses duplicity to persuade the reader that he does not have the freedom to resist the magician.

Hatfield, Henry C. "Thomas Mann's *Mario und der Zauberer*: An Interpretation."
The Germanic Review 21 (1946): 306-312.

Argues that the story is not allegorical, but symbolic, not only on the political level but on the philosophical level as well—the struggle of the free will against the forces of the occult and the subconscious. Concludes that Mario's dignity is more powerful than the free will or the conscious mind, for it brings down the tyrant.

Hunt, Joel A. "Thomas Mann and Faulkner: Portrait of a Magician." *Wisconsin Studies in Contemporary Literature* 8 (Summer, 1967): 431-436.
Argues that the central preoccupation of the story concerns the character of Cipolla and the moral definition of crime. The magician's powers derive from a moral emptiness, symbolized by his physical deformity, which is turned cruelly toward others, and ultimately proves fatal to its possessor.

Jonas, Ilsedore B. *Thomas Mann and Italy.* Translated by Betty Crouse. Tuscaloosa: University of Alabama Press, 1979.
Discusses Mann's holiday stay in Italy in 1926, during which he had the opportunity to observe a nation living under Fascism and which influenced the writing of the story. Discusses how the story is concerned with the psychology of Fascism. Also discusses the many Italian expressions and idioms Mann uses in the story.

Martin, John S. "Circean Seduction in Three Works by Thomas Mann." *Modern Language Notes* 78 (1963): 346-352.
Notes parallels between events and characters in the story and books 10 and 11 of Homer's the *Odyssey*. In "Mario and the Magician" the narrator journeys to a strange land, is seduced, and leaves a wiser man. Cipolla is both seducer and savior, for he seduces the audience and saves them from any responsibility of freely using their will.

Meyers, Jeffrey. "Caligari and Cipolla: Mann's 'Mario and the Magician.' " *Modern Fiction Studies* 32 (Summer, 1986): 235-239.
Argues that the film *The Cabinet of Dr. Caligari* had a direct influence on the atmosphere, plot, characters, and political theme of Mann's story. Discusses Mann's use of a theatrical metaphor, his use of a magician figure, and his political theme of Fascism as being influenced by the film. Notes that Mann hints at this in his essay "On the Film."

Wagener, Hans. "Mann's Cipolla and Earlier Prototypes of the Magician." *Modern Language Notes* 84 (October, 1969): 800-802.
Discusses one of Giovanni Boccaccio's stories in the *Decameron* as source for Mann's magician. Points out the difference between Boccaccio's Cipolla, who is a simple priest, and Mann's Cipolla, who destroys the freedom of will and dignity of the spectators.

"A Railway Accident"

Hermann, John. "Thomas Mann: What Track for the 'Railway Accident.' " *Studies in Short Fiction* 10 (Fall, 1973): 343-346.

Argues for the artistic integrity and aesthetic complexity of the story. Claims that the story is an exemplum for Mann as well as for all others on how the artist prevents his characters from becoming abstractions. Concludes that the story is really about how the writer camouflages the geometry of the fiction with the anecdotes of truth.

"Tonio Kröger"

Basilius, H. A. "Thomas Mann's Use of Musical Structure and Techniques in *Tonio Kröger*." *The Germanic Review* 19 (December, 1944): 284-308.

Discusses Mann's preoccupation and debt to music, particularly how "Tonio Kröger" follows the form of the sonata-allegro. Analyzes four types of musical analogy in the story: allusion to the musical process; exploitation of the tonal and rhythmic properties of words; use of literary leitmotif; and the manipulation of all the musical devices according to the properties of a fugue pattern.

Berendsohn, Walter E. *Thomas Mann: Artist and Partisan in Troubled Times.* Tuscaloosa: University of Alabama Press, 1973.

Discusses the biographical elements of the story and notes how it reflects the central problem of the Romantic, middle-class artist Mann during this period—the tension between art and intellect on the one hand and the naïve life on the other.

Feurlicht, Ignace. *Thomas Mann.* Boston: Twayne, 1968.

Argues that the story has neither the structure nor the content of the traditional novella; it is primarily concerned with the contrast between art and life and the contrast between the artist and ordinary people. Calls it one of Mann's most popular stories, for its adolescent melancholy appeals to the young. Notes that Mann considered it one of his important works.

Heller, Erich. *The Ironic German: A Study of Thomas Mann.* Boston: Little, Brown, 1958.

A long, detailed analysis of the motifs and themes of the story. Claims that the musical leitmotif conveys more effectively than any utterance in the story the foremost problem of the hero: how to defend his work against the encroachment of nonexistence.

Hirschbach, Frank Donald. *The Arrow and the Lyre: A Study of the Role of Love in the Works of Thomas Mann.* The Hague, Netherlands: Martinus Nijhoff, 1955.

Claims that the story combines almost all the ideas and trends of the young Mann. Discusses the story as embodying a struggle between nature and the intellect. Tonio is the truly tragic hero, because he realizes that his greatness stems from the very tension that makes him suffer and because he is willing to make a sacrifice on the altar of love.

McWilliams, James R. *Brother Artist: A Psychological Study of Thomas Mann's Fiction*. Lanham, Md.: University Press of America, 1983.
Argues that Mann's programmatic theory of art as being essentially opposed to life reaches its fullest expression in this short story. This long, detailed analysis concludes that nowhere else does Mann give clearer expression to the notion of the artist's feeling of worthlessness. It is the anguished undertone of self-pity and the sentimental yearning of the hero that give the story its impact.

Wilkenson, E. M. *"Tonio Kröger*: An Interpretation." In *Thomas Mann: A Collection of Critical Essays*, edited by Henry Hatfield. Englewood Cliffs, N.J.: Prentice-Hall, 1964. A detailed explication of the story in terms of the theme of the growth of the artist toward self-knowledge and the related theme of the process of artistic creation. Notes the two ways of experience—seeing and doing—required for artistic maturity. Also discusses the musical leitmotifs, which make up the texture and structure of the story.

Wilson, Kenneth G. "The Dance as Symbol and Leitmotif in Thomas Mann's *Tonio Kröger*." *The Germanic Review* 29 (December, 1954): 282-287.
The thesis of the essay is that the metaphor of life as a dance is the basis of both the structure and the theme of the story. Although the metaphor is thematically widespread, it is structurally important in the first, second, and last episodes. Discusses dancing as a symbolic act throughout the story.

"Tristan"
Feurlicht, Ignace. *Thomas Mann*. Boston: Twayne, 1968.
Notes that the story concerns the antitheses that are typical of Mann's early works. Points out that on one side there is health, life, normality, warmth, simplicity, and usefulness; on the other side there is sickness, death, dream, literature, music, and self-obliteration. Notes the ironic style of the novella and its use of metaphoric motifs.

Hirschbach, Frank Donald. *The Arrow and the Lyre: A Study of the Role of Love in the Works of Thomas Mann*. The Hague, Netherlands: Martinus Nijhoff, 1955.
Shows how in the story the Mann theme of love in the hands of a clever manipulator has been used to destroy a life lie and to test an illusion. Notes its similarity to Henrik Ibsen's play *The Wild Duck*.

ALBERTO MORAVIA
Alberto Pincherle
(1907-   )
Italy

General Biographical and Critical Studies

Baldanza, Frank. "The Classicism of Alberto Moravia." *Modern Fiction Studies* 3 (Winter, 1957-1958): 309-320.
Discussion of Moravia's use of devices of classical Greek tragedy in his prose narrative. Notes that within the pattern of sexuality as a symbolic experience, Moravia borders on, but does not descend into, allegory. Says that "Agostino" and "Luca" are Moravia's first genuine triumphs, for in these works the delicacy of touch and the precision of effect of a great artist emerge.

_____ . "Mature Moravia." *Contemporary Literature* 9 (Autumn, 1968): 507-521.
Discussion of several of Moravia's short-story collections. Comments on the minimalist stories in *Roman Tales* and *The Fetish*, but states that the brevity of the stories is overbalanced by the volume of the works, which gives a panorama of Roman classes and types. Argues that this inclusiveness provides scope to the collections that would otherwise be lacking due to their deficiency in ideological content.

Bergin, Thomas. "The Moravian Muse." *The Virginia Quarterly Review* 29 (Spring, 1953): 215-225.
A general discussion of Moravia's fiction. Says that although some of his stories are surrealistic or fantastic, his world is primarily that of traditional realism. Notes that, as in "Agostino" and "Luca," the type of character who appears most often in his works is the adolescent. Discusses Moravia's style as conventional, if not journalistic. Places him within the Italian literary tradition and comments on his contribution to world literature.

Cottrell, Jane E. *Alberto Moravia*. New York: Frederick Ungar, 1974.
A general introduction to Moravia's life and art. The chapter on the short stories divides Moravia's tales into the early neorealistic stories, the mid-career surrealistic and satiric stories, and the fragmented stories of his later career, which focus on the dehumanization of modern life. Cottrell focuses on Moravia's themes of meaningless middle-class life and the loneliness of the individual.

Dego, Giuliano. *Moravia*. New York: Barnes & Noble Books, 1966.
A chronological introduction to Moravia's works, focusing on the basic themes

of sex, alienation, and moral vice. Points out that Moravia sticks to the natural-ism of events and refuses to accept abstractions. Says that the best stories written since the beginning of his career appear in *Roman Tales* in 1954, for not only are they valid as individual stories, but also they present a panorama of middle-class Roman society.

Heiney, Donald W. *Three Italian Novelists: Moravia, Pavese, Vittorini*. Ann Arbor: University of Michigan Press, 1968.
Discussion of Moravia as a craftsman and an artist. Heiney's primary concern is the novels, and he comments on the short stories as illustrations of themes and techniques that appear in the longer fiction. Argues that the basic premise of Moravia's fiction is human interaction on sexual terms. Discusses several stories briefly, including "Agostino" and "Luca," which Heiney ranks among Moravia's best works.

Lewis, R. W. B. "Alberto Moravia: Eros and Existence." In his *The Picaresque Saint*. Philadelphia: J. B. Lippincott, 1956.
Argues that Moravia presents an image of the world in its sexual aspect, but that much of the time the sex remains hidden. Discusses several elements vitalized by sex in Moravia's world, but also points out the literary or theatrical quality of his work. Analyzes several short works briefly, noting that most of his stories are, by design, pathetic rather than dramatic.

Pacifici, Sergio. "Alberto Moravia's *L'Automa*: A Study in Estrangement." *Symposium* 18 (Winter, 1964): 357-364.
Discusses Moravia's 1963 collection of stories. Argues that the stories as a whole constitute a study in estrangement and a conscious effort to dramatize the kind of automatic life to which the modern individual has fallen prey. Like the characters of Luigi Pirandello, Moravia's automatons want to see themselves live, but they feel as if they are watching a puppet act.

_____ . *Guide to Contemporary Italian Literature: From Futurism to Neorealism*. Cleveland: World Publishing, 1962.
In the chapter on Moravia, Pacifici concurs with the usual critical opinion that in his short stories and novellas Moravia finds the most suitable vehicle for his talent and his themes. Pacifici comments on Moravia's focus on sexuality, the seeming spiritual aridity of his fictional world, his humanism, and his place in modern Italian literature.

Ragusa, Olga. "Alberto Moravia: Voyeurism and Storytelling." *The Southern Review*, n.s. 4 (Winter, 1968): 127-141.
Likens Moravia to a Peeping Tom; his concentration is intense but he is not

emotionally involved. Points out that his stories contain many voyeuristic scenes. Says that his short stories are not typical of the genre, but rather are like journalistic pieces. Comments on several stories in *Roman Tales* and *The Fetish.*

Rebay, Luciano. *Alberto Moravia*. New York: Columbia University Press, 1970.

A helpful introduction to Moravia's fiction, with many brief discussions of the short stories as well as brief comments on "Agostino" as a poetic work and the theme of life being stronger than death in "Luca." No detailed discussion here, but a good first monograph to read on Moravia because of its helpful overall survey.

Ross, Joan, and Donald Freed. *The Existentialism of Alberto Moravia*. Carbondale: Southern Illinois University Press, 1972.

Analysis of the existentialist need of the characters in Moravia's novels and stories to work out their own destinies. The various Moravian existentialist themes discussed include dependence on nature, alienation, sexual dualism, the absurd, nihilism, and bad faith. Passing references are made to the short stories and the novellas.

Selected Titles

"Agostino"

Dego, Giuliano. *Moravia*. New York: Barnes & Noble Books, 1966.

Instead of examining the sexual theme in the story, Dego focuses on the appearance of class differences for the first time in Moravia's work. On the one hand, there is the proletariat filled with envy and violent resentment toward the rich middle class, whereas on the other hand, there is the middle-class Agostino, who, despite his efforts, cannot step down into the working class and who therefore becomes alienated from all concrete and effective relationships.

"Luca"

Ross, Joan, and Donald Freed. *The Existentialism of Alberto Moravia*. Carbondale: Southern Illinois University Press, 1972.

A discussion of the story's focus on alienation manifesting itself in meaning-less suffering. Although the discussion makes some helpful comments about Luca's movement toward nihilism and a death wish, most of the several pages devoted to the story are long quotations illustrating the major stages of Luca's increasing alienation.

VLADIMIR NABOKOV
(1899-1977)
Russia and United States

General Biographical and Critical Studies

Alter, Robert. *Partial Magic: The Novel as a Self-Conscious Genre*. Berkeley: University of California Press, 1975.
Discussion of Nabokov's "game of words" and his position as preeminent practitioner of self-conscious narrative in modern fiction. Although most of this chapter is a discussion of the novel *Pale Fire*, Alter's book is a good introduction to self-reflexive fiction and Nabokov's place in this predominant modern narrative assumption and technique.

Bader, Julia. *Crystal Land: Artifice in Nabokov's English Novels*. Berkeley: University of California Press, 1972.
The introduction to this study of the six English-language novels of Nabokov is valuable in laying out what has been called his "art theme." Argues that the various levels of reality in his works are best seen as the perspective of the game of artifice. Nabokov's characters are not dramatizations of ideas about art; rather they are self-contained worlds, which reshape the reader's conception of art. A helpful discussion of the manifestation of the artistic consciousness in Nabokov's work.

Bitsilli, P. M. "The Revival of Allegory." In *Nabokov*, edited by Alfred Appel, Jr., and Charles Newman. New York: Simon & Schuster, 1970.
A 1936 essay on Nabokov when he was writing under the name of V. Sirin in Europe. Places him within the Russian tradition to which Bitsilli thinks that he belongs. Notes that Sirin's return to the genre of allegory is characterized by a certain estrangement from life, an artistic quality required by allegory.

Burns, Dan E. "*Bend Sinister* and 'Tyrants Destroyed': Short Story into Novel." *Modern Fiction Studies* 25 (Autumn, 1979): 508-513.
Argues that Nabokov's novels are characterized by the same motifs—confusion of identity, movement toward isolation or liberation, and reciprocal worlds—found in his short fiction. Uses the concepts of Northrop Frye to show that such novels as *Bend Sinister* are "romances" and thus more characteristic of the short-story mode than of the novel mode.

Dembo, L. S., ed. *Nabokov: The Man and His Work*. Madison: University of Wisconsin Press, 1967.

A collection of critical essays primarily on the major novels, with some general articles and interviews. The most valuable ones for an understanding of Nabokov's short fiction are the articles on Nabokov and Jorge Luis Borges and on Nabokov's early prose. The book also includes a checklist of criticism on Nabokov, including reviews of the major novels.

Field, Andrew. *Nabokov: His Life in Art*. Boston: Little, Brown, 1967.
In this most frequently cited of all Nabokov studies, Field spends a few pages on the short stories, primarily detailing their publishing history and commenting on the tradition to which they belong. Notes that, as is the case in his novels, many of the characters in his short stories are fixated on the past; cites "The Return of Chorb" as the best-known early example. Summarizes several other stories such as "Spring in Fialta" and "That in Aleppo Once . . . ."

_____ . *Nabokov: His Life in Part*. New York: Viking Press, 1977.
Not to be confused with Field's earlier biography entitled *Nabokov: His Life in Art*, this rambling and personal account of Field playing Boswell to Nabokov's Samuel Johnson, provides additional insights into Nabokov's literary career and his literary obsessions. Of particular interest to the student of the short fiction are the discussions of Nabokov's life in Berlin in the 1920's when he wrote many of his short stories.

_____ . *VN: The Life and Art of Vladimir Nabokov*. New York: Crown, 1986.
In his third book on Nabokov, Field draws upon his earlier research to focus on Nabokov's narcissism. What discussion there is of the stories focuses on their possible biographical sources. For example, Field suggests that "Spring in Fialta" may be a tangential record of his first extramarital affair, although Field offers no real evidence for such interpretations. Very little critical commentary here.

Fowler, Douglas. *Reading Nabokov*. Ithaca N.Y.: Cornell University Press, 1974.
Readings of five Nabokov's novels and three of his stories in terms of such constants as his obsession with human mortality and his moral scheme. Also discusses his use of language, his genius for mimicry, and his creation of character.

Grabes, H. *Fictitious Biographies: Vladimir Nabokov's English Novels*. The Hague, Netherlands: Mouton, 1977.
A close reading of eight English-language novels from the point of view of the obstacles encountered by the writer when transforming autobiographical elements into fiction. Each chapter focuses on a different novel and a different aspect of biography or autobiography; for example, fictitious biography, biogra-

phy as a balance between tragedy and comedy, and autobiography as parody. Grabes does not discuss the short fiction, but he provides a helpful demonstration of Nabokov's use of biography in his fiction.

Green, Geoffrey. *Freud and Nabokov*. Lincoln: University of Nebraska Press, 1988.
Although he admits at the outset that Nabokov hated psychoanalysis and that consequently no one has discussed Nabokov from a Freudian perspective, Green has written a provocative little book in which, instead of trying to apply psychoanalysis either to the mind of Nabokov or to the minds of his characters, he focuses instead on poststructuralist approaches to Freud to show how both Freud and Nabokov were interested in the nature of writing.

Hyde, G. M. *Vladimir Nabokov: America's Russian Novelist*. London: Marion Boyars, 1977.
A fairly routine discussion of the novels in terms of their place in both the Russian nineteenth century tradition and twentieth century Russian Formalism and French structuralism. The author purposely omits the short fiction; however, the book is helpful in placing Nabokov in the literary and theoretical tradition to which he belongs.

Karges, Joann. *Nabokov's Lepidoptera: Genres and Genera*. Ann Arbor, Mich.: Ardis, 1985.
A short monograph on Nabokov's interest in butterflies and moths and its influence on his fiction. Although the focus is primarily on allusions and references in Nabokov's works, the study also focuses on the importance of Nabokov's interest in taxonomy in his fiction. The only references to the short fiction are to two stories which feature lepidoptera: "The Aurelian," which uses butterflies to suggest transcendence, and "Christmas," which uses butterflies to focus on the theme of rebirth and resurrection.

Khodasevich, Vladislav. "On Sirin." In *Nabokov*, edited by Alfred Appel, Jr., and Charles Newman. New York: Simon & Schuster, 1970.
An early discussion (1930's) of Nabokov when he was writing under the name of V. Sirin. Argues that the key to all of his works is that he does not hide his fictional devices but rather displays them for all to see. The major theme of Sirin is the life of the artist and the life of a device in the consciousness of an artist.

Lee, L. L. *Vladimir Nabokov*. Boston: Twayne, 1976.
This general introduction to Nabokov's life and art includes only four pages on the short fiction; Lee says that the stories provide an introduction to the basic themes in the novels. Argues that the stories are mostly conventional, but that they illustrate his delight in language and his focus on the eruption of the

irrational. Also suggests that his stories express deep concern with the moral life.

Maddox, Lucy. *Nabokov's Novels in English*. Athens: University of Georgia Press, 1983.
A general introduction to the themes and techniques of Nabokov's English-language novels. Argues that what makes Nabokov's art so innovative is the way the subjective vision determines structure and style. According to Maddox, Nabokov's characters are by necessity always victims of their own creative imaginations, a point she illustrates with a brief discussion of "That in Aleppo Once. . . ." Says that the world of Nabokov's characters is maddening not because events seem random, but because they seem so carefully designed.

Merrill, Robert. "Nabokov and Fictional Artifice." *Modern Fiction Studies* 25 (Autumn, 1979): 439-462.
Argues that the conventional view of Nabokov's art—that he is a postmodernist—is misleading; for it suggests, wrongfully, that all of his novels are metafictions, and it implies that Nabokov repeatedly worked toward one theme—art. One of the few articles on Nabokov to argue against his self-reflexivity and his art theme. Primarily a discussion of *Lolita* and *Pale Fire*.

Morton, Donald E. *Vladimir Nabokov*. New York: Frederick Ungar, 1974.
This monograph is an introduction to Nabokov's life and art, devoting one chapter to the Russian novels and then a chapter each to such American novels as *Pnin*, *Lolita*, *Pale Fire*, and *Ada or Ardor*. No discussion of the short stories, but a good general introduction to Nabokov's focus on subjectivity and consciousness.

Moynahan, Julian. *Vladimir Nabokov*. Minneapolis: University of Minnesota Press, 1971.
A brief pamphlet-length introduction to Nabokov's life and work, focusing primarily on four novels: *Laughter in the Dark*, *Lolita*, *The Gift*, and *Pale Fire*. Although there is no discussion of the short fiction, this book is a good introduction to Nabokov's fictional techniques and thematic interests. Moynahan's central point is that Nabokov's books are not imitations of reality but rather imitations of imitations.

Nabokov, Vladimir. *Speak, Memory: An Autobiography Revised*. New York: G. P. Putnam's Sons, 1966.
A highly praised autobiography, often referred to by Nabokov's critics and biographers alike. The work is more about atmospheres than it is about events or facts. Indispensable reading for the student of Nabokov. Although often as opaque as one of Nabokov's novels, the work is filled with ideas and insights about Nabokov's theory of fiction.

Naumann, Marina Turkevich. *Blue Evenings in Berlin: Nabokov's Short Stories of the 1920's*. New York: New York University Press, 1978.
This is the only book-length study of Nabokov's short stories; since it deals with the stories written at the beginning of his career, however, many of the best-known stories are not discussed. Naumann discusses the stories from the perspective of Russian Formalism as well as from the point of view of their place in the tradition of Russian literature. The book divides the stories into three categories: the realistic, the realistic-symbolic, and the symbolic.

Parker, Stephen Jan. *Understanding Vladimir Nabokov*. Columbia: University of South Carolina Press, 1987.
An introductory guide to Nabokov for students and nonacademic readers. After an introductory chapter on the self-reflexive aspects of Nabokov's narrative technique, the book focuses on individual analyses of five Russian novels and four American novels. The three pages on the short stories provides brief summary analyses of "Spring in Fialta," "Cloud, Castle, Lake," "Signs and Symbols," and "The Vane Sisters."

Proffer, Carl R., ed. *A Book of Things About Vladimir Nabokov*. Ann Arbor, Mich.: Ardis, 1974.
A collection of essays on all facets of Nabokov's art—from the reaction to his work in Russian émigré criticism to a *Lolita* crossword puzzle. Most of the essays are on individual novels, both Russian and English. The collection contains one article on the short fiction.

Roth, Phyllis A., ed. *Critical Essays on Vladimir Nabokov*, edited by Phyllis A. Roth. Boston: G. K. Hall, 1984.
A collection of previously published essays on individual novels and on general aspects of Nabokov's art. Of particular interest to students of his short stories is an early review of his 1930 collection published under the name V. Sirin and entitled *The Return of Chorb*. Also included is an annotated bibliography of criticism on Nabokov; the selections are limited, but the annotations are extensive.

Rowe, William Woodin. *Nabokov and Others: Patterns in Russian Literature*. Ann Arbor, Mich.: Ardis, 1979.
The only reference to Nabokov's short stories in this collection of essays on Nabokov and other Russian writers is the chapter entitled "Nabokov: The Hounds of Fate," which deals with Nabokov's use of the dog as an emblem of destiny or fate. The stories mentioned briefly in this regard are "That in Aleppo Once . . . ," which features an apparently nonexistent dog; "Cloud, Castle, Lake," in which a fateful dog leads the protagonist into the inn; and "An Affair of Honor," in which a character resembles a dachshund.

_____ . *Nabokov's Deceptive World.* New York: New York University Press, 1971.
Study of the means by which Nabokov creates his artistic deceptions. Chapters focus on negation, linguistic parody in his Russian novels, manipulation of levels of reality, use of sound effects, use of symbolism, and allusions to sports and games. Passing references to the short fiction.

Stegner, Page. *Escape into Aesthetics: The Art of Vladimir Nabokov.* New York: Dial Press, 1966.
Primarily a discussion of the five novels Nabokov wrote in English, with separate chapters on each one. Part of the book, however, is a readable general introduction to Nabokov's literary career and the basic characteristics of his fiction, such as his use of satiric parody, his literary playfulness, his rhetorical achievements, his verbal skill, and his impressionism. Although there are only passing references to the short stories, the general sections are very helpful for understanding Nabokov's fictional art.

Stuart, Dabney. *Nabokov: The Dimensions of Parody.* Baton Rouge: Louisiana State University Press, 1978.
A collection of essays on individual novels focusing on them as a game, a play, a film, a joke, and an autobiography. The book does not deal with such major novels as *Lolita*, *Pale Fire*, or *Ada or Ardor*, nor does it make any mention of the short stories. It is, however, an interesting discussion of the various non-realistic modes of Nabokov's fiction.

Williams, Carol T. "Nabokov's Dozen Short Stories: His World in Microcosm." *Studies in Short Fiction* 12 (Summer, 1975): 213-222.
A discussion of the stories in *Nabokov's Dozen*. Claims that all the stories in the collection are about the quest to unify the two worlds of the mundane and the ecstatic. Although all the stories end with the failure of the quest, all are rich with the beauty encountered along the way. Brief discussions of the best-known stories from the perspective of this central theme and structure.

Selected Titles

"Cloud, Castle, Lake"
Fowler, Douglas. *Reading Nabokov.* Ithaca, N.Y.: Cornell University Press, 1974.
Calls the story a social parable with a fairy-tale atmosphere. Compares the theme of the conflict between the individual and the group to a similar theme in Nabokov's novel *Bend Sinister*. Claims that nowhere in Nabokov's fiction is his moral world presented in so spare and clean a fashion.

"The Return of Chorb"

Green, Geoffrey. *Freud and Nabokov*. Lincoln: University of Nebraska Press, 1988.
Argues that Chorb's behavior in the story is evidence of his desire to undo his wife's death by traveling back to the source of his recollections. Claims that because Chorb seized a substitute for his wife—instead of the repressed image—a new image is found. Thus, like Eurydice, she dies a second death.

Naumann, Marina Turkevich. *Blue Evenings in Berlin: Nabokov's Short Stories of the 1920's*. New York: New York University Press, 1978.
An in-depth analysis of the formal properties of the story as well as its theme of "remembrance of things past." Points out the poetic figures of speech in the story, the importance of the story's atmosphere, its setting, and its character configuration.

"Signs and Symbols"

Andrews, Larry R. "Deciphering 'Signs and Symbols.' " In his *Nabokov's Fifth Arc: Nabokov and Others on His Life's Work*. Austin: University of Texas Press, 1982.
A detailed discussion of the imagery patterns in the story—most of which are concealed clues that the boy commits suicide in the end and that the parents are responsible. The artificiality of the ending of the story, with its withholding of the climax, reminds the reader of the artificiality of the story as a whole.

Carroll, William. "Nabokov's Signs and Symbols." In *A Book of Things About Vladimir Nabokov*, edited by Carl R. Proffer. Ann Arbor, Mich.: Ardis, 1974.
Compares the story to the novel *Pnin* and discusses the deranged boy in the story as one whose self-consciousness resembles the reader's own. Says that the boy's "referential mania" is a disease suffered by all readers of fiction, for the critic analyzes the signs that refer to some meaning outside the work. The story strikes at the very nature of the fictional world and the kind of relationship a reader has to it.

Dole, Carol M. "Innocent Trifles, or 'Signs and Symbols.' " *Studies in Short Fiction* 24 (Summer, 1987): 303-305.
A discussion of the relevance of the "ten fruit jellies in ten little jars" which the couple purchases as a present for their son. By calling the parents innocent, Nabokov uses them as a signpost pointing to his theme of the human impulse to restructure a random world into a meaningful pattern. Says that the story is about creating and interpreting, as well as about a crazed boy and his pitiable parents.

Hagopian, John V. "Decoding Nabokov's 'Signs and Symbols.' " *Studies in Short Fiction* 18 (Spring, 1981): 115-119.

Claims that the central thematic question of the story is whether it is necessarily paranoid to believe that nature and the universe are the enemies of
humankind. Hagopian disagrees with what he calls William Carroll's postmodernist interpretation that the story has an open form. Hagopian has no
doubts that the telephone call at the end of the story is a report of the boy's
suicide.

"Spring in Fialta"

Fowler, Douglas. *Reading Nabokov*. Ithaca, N.Y.: Cornell University Press, 1974.
Argues that the most subtle distinction in this story built on various planes of
the real and the artificial is the difference between life and art. A fully detailed
discussion of the technique of indirection in the story as well as its aesthetic
and sexual themes.

Lee, L. L. *Vladimir Nabokov*. Boston: Twayne, 1976.
Discussion of the story's themes of loss of order in chaos and the past pre-
served in art and lost in time. Analyzes the structure of the story as a series of
waves within a circle of time. Also comments on the characters as doubles and
the repetition of images and themes in the structure of the story.

Monter, Barbara Heldt. " 'Spring in Fialta': The Choice that Mimics Chance." In
Nabokov, edited by Alfred Appel, Jr., and Charles Newman. New York: Simon
& Schuster, 1970.
Says that the key device in all Nabokov's art is his calling attention to the
difference between life and art. Not a detailed analysis of the story, but a
discussion of it as illustrative of Nabokov's basic aesthetic theme. Calls
"Spring in Fialta," with all the Nabokovian artistic preoccupations and stylistic traits packed into a few pages, as clear a masterpiece among his short
stories as *Lolita* is among his novels.

"That in Aleppo Once . . ."

Green, Geoffrey. *Freud and Nabokov*. Lincoln: University of Nebraska Press, 1988.
Argues that the narrator in the story is describing a conflict of opposing drives
which, according to Freudian theory, derive from the distinction between death
instincts and life instincts. The journey of the couple in the story is between
Eros and death. Green's analysis of the story primarily derives from Sigmund
Freud's *Beyond the Pleasure Principle*.

"The Vane Sisters"

Eggenschwiler, David. "Nabokov's 'The Vane Sisters': Exuberant Pedantry and a
Biter Bit." *Studies in Short Fiction* 18 (Winter, 1981): 33-39.
Argues that the reader cannot understand the main techniques of the story

without becoming a diligent pedant, following up the allusions and playing the Nabokovian game. Lays bare the hidden clues in the story, comments on how the reader is betrayed about the character of the narrator, and discusses the allusions to literary and historical lore in the story.

BORIS PASTERNAK
(1890-1960)
Soviet Union

General Biographical and Critical Studies

Anning, N. J. "Pasternak." In *Russian Literary Attitudes from Pushkin to Solzhenitsyn*, edited by Richard Freeborn. New York: Barnes & Noble Books, 1976.
An essay on Pasternak within the framework of his Russian cultural background. No discussions of the short fiction here, but a helpful and readable summary of Pasternak's life and the historical realities of the period within which he lived.

Aucouturier, Michel. "The Legend of the Poet and the Image of the Actor in the Short Stories of Pasternak." In *Pasternak: Modern Judgments*, edited by Donald Davie and Angela Livingstone. London: Macmillan, 1969.
Attempts to show that the stories of Pasternak are worthy of consideration in their own right, rather than simply as experimental efforts at prose by a lyrical poet. Notes that they are works of imagination whose subjects, situations, and characters already reveal Pasternak's fundamental novelistic motifs.

_____ . "The Metonymous Hero or the Beginnings of Pasternak the Novelist." In *Pasternak: A Collection of Critical Essays*, edited by Victor Erlich. Englewood Cliffs, N.J.: Prentice-Hall, 1978.
Discusses the novella "The Childhood of Luvers" and the verse novel *Spektorsky* in terms of the kind of hero created by the process of metonymy. The events of the story are not connected by causality but by pure metonymic contiguity; events are suggested in an allusive fashion.

Berlin, Isaiah. "The Energy of Pasternak." In *Pasternak: A Collection of Critical Essays*, edited by Victor Erlich. Englewood Cliffs, N.J.: Prentice-Hall, 1978.
Says that Pasternak's stories must be understood in the historical context of his life. Describes his prose as overelaborate and euphuistic. The result is an amalgam of inspiration in which moments of beauty and innocence mingle with hysteria and exhibitionism.

Brown, Edward. *Russian Literature Since the Revolution*. Cambridge, Mass.: Harvard University Press, 1982.
A brief introduction to Pasternak's life and art, with some discussion of *Doctor Zhivago* as a poetic novel with a Hamlet-like hero. No discussion of the short stories, but this overview of Pasternak is clear and concise, even though it is too slight to deal with any of his fiction in detail.

de Mallac, Guy. *Boris Pasternak: His Life and Art*. Norman: University of Oklahoma Press, 1981.
A critical biography filled with photographs. Only a few pages on the stories, noting that they represent Pasternak's response to revolutionary events between 1915 and 1924. Says that "The Childhood of Luvers" is the most remarkable of his stories. Notes that the short fiction brought him his first critical recognition as a prose writer. A readable introduction to Pasternak's life and the characteristics of his art.

Dyke, J. W. *Boris Pasternak*. Boston: Twayne, 1972.
A general introduction to Pasternak's works. Discusses the poetry, the autobiographical writings, *Doctor Zhivago*, and the short stories. The chapter on the stories provides summary discussions of Pasternak's five major stories. Says that Pasternak's prose tries to express the unspeakable, that it is filled with vague associations, visions, metamorphic powers, unexpected paradoxes, and mixtures of fact and poetry.

Gifford, Henry. *Pasternak: A Critical Study*. Cambridge. England: Cambridge University Press, 1977.
An introduction to Pasternak's life and work in chronological order. Discusses the short stories in a chapter on Pasternak and the new Russian prose. Says that the stories are an overflow from the poetry, for they deal with the predicament of the artist or the sensibility of the child.

Hingley, Ronald. *Pasternak: A Biography*. London: Weidenfeld & Nicolson, 1983.
A biography with no real critical analyses of the stories. The book does provide information about the sources of the stories and their critical reception. Notes that sensations, not events, are what matters in Pasternak's fiction. Summarizes some of his major themes, such as the similarity between the poet and the actor and the tragic consequences of revolution.

Hughes, Olga R. *The Poetic World of Boris Pasternak*. Princeton, N.J.: Princeton University Press, 1974.
Although this book is primarily a discussion of Pasternak's poetry, the chapter on art and reality, which deals with his view of poetic language and the relationship between art and reality, is helpful for understanding his fiction. Brief discussions of some of the stories such as "The Childhood of Luvers" and "A Tale."

Ivinskaya, Olga. *A Captive of Our Time*. Translated by Max Hayward. Garden City, N.Y.: Doubleday, 1978.
A detailed and heavily documented biography. Brief discussion of the short stories as preparation for *Doctor Zhivago*, arguing that some of the characters

are precursors to characters in that novel. The book also contains several letters of Pasternak, as well as a biographical guide to all the people mentioned in the text.

Jakobson, Roman. "Marginal Notes on the Prose of the Poet Pasternak." In *Pasternak: Modern Judgments*, edited by Donald Davie and Angela Livingstone. London: Macmillan, 1969.
An important essay showing how Pasternak's lyricism in his short stories is characterized by metonymy rather than by metaphor. In Pasternak's prose, the anthropomorphism of the inanimate world is predominant. Jakobson's discussion of Pasternak's metonymic approach to the depiction of reality here is the first appearance of the distinction between metaphor and metonymy that later becomes an important element of structuralist literary theory.

Payne, Robert. *The Three Worlds of Boris Pasternak*. London: Robert Hale, 1961.
A critical/biographical introduction to Pasternak, with chapters on the poetry, the short stories, and *Doctor Zhivago*. In his discussion of the short stories, Payne (who translated the stories into English) notes that in them Pasternak was searching for a prose style. They do not belong in the tradition of Anton Chekhov, but rather are told in a startling mixture of fact and poetry.

Slonim, Marc. *Soviet Russian Literature: Writers and Problems—1917-1967*. New York: Oxford University Press, 1967.
In his discussion of Pasternak, Slonim calls him the voice of the "other Russia," for he reminds readers that even though Communism is a large part of Russian life and history, it does not encompass all Russian people, for a whole world of passion and ideals exists underneath the Communist establishment. Discusses Pasternak's literary career in various periods of his development.

Weidle, Wladimir. "The Poetry and Prose of Boris Pasternak." In *Pasternak: Modern Judgments*, edited by Donald Davie and Angela Livingstone. London: Macmillan, 1969.
Discussion of style in Pasternak's poems and stories. Points out that in comparison to the vacuous prose style of other Russian writers at the time, Pasternak's is conscious, sober, and real. Argues that his prose style is a more perfect tool than the style of his poetry.

Selected Titles

"Aerial Ways"
Dyke, J. W. *Boris Pasternak*. Boston: Twayne, 1972.
Suggests that what is striking in the story is the artistic projection of various

levels of reality, for in it psychodisturbances are rivaled by mysterious natural events. The style of the story is like a modern symphony in which numerous nonmelodic circles interweave into an opaque opus.

Kestner, Joseph. "The Spatiality of Pasternak's 'Aerial Ways.' " *Studies in Short Fiction* 10 (Summer, 1973): 243-251.
An analysis of how the story makes use of the spatial arts of the pictorial, the sculptural, and the architectural. Argues that in the story one experiences the most rigid reduction of the situation to the essentials of the narrative. Claims that like most of Pasternak's prose, this story is empty of action and has dispensed with the object.

Payne, Robert. *The Three Worlds of Boris Pasternak*. London: Robert Hale, 1961.
Says that the story is actually five separate fragments, only loosely connected, of the despair in Russia in 1925. Notes that this was Pasternak's favorite story; says that it is the story that most clearly describes his relationship to the Communists. Payne claims that nothing Pasternak ever wrote seems so hard and close-packed as this story.

"The Childhood of Luvers"
Dyke, J. W. *Boris Pasternak*. Boston: Twayne, 1972.
Claiming that this is the most perfect of Pasternak's short stories, Dyke discusses the story as a fragmented stream of consciousness. Argues that what is characteristic of the events that occur to the young girl is how they affect her maturing process and how they reveal the perception changes from the particular to the general in direct proportion with the experience that she acquires.

Gifford, Henry. *Pasternak: A Critical Study*. Cambridge, England: Cambridge University Press, 1977.
A brief summary discussion of the story, arguing that it is more straightforward than many of his other stories, for it attempts to reflect the charm of a child's imagination. Says that the story is flawless in its presentation of an innocent awareness growing into a full knowledge of life.

Payne, Robert. *The Three Worlds of Boris Pasternak*. London: Robert Hale, 1961.
Payne says that this is the most perfectly accomplished of all of Pasternak's stories, for here he displays a full command of the prose medium. At first reading, the story gives the effect of a prodigious conjuring trick—an effect created by the invention of long complex sentences, which outline the thoughts of the girl.

"The Last Summer"
Dyke, J. W. *Boris Pasternak*. Boston: Twayne, 1972.
Describes the complex frame-story structure of this autobiographical fiction.

Says that it is a modern story in that it ignores events and the details of things to focus instead on moods and images. Likens the story to an abstract painting or a symphony with infinite allusions.

"Letters from Tula"
Dyke, J. W. *Boris Pasternak*. Boston: Twayne, 1972.
Tries to show that the novel *Doctor Zhivago* is contained in miniature in this story by focusing on the relationship of the poet to the old man. Discusses Pasternak's reclaiming of Leo Tolstoy as the antithesis to glamorous and blatant modernism. Says that this story is the most characteristic story Pasternak ever wrote.

Payne, Robert. *The Three Worlds of Boris Pasternak*. London: Robert Hale, 1961.
Discusses the story as an allegory that succeeds brilliantly as an improvisation in a new form. Interested in the style of the story, Payne quotes generously from it and concludes that nearly all of *Doctor Zhivago* is contained in the work in embryo.

"The Mark of Apelles"
Dyke, J. W. *Boris Pasternak*. Boston: Twayne, 1972.
Dyke calls this the most complex of Pasternak's stories. Says that it was influenced by his translations of the works of Heinrich von Kleist. Argues that the story deals with Pasternak's attempt to extend the artistic atmosphere to the realities of life. Concludes that the story is the beginning of Pasternak's long struggle to find a unity between life and art.

Payne, Robert. *The Three Worlds of Boris Pasternak*. London: Robert Hale, 1961.
Discusses the story as Pasternak's version of a Greek myth, but notes that the style and mood are borrowed from Heinrich von Kleist's *The Marquise of O . . . .*. Argues that in the story Pasternak is trying to say things never said before and that for him words and images posses magical properties. Notes that the particular virtues of Pasternak's style are not fully apparent yet.

CESARE PAVESE
(1908-1950)
Italy

General Biographical and Critical Studies

Biasin, Gian-Paolo. *The Smile of the Gods: A Thematic Study of Cesare Pavese's Works*. Translated by Yvonne Freccero. Ithaca N.Y.: Cornell University Press, 1968.
Each of the chapters in this study deals with a different thematic concern of Pavese, such as solitude, violence, or love; each begins with a brief discussion of how the short stories embody these themes, although the majority of the chapters discusses the novels. In spite of the thematic focus, the study also deals briefly with the structure of the stories; for example, the relationship between dialogue and narrative in "Wedding Trip" and the lucidity of introspection in "Suicides." Biasin argues that Pavese's themes are more explicit in his short stories than in his novels.

Heiney, Donald W. *Three Italian Novelists: Moravia, Pavese, Vittorini*. Ann Arbor: University of Michigan Press, 1968.
Argues that Pavese's fiction is highly poetic — a fact not easily appreciated in translations. Little comment here on the short stories, but a helpful discussion of Pavese's narrative techniques and his efforts to unify style and theme in his fiction. Also deals with the theme of the contrast between nature and civilization in Pavese's fiction.

Lajolo, Davide. *An Absurd Vice: A Biography of Cesare Pavese*. Translated by Mario Pietralunga and Mark Pietralunga. New York: New Directions, 1983.
A popular biography, originally a best-seller in Italy when it was published in 1960. Includes numerous letters. Lajolo says that in his short stories Pavese entrusted his true self; he quotes from the story "Suicides" to reflect Pavese's flight from solitude, his delusions, and his remorse.

Thompson, Doug. *Cesare Pavese: A Study of the Major Novels and Poems*. Cambridge, England: Cambridge University Press, 1982.
Although, as the title suggests, this study does not really deal with the short fiction, its concluding chapter is valuable in pointing out the concept of antithesis that runs throughout all Pavese's work. The study focuses on individual novels to chart Pavese's search for style and his development of his theory of myth.

LUIGI PIRANDELLO
(1867-1936)
Italy

General Biographical and Critical Studies

Büdel, Oscar. *Pirandello*. London: Bowes & Bowes, 1966.
    Brief introduction to the man and his life. Passing comments on the short
    stories, which Büdel says depict man's ensnarement in the strange and in-
    congruous ways of life. Claims that Pirandello does so well in the short story
    because his characters are never types. Although the focus is primarily on the
    plays, Büdel's discussion of themes is a good introduction to Pirandello's major
    concerns.

Caputi, Anthony. *Pirandello and the Crisis of Modern Consciousness*. Urbana:
    University of Illinois Press, 1988.
    Argues that the importance of Pirandello's work lies in his recognition that the
    twentieth century, because of the loss of traditional structures and values,
    focuses on consciousness as its chief source of value. Most of the book focuses
    on the drama, but in one chapter several summary analyses of the stories deal
    with the mania to live in face of life's arcane forces.

Castris, A. L. de. "The Experimental Novelist." In *Pirandello: A Collection of
    Critical Essays*, edited by Glauco Cambon. Englewood Cliffs, N.J.: Prentice-
    Hall, 1967.
    Discusses Pirandello's fiction in terms of modern man's rebellion against the
    false forms of individuation and the false masks of society that warp his will;
    however, finding the escape impossible, for outside society there is nothing, the
    Pirandellian hero returns to life with bitterness. Although there is no discus-
    sion of the short fiction in this essay, it provides some stimulating ideas about
    Pirandello's fictional themes.

Howe, Irving. Foreword to *The Merry-Go-Round of Love*, by Luigi Pirandello. New
    York: New American Library, 1959.
    A brief introduction to Pirandello's life and art as a short-story writer. Places
    his stories in the main tradition of nineteenth century European realism.
    Claims that Pirandello does not engage in "fine writing," but, more than most
    modern short-story writers, depends on action. Says his stories are quite
    conventional, containing no Joycean flashes of insight, but that they read like
    compressed scenarios.

Matthaei, Renate. *Luigi Pirandello*. Translated by Simon Young and Erika Young.
    New York: Frederick Ungar, 1973.

The focus of this study is on the plays, but the biographical sketch and the brief account of Pirandello's fictional work before he began writing plays make the book a helpful introduction. Emphasizes Pirandello's disillusionment, first with socialism and then with Fascism, and the cynicism that resulted.

May, Frederick. Introduction to *Short Stories*, by Luigi Pirandello, edited by May. London: Oxford University Press, 1965.

Says that all of Pirandello's works are of a piece, that the stories deal with the same themes encountered in the plays, that is the nature of identity, reality and illusion, and the impossibility of communication. Argues that Pirandello's most important contribution to the short story is his use of dialogue. Discusses a number of stories briefly in terms of both their themes and their style. Informed, sensitive, and readable, this text is the best brief introduction to Pirandello as a short-story writer.

Mooestrup, Jorn. *The Structural Patterns in Pirandello's Work*. Odense, Denmark: Odense University Press, 1972.

A discussion of the five basic periods in the development of Pirandello's career. Short stories from each of the periods are briefly summarized and characterized as to their generic type. Although there are no detailed discussions of any of the stories, this book is one of the few studies of Pirandello that devotes as much space to his fiction as to his plays.

Poggioli, Renato. "Pirandello in Retrospect." In *The Spirit of the Letter: Essays in European Literature*. Cambridge, Mass.: Harvard University Press, 1965.

Extended comparison of Pirandello with his spiritual father, Giovanni Verga. Poggioli says that Verga's shepherds and Pirandello's petit-bourgeois represent the artistic synthesis of two contrasting generations and reflect the social evolution of Sicily since the 1900's. Briefly discusses Pirandello's short story "The Jar" and Verga's story "Property" to indicate this social evolution.

Ragusa, Olga. *Luigi Pirandello*. New York: Columbia University Press, 1968.

The primary focus is on the plays and novels, but the monograph contains passing references to the short stories. The discussion of Pirandello's fictional world and fictional creation of characters makes this a helpful introduction to his typical themes and techniques.

Reynolds, Mary T. "Joyce and Pirandello." In *Pirandello*, edited by Anne Paolucci. New York: Griffon House, 1987.

Reviews the possible meetings and mutual acquaintances of the two men, as well as the readings they had in common. More important, Reynolds notes the similarity of fictional method and theme, as well as the strong biographical element in their writings. Shows how both writers are major ironists of the modern movement.

Starkie, Walter. *Luigi Pirandello: 1967-1936*. Berkeley: University of California Press, 1965.

Treats Pirandello as a futurist, a regionalist, and one of the intellectual chiefs of Italy in the early twentieth century. Includes a brief section on the short stories, noting that there are traces of a kinder Pirandello in the stories than in the plays. Also claims that Pirandello's characters often seem abnormal because he interprets them so completely. More than just plot summary, this chapter is an incisive critical discussion of the characteristics of Pirandello's stories.

Ulrich, Leo. "Pirandello Between Fiction and Drama." In *Pirandello: A Collection of Critical Essays*, edited by Glauco Cambon. Englewood Cliffs, N.J.: Prentice-Hall, 1967.

A careful analysis of a short story ("Mrs. Frola and Her Son-in-Law") as a monologue that contains the seeds of the play *Right You Are (If You Think So)*. The emphasis of the analysis is on the speaker of the short story, which Ulrich calls less a story than a dramatic structure. Argues that the play is already potentially in the short work, which Ulrich defines as an "author monologue," a little genre unto itself.

ALAIN ROBBE-GRILLET
(1922-   )
France

General Biographical and Critical Studies

Clayton, John J. "Alain Robbe-Grillet: The Aesthetics of Sadomasochism." *The Massachusetts Review* 18 (Spring, 1977): 106-119.
The title of this article is misleading; Clayton does not deal with the theme of sadomasochism in Robbe-Grillet, but rather his self-reflexive technique of making the reader an accomplice in the narration. Clayton does not approve of Robbe-Grillet's turning the world into an art object, for such aestheticization imposes a totalitarian order on the world and is life-denying in its spirit.

Fletcher, John. *Alain Robbe-Grillet*. New York: Methuen, 1983.
A short monograph focusing on the themes of love, loss, and eroticism in Robbe-Grillet's works. Suggests that the stories in *Snapshots* are, like Kafka's stories, condensed versions of his novels; they are practice pieces, five-finger exercises, says Fletcher, for the composition of *The Voyeur* and *In the Labyrinth*. Singles out "The Secret Room" as representative of Robbe-Grillet's sadistic view of the female.

Heath, Stephen. *The Nouveau Roman: A Study in the Practice of Writing.* London: Elek Books, 1972.
Argues that the novels of Robbe-Grillet must be read at the level at which reading itself is posed as a problem. Although the long chapter on Robbe-Grillet contains no discussion of his short stories, it is one of the best discussions of the theoretical background of the *New Novel*. A demanding but rewarding analysis.

Leki, Ilona. *Alain Robbe-Grillet*. Boston: Twayne, 1983.
A general introduction to Robbe-Grillet, focusing primarily on his contribution to the French New Novel, or *le nouveau roman*. After an introductory chapter on the beginnings of the New Novel, Leki devotes a chapter to each of Robbe-Grillet's major novels and adds one final brief chapter on his films. Although there is no discussion of the short stories, this book offers a good orientation to the nature of Robbe-Grillet's fiction.

Mercier, Vivian. *The New Novel: From Queneau to Pinget*. New York: Farrar, Straus & Giroux, 1971.
In the chapter on Robbe-Grillet, Mercier discusses the major works and how they are examples of the New Novel. Argues that the stories in *Snapshots* are

not short stories at all, but rather sketches and brief prose descriptions. Notes that "The Secret Room" is the most explicit manifestation of the fetishistic sadism that is found in many of Robbe-Grillet's works.

Morrissette, Bruce. *Alain Robbe-Grillet*. New York: Columbia University Press, 1965.
A short monograph by one of the best-known critics of Robbe-Grillet. Morrissette devotes three pages to the stories in *Snapshots*, more than most critics, noting that they illustrate original formal techniques. Focuses on how the techniques, such as the suppressed first-person point of view, appear in later novels. Morrissette points out that although the stories have been given little attention by critics, as samples of Robbe-Grillet's writing techniques and thematic obsessions they are a rich source of material.

––––––––––––– . "Games and Game Structures in Robbe-Grillet." *Yale French Studies* no. 41 (1968): 159-167.
A brief survey of the game playing and gamelike patterns in Robbe-Grillet's fiction, specifically games of which the characters and the readers are unaware. Morrissette says that games represent structural freedom for Robbe-Grillet, the absence of traditional rules of previous fiction, as well as an invitation to create new models of structure.

––––––––––––– . *The Novels of Robbe-Grillet*. Ithaca, N.Y.: Cornell University Press, 1975.
In this updated and expanded version of Morrissette's important and frequently cited 1965 study of Robbe-Grillet, he begins with a discussion of the theory of the New Novel and then devotes a chapter to each of Robbe-Grillet's major novels published through 1974. The only comments on the short stories appear in the chapter on *La Maison de rendezvous*, in which Morrissette notes the similarity between the theme of erotic violence in the novel and "The Secret Room."

Roudiez, Leon S. *French Fiction Today: A New Direction*. New Brunswick, N.J.: Rutgers University Press, 1972.
Although the chapter on Robbe-Grillet focuses on the novels and makes no mention of the short stories in *Snapshots*, Roudiez's discussion of Robbe-Grillet's basic narrative techniques and how they develop from *The Erasers* to *La Maison de rendezvous* is clear and helpful. A good introduction to narrative assumptions and devices that inform Robbe-Grillet's fiction.

Stoltzfus, Ben F. *Alain Robbe-Grillet: The Body of the Text*. London: Associated University Press, 1985.
A poststructuralist, Marxist, Freudian analysis of Robbe-Grillet's novels, par-

ticularly since 1965. Stoltzfus is primarily interested in what he calls the dual emphasis of Robbe-Grillet's fiction—the formalist, self-reflexive reference to the work itself and the work's attempts to subvert established ideology. He argues that the short stories in *Snapshots* are Robbe-Grillet's first and most emphatic use of the artwork reflecting its own reflection, thus dissolving reality and substituting consciousness in its place.

——————. *Alain Robbe-Grillet and the New French Novel*. Carbondale: Southern Illinois University Press, 1964.
The first book published in English on Robbe-Grillet. Discusses Robbe-Grillet's place in the tradition of Western narrative and the existential basis of the French New Novel in general. In a brief comment on Robbe-Grillet's short stories, Stoltzfus notes that they are snapshots of the affective life of the psyche. Moreover, he says that the way Robbe-Grillet alternates passages in the stories between objective descriptions and subjective involvement emphasizes his basic theme of the separation between human consciousness and things.

Szanto, George H. *Narrative Consciousness*. Austin: University of Texas Press, 1972.
In his chapter on Robbe-Grillet, Szanto argues that narrative consciousness moves beyond Franz Kafka and Samuel Beckett to completeness. Claims that although Robbe-Grillet's works display no formal organization they are highly organized according to the narrative consciousness of the protagonist.

JEAN-PAUL SARTRE
(1905-1980)
France

General Biographical and Critical Studies

Ames, Van Meter. "Back to the Wall." *Chicago Review* 13 (1959): 128-143.
A discussion of Sartre's collection of stories *The Wall* from the point of view of his philosophy. Ames argues that although the stories may at first reading seem to suggest a nihilistic attitude, the capacity of human beings to learn, to forgive, and to start over shine through all of them. Despite the disturbing nature of the stories, Ames believes that it is better to know what is missing in life than to ignore the absence.

Barnes, Hazel E. *Sartre*. Philadelphia: J. B. Lippincott, 1973.
A study of Sartre's philosophy, with chapters on how his thought is embodied in his drama. In her brief discussion of the stories, Barnes notes that they indicate the transitional nature of Sartre's thought in the 1930's. Whereas "The Childhood of a Leader" might be read as a commentary on the philosophy in *Being and Nothingness*, other stories reflect Sartre's study of such psychologists as Alfred Adler and Wilhelm Stekel.

Brosman, Catherine Savage. *Jean-Paul Sartre*. Boston: Twayne, 1983.
An introduction to Sartre, with chapters on his life, his philosophy, his fiction, and his drama. A brief discussion of the five stories in *The Wall and Other Stories* appears in the chapter on the early fiction. In these sketchy summaries, Brosman notes that all the stories are ironic and place characters in extreme situations against the wall of circumstances. Brosman illustrates how the stories reflect basic Sartrean views of facticity, contingency, and bad faith.

Champigny, Robert. *Stages on Sartre's Way*. Bloomington: Indiana University Press, 1959.
A study of Sartre's fiction and drama published between 1938 and 1952. The focus is on the development of Sartre's view of the moral question in *Being and Nothingness*. Although there is no discussion of the short stories here, the discussion of such works as *Nausea* and *Being and Nothingness*, which were written during the same period, is helpful in putting the stories in the context of Sartre's developing thought.

Cranston, Maurice. *Jean-Paul Sartre*. New York: Grove Press, 1962.
A short introductory volume which includes chapters on Sartre's life, his major works, his critical theories, his psychoanalysis, his ethics, and his political

plays. Cranston's brief commentary on the stories focuses primarily on "The Wall," which he says is one of his least characteristic fictions; in fact, with its neat plot and ironic final twist, it belongs to a tradition of fiction typical of Guy de Maupassant, which Sartre repudiated.

Howells, Christina. *Sartre: The Necessity of Freedom*. Cambridge, England: Cambridge University Press, 1988.
A full-scale introductory study of Sartre, examining the development of his philosophical thought as well as his drama, fiction, and literary criticism. An original and perceptive study of Sartre intended for the nonspecialist. No discussion of the short stories except for a brief remark that the stories in *The Wall and Other Stories* are focused, centered, and often told retrospectively.

Masters, Brian. *Sartre: A Study*. London: Heinemann, 1970.
A preliminary and general introduction to Sartre's fiction. The focus is on the existential themes of absurdity, freedom, contingency, and bad faith found in Sartre's work. Although there are passing references to the stories in this running commentary on quoted passages, the primary emphasis is on the novels.

Peyre, Henri. *Jean-Paul Sartre*. New York: Columbia University Press, 1968.
In this brief monograph Peyre says there may not be another volume of short stories in French literature of the last hundred years as remarkable as *The Wall and Other Stories*. He argues that because the stories are early works, they are not marred by philosophy or obtrusive symbolism as are Sartre's novels, but rather are as concrete as the stories of Ernest Hemingway. Peyre's actual discussions of the stories are less analysis than summary and praise.

Plank, William. *Sartre and Surrealism*. Ann Arbor, Mich.: UMI Research Press, 1981.
A short study of Sartre's anti-Surrealism in his stories and his Surrealism in *Nausea*. Claims that the five stories in *The Wall and Other Stories* demonstrate the efforts of five people to escape the human condition but are stopped by a wall. In varying ways the stories attempt to discredit, often by satire, the ways that the Surrealists approached the problem of man's existence.

Thody, Philip. *Jean-Paul Sartre*. London: Hamish Hamilton, 1960.
This study of Sartre's literary works and his political ideas contains a chapter on the short stories, pointing out how each illustrates one of Sartre's favorite philosophical ideas, for example, bad faith, the attempt at humanization of death, the extreme confines of anti-humanism, and the escape from super-fluidity. Thody notes that it is not only the ideas expressed in the stories that make them among his most interesting works, but also the evidence they give of his sensitive observation of social behavior.

Selected Titles

"The Childhood of a Leader"
Ames, Van Meter. "Back to the Wall." *Chicago Review* 13 (1959): 128-143.
   Suggests that the story illustrates George Herbert Mead's account of the development of the self by means of assuming many roles. Analyzes the story in
   terms of Sartre's concept in *Being and Nothingness* that man is always moving
   away from what he is no longer to what he is not yet.

Plank, William. *Sartre and Surrealism*. Ann Arbor, Mich.: Research Press, 1981.
   Argues that the story is more than a dramatization of some Sartrean ideas, that
   it is a kind of intellectual history of the interwar years and a satire on some of
   the major ideologies of the time. Claims that the story is almost a continuous
   mockery of Surrealism, a burlesque history of the preoccupations of the movement. A detailed analysis of the story as satire on Surrealism.

Smith, Madeleine. "The Making of a Leader." *Yale French Studies* 1 (1948): 80-83.
   Although this short essay argues that the story is a kind of case history or
   social document, it points out that the history of the protagonist is told as if he
   were a physiological thing; his emerging personality is bound up with the
   history of his bodily sensations. Smith says that the story emphasizes the
   human fundamental urges, such as prejudice, that we all have to fight in our
   neighbors, ourselves, and our children.

Thody, Philip. *Jean-Paul Sartre*. London: Hamish Hamilton, 1960.
   Calling this story the most obviously political of Sartre's prewar writings,
   Thody says that it is a social satire of the bourgeoisie as seen from the inside.
   The close relationship between this story and Sartre's essay on anti-Semitism
   shows how easily Sartre's political and philosophical ideas intermingle and
   how his dislike of the bourgeoisie springs from both philosophical and political
   reasons.

"Erostratus"
Ames, Van Meter. "Back to the Wall." *Chicago Review* 13 (1959): 128-143.
   Discussion of the story in terms of Sartre's psychology, especially his notion of
   the human desire to be a thing under the petrifying gaze of the other. The story
   reveals the pit beneath men of good will and the sick and self-defeating
   outlook of the man of ill will.

Plank, William. *Sartre and Surrealism*. Ann Arbor, Mich.: UMI Research Press,
   1981.
   Although Surrealism is not explicitly mentioned in this story, says Plank, the
   protagonist's plan is to perform the "Surrealist act" as defined by André
   Breton. Describing the protagonist Hilbert as surrealist material, Plank argues

that Hilbert's attitude toward language particularly makes him nearer to the Surrealist than to the existentialist.

Thody, Philip. *Jean-Paul Sartre*. London: Hamish Hamilton, 1960.

In this story, Thody claims, Sartre so excels at describing the abnormal that one can see his early short fiction as an attempt to liberate himself from his obsessions and neglect the philosophical overtones in each of his stories. In this satirical story, Sartre shows that the anti-Humanist attitude is just as pointless as that of the Humanist. The protagonist in the story illustrates the sadistic need to dominate the other by forcing the other to be completely identified with the body.

Woodle, Gary. "Erostrate: Sartre's Paranoid." In *Critical Essays on Jean-Paul Sartre*, edited by Robert Wilcocks. Boston: G. K. Hall, 1988.

Argues that the story is not only an indispensable introduction to Sartre's novel *Nausea*, but also that it anticipates many of his works in general. The protagonist Hilbert is more than a paranoid type; he is an antiChrist and a study in bad faith. In its broadest significance, says Woodle, the story represents the foundation in fiction for what will later become an existentialist humanism, which comprehends the human situation as demanding a fluid relationship with others.

"Intimacy"

Ames, Van Meter. "Back to the Wall." *Chicago Review* 13 (1959): 128-143.

Argues that although the story may be read as a heartless satire on intimacy, the pair in this story do love, in their fashion, even if it leaves much to be desired. Suggests that the story reflects Sartre's tendency to turn the tables on the normal and the adjusted and sympathize with the lame and the losers.

Morris, Edward. "Intimacy." *Yale French Studies* 1 (1948): 73-79.

Discusses the underlying patterns of the story as a way to reveal Sartre's talent for expressing thematic richness through banal reality and seemingly indifferent details. Comparing Lulu in the story with Molly Bloom in James Joyce's *Ulysses*, Morris suggests that the story follows a five-act dramatic structure in which there is an absence of action and a final irresolution. By using Joyce's parody of the faithful wife, Sartre is actually parodying a parody.

Thody, Philip. *Jean-Paul Sartre*. London: Hamish Hamilton, 1960.

According to Thody, the story examines a concept at the center of Sartre's moral philosophy—that man is always free to make whatever decision he likes and live his life as he pleases, that is, he is free to adopt whatever attitude he pleases toward his situation. The central female figure in the story is an illustration of Sartre's view of bad faith, says Thody, for she tries to hide her freedom and responsibility from herself.

"The Room"

Greenlee, James. "Sartre's 'Chambre': The Story of Eve." *Modern Fiction Studies* 16 (Spring, 1970): 77-84.

Argues that the reader must approach the story as if it were the work of one of the "new novelists" whose techniques Sartre anticipates. Analyzes the narrative technique to show how central Eve is in the story. Eve's selection and interpretation of events are more important than the events themselves.

Plank, William. *Sartre and Surrealism*. Ann Arbor, Mich.: UMI Research Press, 1981.

Although this story is not a close-knit satire on the Surrealist use of abnormal mental states, Pierre, the madman in the story, is like the Surrealist in his special relationship with objects; for both, objects lose their stability and become threatening. Moreover, his speech at times sounds like automatic writing and his invention of a spiderlike device suggests the same function as the surrealistic object—to break through the ordinary world and weaken the barrier between reason and nonreason.

Simon, John K. "Madness in Sartre: Sequestration and the Room." *Yale French Studies* 30 (1964): 63-67.

Compares the story with Sartre's *The Condemned of Altona*; argues that both suggest that insanity is a potential form of truth. Points out that since the narration of the story forces the reader to approach the madman only through Eve, the reader is left on the threshold of madness.

—————— . "Sartre's Room." *Modern Language Notes* 79 (December, 1964): 526-538.

An analysis of the story in terms of its reaction against the Proustian idea that the human mind can control its surroundings through a subjective process. Simon argues that in spite of this negative comment on Proustian solipsism, the kind of sequestration Sartre describes in the story has certain heroic elements, for the paranoiac makes an admirable effort to objectify the animate and animate objects so they can participate in a unified system.

Thody, Philip. *Jean-Paul Sartre*. London: Hamish Hamilton, 1960.

Suggests that the story illustrates that the human mind can no more deliberately escape from its own humanity into madness than it can think its own death. Also points out that the story illustrates Sartre's idea in *Being and Nothingness* that when two lovers know they are being observed by a third person, their love is destroyed.

"The Wall"

Braun, Sidney. "Source and Psychology of Sartre's 'Le Mur.' " *Criticism* 7 (1965): 45-51.

Discussion of the source of the story as well as the concepts underlying its psychological study of fear in the works of Georges Dumas. Discusses aspects of fear in the story, such as its effects on the body and its nonreflective emotional consciousness. At the heart of the story, says Braun, fear exists by virtue of such concrete facts of consciousness as the Look.

Carson, Ronald A. *Jean-Paul Sartre*. Valley Forge, Pa.: Judson Press, 1974.

In this brief monograph, Carson analyzes the story as a meditation on death. Primarily a plot summary with a final comment that the coincidence that ends the story is a reflection of the absurdity of existence. Generally, this monograph is a simple summary of Sartre's thought and art.

Thody, Philip. *Jean-Paul Sartre*. London: Hamish Hamilton, 1960.

Argues that the plot of the story and the description of the protagonist's reaction to the idea of his own death refute the idea that man can control and decide the significance of his own mortality. The story is an ironic illustration of the idea that man can never count on anything but his own actions.

148

BRUNO SCHULZ
(1892-1942)
Poland

General Biographical and Critical Studies

Updike, John. "Polish Metamorphoses." In *Hugging the Shore: Essays and Criticism*. New York: Alfred A. Knopf, 1983.
This essay, which originally appeared as an introduction to the Penguin edition of *Sanitorium Under the Sign of the Hourglass*, is primarily an appreciation of Schulz. Updike notes the verbal brilliance and beauty of Schultz's work, but points out the cruelty of myth that lies behind it. Compares Schulz with Franz Kafka and others.

Wieniewska, Celina. Translator's Preface to *Sanitorium Under the Sign of the Hourglass* by Bruno Schulz. New York: Walker, 1977.
Calls the collection a poetic re-creation of Schulz's autobiography—the memories of a child through the eye of an artist. Discusses some of the biographical elements in the stories. Also provides a brief biographical sketch of Schulz's life and career.

_____ . Translator's Preface to *The Street of Crocodiles*, by Bruno Schulz. New York: Walker, 1963.
A thumbnail sketch of Schulz's brief literary career. Notes that the world of his work is basically a private world, dominated by his father. Discusses the influence that Franz Kafka, Thomas Mann, and Sigmund Freud had on his work. Says that his prose is as memorable as the brush strokes of Marc Chagall.

ISAAC BASHEVIS SINGER
(1904-   )
Poland and United States

General Biographical and Critical Studies

Alexander, Edward. *Isaac Bashevis Singer*. Boston: Twayne, 1980.
A chapter on the short stories in this introduction to Singer's literary career and his major works discusses representative stories in four of what Alexander calls Singer's favorite modes: apocalypse, Jewish survival, love and perversion, autobiography. Notes that as opposed to Singer's novels, which are within the tradition of nineteenth century realism, the short stories are read as modernist excursions into diabolism, perversity, and apocalypse.

Buchen, Irving H. *Isaac Bashevis Singer and the Eternal Past*. New York: New York University Press, 1968.
Argues that Singer is a master of the short story because he believes that caricature is the norm rather than the exception. Suggests that his short stories differ from his novels by having an untraditional feminine point of view. Discusses the stories as the normalizing of dislocation.

Eisenberg, J. A. "Isaac Bashevis Singer: Passionate Primitive or Pious Puritan." In *Critical Views of Isaac Bashevis Singer*, edited by Irving Malin. New York: New York University Press, 1969.
Points out that the difficulties of reading Singer are due to his creation of a strange and incongruous world, his fusing of the two different worlds of the bourgeois and the supernatural. Discusses the basic moral themes in Singer's stories as well as his deep involvement with the sensual and the passionate.

Fixler, Michael. "The Redeemers: Themes in the Fictions of Isaac Bashevis Singer." In *Critical Views of Isaac Bashevis Singer*, edited by Irving Malin. New York: New York University Press, 1969.
Says that Singer, obsessed by essentially religious themes, is most at home in archaic, prerational traditions and in native Yiddish folklore from his homeland in Poland. Discusses the basic religious themes in Singer; compares him to Thomas Mann in his ability to create stories that resonate with both pathological and supernatural overtones.

Friedman, Melvin J. "Isaac Bashevis Singer: The Appeal of Numbers." In *Critical Views of Isaac Bashevis Singer*, edited by Irving Malin. New York: New York University Press, 1969.

Argues that Singer's real subject is the constant reminder of the disproportion between the ethic the Jews have fashioned for themselves and the abuse it has suffered at various moments in their history. Says that Singer does not have enough ideological base in his short stories.

Gass, William H. "The Shut-In." In *The Achievement of Isaac Bashevis Singer*, edited by Marcia Allentuck. Carbondale: Southern Illinois University Press, 1969.
This brief essay discusses the unstated philosophic framework of Singer's tales. Says that his fiction possesses a magnificent ontological equality, for it has the material solidity that it claims for everything. Calls Singer a shut-in because of the primitive materiality of his approach.

Hochman, Baruch. "I. B. Singer's Vision of Good and Evil." In *Critical Views of Isaac Bashevis Singer*, edited by Irving Malin. New York: New York University Press, 1969.
Claims that Singer comes into his own with his vision of the grotesque world of the archaic shtetl, for within this world he makes no effort to be realistic but reformulates the world to suit his artistic needs. Says that he is at his best in the short tales.

Howe, Irving. Introduction to *Selected Short Stories of Isaac Bashevis Singer*. New York: Random House, 1966.
Often called one of the best introductory essays on Singer's short fiction, this discussion focuses on Singer's love of the grotesque, the demonic, the erotic, and the quasi-mystical. Discusses the influence of Singer's culture and tradition on his fiction, but also discusses how his stories differ from others in the Yiddish tradition. Comments on the combination of modernism and Yiddish traditionalism in his stories.

Kresh, Paul. *Isaac Bashevis Singer: The Magician of West 86th Street*. New York: Dial Press, 1979.
A detailed critical biography with brief discussions of many of the stories. Recounts a class session in which Singer talks to students about the story "Yentl the Yeshiva Boy." Says that "Gimpel the Fool" is Singer's world in microcosm. Notes that most of Singer's stories have the seemingly artless art of the folktale.

Mintz, Samuel I. "Spinoza and Spinozism in Singer's Short Fiction." In *Critical Views of Isaac Bashevis Singer*, edited by Irving Malin. New York: New York University Press, 1969.
Says that Singer's use of Spinoza's philosophy is a way of focusing on the

tension between rationalism and the spirit world of demons. Discusses this idea in "The Spinoza of Market Street" and "Caricature."

Siegel, Ben. *Isaac Bashevis Singer*. Minneapolis: University of Minnesota Press, 1969.
A short monograph introduction. Helpful for providing an understanding of the European tradition from which Singer's stories spring. Particularly helpful is the brief discussion of the collection *Gimpel the Fool and Other Stories*. Siegel says that Singer's tales transcend the regional to explore the individual's moral fiber under severe testing circumstances.

Wolkenfeld, J. S. "Isaac Bashevis Singer: The Faith of His Devils and Magicians." In *Critical Views of Isaac Bashevis Singer*, edited by Irving Malin. New York: New York University Press, 1969.
Traces the theme of faith through his fiction, citing "Gimpel the Fool" as the clearest case in point. Says that in its insistence on the lonely necessity to decide how to live and in its conclusion that man has to choose without certitude, Singer's work is meaningful for both Jew and non-Jew.

Selected Titles

"The Gentleman from Cracow"
Alexander, Edward. *Isaac Bashevis Singer*. Boston: Twayne, 1980.
Analyzes the story as one of Singer's apocalyptic tales in which the theory that "worse is better" is endorsed by the action. Says that the story reflects the paradox that out of evil must come good and that even the most enterprising of devils is a servant of heaven.

"Gimpel the Fool"
Alexander, Edward. *Isaac Bashevis Singer*. Boston: Twayne, 1980.
Discusses the basic theme of this, Singer's best-known story. Points out that what characterizes Gimpel is his readiness to believe everything that he is told, no matter how fantastic. Notes his descent from the schlemiels of the classical Yiddish writers, but also notes that he differs from them by choosing to be fooled. Argues that if worldliness disbelieves everything, then this story is Singer's most powerful attack on worldliness.

Buchen, Irving H. *Isaac Bashevis Singer and the Eternal Past*. New York: New York University Press, 1968.
Points out that Gimpel's gullibility is actually the overflow of faith. Argues that the aim of the story is to invest the strange with the familiar. The wisdom of Gimpel dictates that surrender often requires greater strength than self-reliance and that certain illusions are more real than the facts of life.

Siegel, Paul N. "Gimpel and the Archetype of the Wise Fool." In *The Achievement of Isaac Bashevis Singer*, edited by Marcia Allentuck. Carbondale: Southern Illinois University Press, 1969.

Says that the story is a masterpiece of irony and compares Gimpel to other fools in literature, especially the wise fool of Desiderius Erasmus' *The Praise of Folly*. The essay is an extended comparison of the wise fool in both works.

"The Little Shoemaker"

Alexander, Edward. *Isaac Bashevis Singer*. Boston: Twayne, 1980.

Describes the story as one of Singer's most beautiful and most ambitious tales. Both a mourning over what has been lost and a celebration over what has survived, it tries to encompass the enormous upheavals of the Jewish people in modern times. Stresses more than any other Singer story the degree to which the disastrous events that have befallen the Jews resemble the fantastic tales of the Bible.

"The Spinoza of Market Street"

Buchen, Irving H. *Isaac Bashevis Singer and the Eternal Past.* New York: New York University Press, 1968.

Says that the story depicts one of Singer's scholarly Jews who, in turning from the religious to the secular, encounters the face of his own mortality. Says that Dr. Fischelson will probably live out his life believing that he has betrayed Spinoza, whereas the reverse is true.

"Yentl the Yeshiva Boy"

Alexander, Edward. *Isaac Bashevis Singer*. Boston: Twayne, 1980.

Calls the story one of Singer's most balanced and restrained treatments of how even the noblest of human impulses may lead to perversion. Points out that Singer's resistance to Yentl's ambition comes from two sources: his traditionalist view that Judaism depends on separation and distinction and his view of homosexuality's inability to propagate the race and perpetuate the Jewish people.

Buchen, Irving H. *Isaac Bashevis Singer and the Eternal Past*. New York: New York University Press, 1968.

Says that what Yentl does not foresee in the story is what happens when a familiar personality resides in an alien body. Singer cannot approve of Yentl's act because it precludes the family and thus terminates the community. Behind Yentl's scholarship lies the ultimate perversion—the refusal to be dependent and vulnerable.

ALEXANDR SOLZHENITSYN
(1918-   )
Soviet Union

General Biographical and Critical Studies

Anning, N. J. "Solzhenitsyn." In *Russian Literary Attitudes from Pushkin to Sol-zhenitsyn*, edited by Richard Freeborn. New York: Barnes & Noble Books, 1976.
Briefly summarizes Solzhenitsyn's life and literary career, including the reception of "One Day in the Life of Ivan Denisovich." Mentions the stories' ironic overtones, which are meant to suggest a moral. Points out that many of the stories are drawn from experience but differ from the novels by being more compressed and more polished linguistically.

Barker, Francis. *Solzhenitsyn: Politics and Form*. New York: Barnes and Noble Books, 1977.
Barker divides Solzhenitsyn's writings into two periods: the first including the early works such as "One Day in the Life of Ivan Denisovich," *The First Circle*, and *Cancer Ward*, which Barker calls the "democratic" novels; and the second, including those works beginning with *August 1914*, which he says define a specific ideology. The one-dimensionality of "One Day in the Life of Ivan Denisovich," its ideological and tonal flatness, constitutes its aesthetic decisiveness.

Burg, David, and George Feifer. *Solzhenitsyn*. Briarcliff Manor, N.Y.: Stein & Day, 1972.
A popular biography, much less ambitious than the more detailed life of Solzhenitsyn by Michael Scammel. There is little critical analysis of the short fiction here, but the study does place some of the stories in their auto-biographical and historical contexts. A very readable life of the man, even if, as Burg and Feifer admit, it is limited by the difficulty of gaining access to either Solzhenitsyn or to his Russian background.

Carter, Stephen. *The Politics of Solzhenitsyn*. New York: Holmes & Meier 1977.
This study, although admitting at the outset that Solzhenitsyn is more concerned with moral, religious, and aesthetic values than with politics, attempts to place him within the Soviet context of his political thought. The first half of the book discusses Solzhenitsyn's political thought by means of a close textual analysis of *The Gulag Archipelago, 1918-1956*, while the second focuses on Solzhenitsyn's speeches and other political works. No discussion of the short fiction, except for brief remarks on "One Day in the Life of Ivan Denisovich."

Clément, Oliver. *The Spirit of Solzhenitsyn*. Translated by Sarah Fawcett and Paul
Burns. London: Search Press, 1976.
After the initial chapters, which focus on the influence the prison camp, the
war, cancer, and the threat of death had on Solzhenitsyn's thought and art, this
study emphasizes the themes of erotic love, Christian mysticism, and history in
Solzhenitsyn's work. Passing references to the short stories indicate how they
embody these various themes.

Curtis, James M. *Solzhenitsyn's Traditional Imagination*. Athens: University of
Georgia Press, 1984.
A study of the relationships between Solzhenitsyn's work and the Russian
literature of the past, such as that of Leo Tolstoy, Fyodor Dostoevski, and
Anton Chekhov; also compares him to such twentieth century writers as John
Dos Passos and Ernest Hemingway.

Dunlop, John B. "Solzhenitsyn's 'Sketches.' " In *Aleksandr Solzhenitsyn: Critical
Essays and Documentary Materials*, edited by Dunlop, Richard S. Haugh, and
Alexis Klimoff. Belmont, Mass.: Nordland, 1973.
A discussion of Solzhenitsyn's very brief stories or sketches, lyric prose pieces
of fifteen to twenty lines. Says that they are primarily concerned with the
spiritual inadequacy of modern life and Solzhenitsyn's romantic and religious
attitude toward nature.

Dunlop, John B., Richard S. Haugh, and Alexis Klimoff, eds. *Aleksandr Solzhenitsyn: Critical Essays and Documentary Materials*. Belmont, Mass.: Nordland,
1973.
An extremely valuable collection of critical essays as well as statements by
Solzhenitsyn. Part 1 contains general essays on his life and art; Part 2 contains
essays on the individual novels, particularly *August 1914*. The documents include Solzhenitsyn's Nobel lecture, as well as annotated bibliographies of both
Soviet and Western responses to his work.

Dunlop, John B., Richard S. Haugh, and Michael Nicholson, eds. *Solzhenitsyn in
Exile*. Stanford, Calif.: Hoover Institution Press, 1985.
A second collection of critical essays and documentary material on Solzhenitsyn, with most of the essays being on *The Gulag Archipelago 1918-1956*. The
first half of the book surveys the reception of Solzhenitsyn in England, the
United States, West Germany, France, and Yugoslavia, mostly since 1974. Also
includes an annotated bibliography of criticism on Solzhenitsyn's fiction.

Ericson, Edward E., Jr. *Solzhenitsyn: The Moral Vision*. Grand Rapids, Mich.: Wm.
B. Eerdmans, 1980.
An analysis of Solzhenitsyn's work from the point of view of his Christian

vision. Contains individual chapters on the major novels as well as the short stories and prose poems. The prose poems show Solzhenitsyn's gentle, reflective side and introduce some of the themes of his longer works. Ericson examines the prose poems in terms of such basic themes as joy in nature, respect for simple peasant ways, and the despiritualization of the modern individual.

Erlich, Victor. "The Writer as Witness: The Achievement of Aleksandr Solzhenitsyn." In *Aleksandr Solzhenitsyn: Critical Essays and Documentary Materials*, edited by John B. Dunlop, Richard S. Haugh, and Alexis Klimoff. Belmont, Mass.: Nordland, 1973.
Notes that the Western literary critic may have difficulty with Solzhenitsyn's old-fashioned nineteenth century realism. A brief survey of his work, arguing that his most salient quality is his relentless veracity. The real hero of all of his stories, like those of Leo Tolstoy, is truth.

Grazzini, Giovanni. *Solzhenitsyn*. Translated by Eric Mosbacher. London: Michael Joseph, 1971, 1973.
A social and biographical account of Solzhenitsyn's literary career and his political troubles from the publication of "One Day in the Life of Ivan Denisovich" to the awarding of the Nobel Prize in Literature. As with many books on Solzhenitsyn, the focus is less on analysis of the works than on the political repercussions of their publication. What comments there are on the short fiction are limited to their reception and social and political impact.

Klimoff, Alexis. "Solzhenitsyn in English: An Evaluation." In *Solzhenitsyn: A Collection of Critical Essays*, edited by Kathryn Feuer. Englewood Cliffs, N.J.: Prentice-Hall, 1976.
A review and evaluation of the major English translations of Solzhenitsyn's fiction, especially those translations which have had the greatest impact on the English-speaking world. Discusses the problems that Solzhenitsyn's prose creates for translators.

Kodjak, Andrej. *Alexander Solzhenitsyn*. Boston: Twayne Publishers, 1978.
A general introduction to Solzhenitsyn's works, with separate chapters on "One Day in the Life of Ivan Denisovich" and the short stories. Also contains a short bibliography of both primary and secondary sources. Notes that although the short stories and the novels were written during roughly the same period, they differ in that the stories do not deal with prison life.

Krasnov, Vladislav. *Solzhenitsyn and Dostoevsky: A Study in the Polyphonic Novel*. Athens: University of Georgia Press, 1980.

This study of Solzhenitsyn's three major novels—*The First Circle*, *Cancer Ward*, and *August 1914*—makes clear their similarities to the novels of Fyodor Dostoevski and shows how they are polyphonic novels, as that term is defined by the Russian critic, Mikhail Bakhtin. The basic Bakhtin thesis is that in a polyphonic novel the author expresses himself not through one character or another, but through the structure of the novel itself. Although there is no discussion of the short stories, this book provides a helpful study of Solzhenitsyn's narrative style.

Labedz, Leopold, ed. *Solzhenitsyn: A Documentary Record*. New York: Harper & Row, 1971.
A collection of reviews, interviews, newspaper articles, and commentaries on Solzhenitsyn's literary career and political struggles in the Soviet Union through his winning Nobel Prize in 1970. The first two sections on the reception of his early work are the most helpful for studying his short stories, including "One Day in the Life of Ivan Denisovich."

Medvedev, Zhores A. *Ten Years After Ivan Denisovich*. New York: Alfred A. Knopf, 1973.
A series of personal observations, analyses, and social and biographical commentaries on Solzhenitsyn's literary career and political misfortunes in the ten years since the publication of "One Day in the Life of Ivan Denisovich." Although there is no literary analysis here, Medvedev, who knew Solzhenitsyn, provides a helpful summary of the reception of "One Day in the Life of Ivan Denisovich" in the Soviet Union, as well as the political pressure that caused it to be rejected for the award of the Lenin Prize.

Modern Fiction Studies 23 (Spring, 1977).
A special issue devoted to Solzhenitsyn. The focus is primarily on the novels, with essays on *Cancer Ward*, *The First Circle*, and *August 1914*; however, there is one essay on "One Day in the Life of Ivan Denisovich." The general essays comparing Solzhenitsyn with Fyodor Dostoevski and commenting on polyphonic structure and political implications in the fiction generally are helpful for understanding the short stories.

Moody, Christopher. *Solzhenitsyn*. Edinburgh: Oliver & Boyd, 1973.
A short monograph introduction to the life and work of Solzhenitsyn. The biographical chapter recounts Solzhenitsyn's troubles with Soviet censorship. There are individual chapters on *Cancer Ward*, *The First Circle*, and *August 1914*, as well as detailed chapters on many of the short stories.

Rzhevsky, Leonid. *Solzhenitsyn: Creator and Heroic Deed*. Translated by Sonja Miller. Tuscaloosa: University of Alabama Press, 1978.

A relatively thin book on various aspects of Solzhenitsyn's art, such as his enlivening the bookish literary Russian language of the 1930's, his use of autobiography in *Cancer Ward*, and the nature of his "significant" realism in his prose poems.

Scammel, Michael. *Solzhenitsyn: A Biography* New York: W. W. Norton, 1984.
This monumental biography of almost a thousand pages is based, in addition to Scammel's extensive research on Russian history, politics, and culture, on discussions with Solzhenitsyn and correspondence with his estranged first wife, Natalya Reshetovskaya. What discussions there are of the short fiction focus on the historical and biographical sources of the stories, as well as on the literary and political tradition to which they belong.

Zamoyska, Hélène. "Solzhenitsyn and the Grand Tradition." In *Aleksandr Solzhenitsyn: Critical Essays and Documentary Materials*, edited by John B. Dunlop, Richard S. Haugh, and Alexis Klimoff. Belmont, Mass.: Nordland Publishing Co., 1973.
A brief discussion of three of Solzhenitsyn's stories in terms of his mixture of traditions, especially the "Grand Tradition" of the respect for truth, and innovation. Focuses on how his characters are exploited and victimized either by the Soviet system or by their own prejudices.

Selected Titles

"The Easter Procession"
Kodjak, Andrej. *Alexander Solzhenitsyn*. Boston: Twayne, 1978.
Says that the story's didacticism is typical of Solzhenitsyn's prose poems and resembles Leo Tolstoy's didactic stories. Notes the theme of anti-Semitism in the story. Says that Solzhenitsyn appeals to conscience of Russians concerning the younger generation they have reared.

Moody, Christopher. *Solzhenitsyn*. Edinburgh: Oliver & Boyd, 1973.
Calls the story a symbolic reenactment of the Passion of Christ. Notes that Solzhenitsyn uses the same Christian imagery that Boris Pasternak does in *Doctor Zhivago* to communicate a similar message.

"For the Good of the Cause"
Ericson, Edward E., Jr. *Solzhenitsyn: The Moral Vision*. Grand Rapids, Mich.: Wm. B. Eerdmans, 1980.
This is one of Solzhenitsyn's most overtly political and least aesthetically pleasing works, says Ericson. Characterization is sacrificed to thematic issues, and the large cast of characters overwhelms this novella-length work.

Kodjak, Andrej. *Alexander Solzhenitsyn*. Boston: Twayne, 1978.
> Argues that the story deals with more than just the Soviet educational system. The real theme is the perpetuation of the Stalinist methods of rule in post-Stalinist Soviet Union. Discusses the story in terms of its two-part structure — the first three chapters, which set up the problem, and the last three, which develop the basic theme.

Moody, Christopher. *Solzhenitsyn*. Edinburgh: Oliver & Boyd, 1973.
> Notes that it is one of his few stories that deal with events in the 1960's. Calls it an overtly political story, an undisguised attack on the way in which the central bureaucracy makes undemocratic decisions without concern for the interests of the people.

Zekulin, Gleb. "Solzhenitsyn's Four Stories." *Soviet Studies* 16 (July, 1964): 45-62.
> Argues for the artistic merits of the story. Claims that its most striking feature is its apparent triviality and ordinariness, which might be dismissed by an inattentive reader. Concludes that Solzhenitsyn, more than any other contemporary Soviet writer, asks his readers to think about problems that were long forbidden.

"Incident at Krechetovka Station"

Ericson, Edward E., Jr. *Solzhenitsyn: The Moral Vision*. Grand Rapids, Mich.: Wm. B. Eerdmans, 1980.
> Ericson says there is a Chekhovian slice-of-life quality to this story, but points out that its central issue centers on the life-debasing nature of the Communist ideology, as exemplified by the central character. The simplistic ethic on which the protagonist has been reared allows no room for the moral ambiguity of the situation with which he is confronted.

Kodjak, Andrej. *Alexander Solzhenitsyn*. Boston: Twayne, 1978.
> Argues that the theme of the story is similar to that of the novel *The First Circle*. Both expose the fanaticism of the Communist Party's deification of Joseph Stalin, who is in fact responsible for the cruelty and stupidity of the bureaucratic machine. Although everyone acts as he is supposed to in Stalin's system, it is the system itself that is to blame.

Moody, Christopher. *Solzhenitsyn*. Edinburgh: Oliver & Boyd, 1973.
> Says that the protagonist of the story, Lieutenant Zotov, is one of Solzhenitsyn's most sympathetically drawn characters. Although he holds conventional Stalinist assumptions about life, he possesses human qualities that Solzhenitsyn admires.

Zekulin, Gleb. "Solzhenitsyn's Four Stories." *Soviet Studies* 16 (July, 1964): 45-62.
> Argues that the main interest in the story lies in the portrayal of the protagonist

Zotov. Says that the story focuses on the tragedy that arises from the conflict between the character's sincerity and honesty and his leaning toward mistrust and doubt.

"Matryona's House"

Ericson, Edward E., Jr. *Solzhenitsyn: The Moral Vision*. Grand Rapids, Mich.: Wm. B. Eerdmans 1980.

Discusses the protagonist of the story as representative of unthinking natural piety, which for Solzhenitsyn exemplifies the best of old Russia. What Solzhenitsyn pictures here, says Ericson, is what he has stated directly in later works—that evil lies in human nature, but that when one is simple and at one with the natural world, one embodies the spiritual values that Russia must cultivate.

Jackson, Robert Louis. " 'Matryona's Home': The Making of a Russian Icon." In *Solzhenitsyn: A Collection of Critical Essays*, edited by Kathryn Feuer. Englewood Cliffs, N.J.: Prentice-Hall, 1976.

Discusses the theme of disfiguration of the countryside in the story, from the ancient peasant with an ax to the modern excavators with their machines. Notes that the story follows in the tradition of Fyodor Dostoevski and Leo Tolstoy. Says that the railroad crossing in the story is a tragic junction between all forces in Russian life.

Kodjak, Andrej. *Alexander Solzhenitsyn*. Boston: Twayne, 1978.

Argues that the usual interpretation of the story—that it is a reflection of the dismal rural life resulting from Stalin's collectivization of the countryside—ignores much of the text. Claims that the story is really about Matryona, offering a profound portrait of her personality as the only righteous member of her community.

Moody, Christopher. *Solzhenitsyn*. Edinburgh: Oliver & Boyd, 1973.

Discusses the story as an indictment of life in the Russian village in the tradition of Anton Chekhov and Ivan Bunin. Sees Matryona as a kind of holy innocent, a Christlike figure who not only labors for others without reward, but also helps those who rob her. The story provides a picture of goodness and truth at the mercy of evil and falsehood.

Rzhevsky, Leonid. *Solzhenitsyn: Creator and Heroic Deed*. Tuscaloosa: University of Alabama Press, 1978.

A brief discussion of the power of the central character in the story. Notes the plain and sincere narrative manner, the warmth with which the narrator describes village life, and the peasantlike speech of the narrator. Discusses forerunners to Matryona in works by Fyodor Dostoevski and Nikolai Leskov.

Zekulin, Gleb. "Solzhenitsyn's Four Stories." *Soviet Studies* 16 (July, 1964): 45-62.

Says that all the information in the story indicates implicitly that the life of the small peasant farmers is as dreary as that of their forefathers, in spite of the mechanization of agricultural work. The most striking aspect of the story is the calm and detachment of its presentation.

"One Day in the Life of Ivan Denisovich"

Allaback, Steven. *Alexander Solzhenitsyn*. New York: Taplinger, 1978.

Analysis of the four major novels and "One Day in the Life of Ivan Denisovich." A long but relatively simple summary analysis of the action in the novella; Allaback disagrees with the common approach that it is the story of an entire political system. Instead, he says that the character Shukhov is the most consistently alive character in all Solzhenitsyn's fiction, for the reader does not see the author pulling the strings, as one does in such novels as *The First Circle*.

Brown, Edward J. *Russian Literature Since the Revolution*. Rev. ed. Cambridge, Mass.: Harvard University Press, 1982.

Notes that a structural feature of the story, which is common to all Solzhenitsyn's fiction, is the collapse of both space and time into a severely constricted space. As a result of this structure, there are two lines of time as well as space—the limited time of the actual day, and the sweep of history. Also discusses the language and style of the story, as well as its basic motif of survival.

Curtis, James M. *Solzhenitsyn's Traditional Imagination*. Athens: University of Georgia Press, 1984.

Analyzes the story to show that Solzhenitsyn works against the historical dynamics and style of Leo Tolstoy's works. Solzhenitsyn reacts against the pastoral conventions that Tolstoy used to present the life of the peasant; by narrating the story through Ivan's consciousness, Solzhenitsyn makes him less symbolic and more individual.

Ericson, Edward E., Jr. *Solzhenitsyn: The Moral Vision*. Grand Rapids, Mich.: Wm. B. Eerdmans, 1980.

After summarizing the reception of the novella, Ericson analyzes the story in terms of narrative style. He claims that its most memorable technical trait is its understatement and points out that while Solzhenitsyn tells the story in the third person, he creates the illusion that the reader is inside the mind of Shukhov. Ericson also notes that the story embodies one of Solzhenitsyn's most significant themes—the human capacity to endure pain with some vestiges of humanity intact.

Kern, Gary. "Ivan the Worker." *Modern Fiction Studies* 23 (Spring, 1977): 5-30.
An extensive discussion of the structure of the work and how the structure reveals the work's themes. Discusses the metaphorical scheme based on animal images in the story. Shows how the imagery relates to the social and religious alienation in the work. The essay outlines the structure of the story from the smallest units to the broader philosophic implications and consequences of pattern.

Kodjak, Andrej. *Alexander Solzhenitsyn*. Boston: Twayne, 1978.
Kodjak's chapter on the novella focuses on the dual perspective created by the narrator-commentator of the work and the code that the protagonist uses to protect himself from his three mortal enemies: starvation, exhaustion, and annihilation by the authorities. The application of the code is the central theme of the story, reflected in Denisovich's struggle for dignity and respect against the powers that would dehumanize him.

Lukács, Georg. *Solzhenitsyn*. Translated by William David Graf. Cambridge, Mass.: MIT Press, 1969.
An influential discussion of the novella from the point of view of its generic characteristics and its difference from the novel form. Notes that Solzhenitsyn's achievement in the story is the transformation of an uneventful day in a camp into a symbol of a past that has not yet been overcome, even though the story shows no overt trace of symbolism at all, but is presented as a genuine, realistic slice of life.

Moody, Christopher. *Solzhenitsyn*. Edinburgh: Oliver & Boyd, 1973.
Discusses Solzhenitsyn as an old-fashioned writer who has made no contribution to the advancement of the novel or the short story as genres. Notes that there is no romanticism in the descriptions of Denisovich's day, but that the language is colorful and rhythmical because it reflects the cadences of peasant speech. Also notes the two narrative voices of the story, with no clear syntactical dividing line between them.

Nielsen, Niels C., Jr. *Solzhenitsyn's Religion*. Nashville: Thomas Nelson, 1975.
A general, nonacademic study of Solzhenitsyn's Christian point of view and his place in the traditions of the Russian Orthodox church. Argues that the story contains most of the major themes of Solzhenitsyn's writings. Comments on the different kinds of religion embodied in the story and emphasizes the story as a testament of Solzhenitsyn's Christian faith.

Rothberg, Abraham. *Aleksandr Solzhenitsyn: The Major Novels*, Ithaca, N.Y.: Cornell University Press, 1971.
A long, but general, analysis of the story in terms of its action and theme.

Discusses the convicts' hatred of the machinery that enslaves them and Denisovich's notions of dignified conduct, which sustains him. Notes that the story reflects Solzhenitsyn's belief that the imprisonment of the body cannot enslave the spirit.

Zekulin, Gleb. "Solzhenitsyn's Four Stories." *Soviet Studies* 16 (July, 1964): 45-62.
Discusses the kinds of direct and indirect information that the story communicates. Comments on its presentation of people's attitudes toward work. Notes how the story presents a short survey of Soviet history from the angle of the various generations of inmates in the camp.

ITALO SVEVO
Ettore Schmitz
(1861-1928)
Austria and Italy

General Biographical and Critical Studies

Biasin, Gian-Paolo. *Literary Diseases: Theme and Metaphor in the Italian Novel.* Austin: University of Texas Press, 1975.

Discusses how Svevo deals with disease in his major novels, especially *Confessions of Zeno*. Although there is only passing mention of the short stories, this is a probing study from a poststructuralist point of view of one of Svevo's most pervasive philosophic and psychological themes.

Champagne, Roland A. "A Displacement of Plato's *Pharmakon*: A Study of Italo Svevo's Short Fiction." *Modern Fiction Studies* 21 (Winter, 1975-1976): 564-572.

Discusses Svevo's short stories as commentaries on the act of writing as an act of ambivalence. Champagne shows how Svevo's short fiction presents time as a grammatical entity in which the linear sequence of events is broken up and space is presented relative to the narrator. These creative presentations of time and space preclude a mimetic aesthetics.

De Lauretis, Teresa. "Discourse and the Conquest of Desire in Svevo's Fiction." *Modern Fiction Studies* 18 (Summer, 1972): 91-109.

Although the focus of this discussion is Svevo's novels, it is valuable in charting how all of his fiction presents the same basic human experiences of unrequited love, struggle with a master figure, disease, and death. Shows that one of the most diffuse motifs in Svevo's fiction is disease as a metaphor for existence, related in a two-way causal connection to the motifs of guilt and death.

Furbank, P. N. *Italo Svevo: The Man and the Writer*. Berkeley: University of California Press, 1966.

Half this study is devoted to Svevo's life, the rest to the major works. Only passing comments on the short stories. Notes that "The Hoax" is based on a real-life incident and that it develops a favorite pattern in Svevo's stories of accidentally profiting from the discovery of the hoax.

Gatt-Rutter, John. *Italo Svevo: A Double Life*. Oxford, England Clarendon Press, 1988.

A lengthy, detailed biography of Svevo who lived the life of his everyday

persona as Ettore Schmitz and his literary persona as Italo Svevo. Focuses on
the conflict between his life as a bank clerk and his life as a writer, between
his Jewish origins and his aesthetic convictions, between his Austrian background and his Italian nationality. The study also attempts to draw a relationship between the life and the literary works and to define the role of writing in
Svevo's life. Only passing references to the short stories, but essential for
understanding Svevo's work in general.

Lebowitz, Naomi. *Italo Svevo*. New Brunswick, N.J.: Rutgers University Press, 1978.
A study of the development of Svevo's fiction and the cultural atmosphere
within which he worked. Discusses the fable-like nature of some of his novellas and the burlesque nature of some of his short stories. Notes the closed form
of his major stories such as "The Hoax" and "Generous Wine."

Mancini, Albert N. "*Short Sentimental Journey and Other Stories.*" *Studies in Short
Fiction* 6 (Fall, 1969): 659-664.
An important review article that argues for Svevo's importance as a short-story
writer. Provides brief discussions of several stories in the collection not only in
terms of their plots, but also their styles and techniques. Discusses Svevo's use
of the fable form as well as his anecdotal technique in the novellas.

Poggioli, Renato. "A Note on Italo Svevo." In his *The Spirit of the Letter: Essays in
European Literature*. Cambridge, Mass.: Harvard University Press, 1965.
A short but stimulating discussion. Poggioli briefly comments on the influence
of Sigmund Freud on Svevo, his stream of consciousness technique, his bourgeois protagonists, and the conflict between the bourgeois spirit and the literary mind, which is often his theme. Argues that in the literary vocation of his
heroes Svevo sees an attempt to escape from life and even consciousness.

Roditi, Edouard. "Italo Svevo." In *The Golden Horizon*, edited by Cyril Connolly.
London: Weidenfeld & Nicolson, 1953.
An introduction to Svevo's work, placing him in the central European tradition
of Robert Musil and Franz Kafka rather than in the Italian tradition. Says that
his heroes all seem to be tormented with a lust for self-improvement, although
many of them are "hopeless" like those of Musil and Kafka. Argues that
Svevo's plots follow dialectical schemes that resolve contraries through endless
dilemmas and reversals.

Weiss, Beno. *Italo Svevo*. Boston: Twayne, 1987.
An introductory account of Svevo's life, prose fiction, and drama. Includes a
brief chapter on the short stories, which Weiss calls minor writings. Argues
that "The Hoax" is important because it provides an insight into Svevo's self-
image as an author, that "Generous Wine" is full of psychological insights

about old age, and that "This Indolence of Mine" focuses on the attempt to hoodwink nature by means of sexuality. No detailed discussions here; Weiss does suggest that the stories illustrate Svevo's literary experimentalism.

Selected Title

"The Hoax"

Bondanella, Peter E. " 'The Hoax': Svevo on Art and Reality." *Studies in Short Fiction* 10 (Summer, 1973): 263-269.

Claims that the story proposes a view of reality that places Svevo in the ranks of precursor of the Italian absurd. Demonstrates that "The Hoax" contains an important expression of Svevo's opinions about the nature of art and how it deals with the absurdity of the human condition. Focuses on two basic issues in the story: the incomprehensibility of life and the response of the artist to that fact. Argues that Svevo rejects representational realism as the proper goal of the artist.

Lebowitz, Naomi. *Italo Svevo*. New Brunswick, N.J.: Rutgers University Press, 1978.

Argues that the fables of the protagonist represent literary atrophy. Says that the well-defined twist of the plot and its logical preparation make the story like the classic joke; it ends with a victory of the fable's organization over the chaotic nature of experience.

Robison, Paula. "*Una Burla Riuscita*: Irony as Hoax in Svevo." *Modern Fiction Studies* 18 (Spring, 1972): 65-80.

Says that the story reveals that Svevo has a view of art similar to that of Sigmund Freud, that is, art as sublimation, the connection between art, fantasy, and the unconscious, and the psychic functions of comedy and wit as a means of asserting the ego. This is a detailed analysis of the story demonstrating how these Freudian principles govern the artistic endeavors of the story's protagonist.

MIGUEL DE UNAMUNO
(1864-1936)
Spain

General Biographical and Critical Studies

Kerrigan, Anthony. Introduction to *Abel Sánchez and Other Stories*, by Miguel de Unamuno y Jugo. Chicago: Henry Regnery, 1965.
A brief introduction to Unamuno's life and thought. Claims that the most startling characteristic of Unamuno is his urge toward immortality. Comments briefly on the notion of the tragic sense in the three stories in the collection, arguing that in Unamuno's existential world the protagonists of the stories are immunized against the trivial by their concern over the immortal life of their village.

Lacy, Allen. *Miguel de Unamuno: The Rhetoric of Existence*. The Hague, Netherlands: Mouton, 1967.
This three-part study presents a summary of Unamuno's early life, focusing on what led him to his philosophy, a discussion of the philosophy of language that underlies his work, and an analysis of the nature of discourse in Unamuno's *The Tragic Sense of Life in Men and Peoples*. Although the emphasis of the book is on the philosophy rather than on the fiction, the study is important for understanding the primacy of language in Unamuno's thought and writing.

Marías, Julián. *Miguel de Unamuno*. Translated by Frances M. López-Morillas. Cambridge, Mass.: Harvard University Press, 1966.
Discussion of many aspects of Unamuno's work: religion, philosophy, and fiction. Argues that the basic problem in reading Unamuno is trying to determine how his philosophical ideas are interwoven into his art. A valuable chapter on Unamuno's narratives focuses on the relation between fiction and reality.

Nozick, Martin. *Miguel de Unamuno*. Boston: Twayne, 1971.
General introduction focusing on how Unamuno's "tragic sense of life" deals with both religious doubts and ideological crises. A chapter on "Fiction as Philosophy" focuses on both the plays and the fiction. Includes a brief summary discussion of the short stories as being alternately romantic and macabre. Briefly notes that "The Madness of Doctor Montarco" dramatizes one of the paths that Unamuno's life might have taken.

Rubia Barcia, José, and M. A. Zeitlin. *Unamuno: Creator and Creation*. Berkeley: University of California Press, 1967.

A collection of papers on Unamuno presented at University of California at Los Angeles in 1964. The topics include the life of the man, as well as his moral, political, and philosophical ideas. The most valuable paper for an understanding of his fiction, although it does not mention the short stories, is "The Novel as Self-Creation," which discusses the self-reflexive nature of his narrative art.

Rudd, Margaret Thomas. *The Lone Heretic: A Biography of Miguel de Unamuno y Jugo.* Austin: University of Texas, 1963.

Since this is the only biography of Unamuno in English, it is essential reading, but many critics suggest that it should be read with caution. Only passing comments on the short fiction and its relation to Unamuno's life. Says that "Saint Manual Bueno, Martyr" presents the religious dilemmas of Unamuno himself, for it was conceived when he believed that he was losing his faith. Suggests that "Abel Sánchez" is important to understanding his work, for much of his writings reveal a basic Cane and Abel contradiction in the individual.

Valdés, Mario J. *Death in the Literature of Unamuno.* Urbana: University of Illinois Press, 1966.

A study of the theme of death in the works of Unamuno, focusing on the relationship between the philosophy of Unamuno in relation to death and the aesthetic experience of death in his fiction and drama. A brief discussion of the short fiction focuses on the stories as a storehouse of themes, plots, characters, and ideas that he would develop more fully later.

Selected Titles

"Abel Sánchez"

Kinney, Arthur. "The Multiple Heroes of Abel Sánchez." *Studies in Short Fiction* 1 (1964): 251-257.

Argues that the story treats two of Unamuno's most basic concepts: that the most rewarding life is one of struggle and that the end of life is worldly fame and immortality. Further suggests that these concepts are paradoxically embodied in the two central characters in the story and that the story deals with the existential search for absolutes that are ultimately contingent.

Marías, Julián. *Miguel de Unamuno.* Translated by Frances M. López-Morillas. Cambridge, Mass.: Harvard University Press, 1966.

Says that in this story Unamuno attempts for the first time to descend to the profoundest depths of the human soul. Claims that "hatred" is actually the

principal character of the work and that the terrifying descriptions of hatred in
it are not psychological but rather existential.

Nozick, Martin. *Miguel de Unamuno*. Boston: Twayne, 1971.
Discusses the various metaphysical, national, and psychological implications of
the story and how they are interwoven into the texture of the work. Argues that
Unamuno is not in control of the structure of the story, which is loosely
episodic. Also suggests that the story reflects Unamuno's inability to make use
of indirection, suggestion, and understatement.

Valdés, Mario J. *Death in the Literature of Unamuno*. Urbana: University of Illinois
Press, 1966.
Discusses the work as a tragic story of a man who struggles with his passions
as he searches for inner freedom. Mostly a summary of the story, tracing the
efforts of the protagonist to free himself from his alter ego. Concludes that
because of his obsession, Joaquín Monegro was never able to achieve the inner
freedom of being aware that he is his own maker.

"Saint Manuel Bueno, Martyr"
Longhurst, C. A. "The Problem of Truth in 'San Manuel, Bueno, Mártir.' " *The
Modern Language Review* 76 (July, 1981): 581-597.
A detailed analysis of the story in terms of the equivocal and contradictory
image the reader receives of Don Manuel as a result of the narrator's own
ambiguous relation to him. Longhurst argues that it is the story's infrastructure
that gives it a special quality, for it moves away from an extraliterary reality
and towards the fictive form itself.

Marías, Julián. *Miguel de Unamuno*. Translated by Frances M. López-Morillas.
Cambridge, Mass.: Harvard University Press, 1966.
Argues that death and the necessity for surviving are the central themes of the
story. Furthermore, Marías suggests that for the first and only time Unamuno
overcomes the abstraction of the self by grounding it in the concrete world of
the person. The formula for the basic structure of the story is thus the notion
of the person in his world.

Nozick, Martin. *Miguel de Unamuno*. Boston: Twayne, 1971.
A long discussion of Unamuno's most admired work of fiction. Examines the
story as a major statement of all the conflicts in Unamuno: desire for seclusion
versus the pull toward active life; the nostalgia for serenity versus the need for
progress; the obligation to speak versus the guilt created by self-assertion.

Valdés, Mario J. *Death in the Literature of Unamuno*. Urbana: University of Illinois
Press, 1966.

A summary commentary on the story, focusing on Don Manuel's inner struggle as he embodies the strife of all of his people. Every moment of his life he must fight the struggle between the desire to commit suicide and the assertion of his inner freedom. Argues that like Jesus Christ, Don Manuel wants to use the burdens of the tragic sense of his people to achieve the true essence of his martyrdom.

MIKHAIL ZOSHCHENKO
(1895-1958)
Soviet Union

General Biographical and Critical Studies

Brown, Edward J. "Zoshchenko and the Art of Satire." In his *Russian Literature Since the Revolution*. Cambridge, Mass.: Harvard University Press, 1982.
Argues that although Zoshchenko's work fits the concept of satire in a general way, it is in no sense a humorous attack on a specific social organization or way of life. Situational and linguistic absurdities from Soviet life are the subjects of many of his short tales. Brown says that no one has ever spoken the language of Zoshchenko's characters; it is an invented speech made up of newspaper rhetoric. Also notes that the stories follow a formal pattern.

Fen, Elisaveta. Preface to *The Woman Who Could Not Read and Other Tales*, by Mikhail Zoshchenko. Westport, Conn.: Hyperion Press, 1973.
A brief discussion of Zoshchenko as a short-story writer par excellence. Comments briefly on the nature of his whimsy and humor and places him within the tradition of earlier Russian humorists.

_____ . Preface to *The Wonderful Dog and Other Tales* by Mikhail Zoshchenko. Westport, Conn.: Hyperion Press, 1973.
Notes that the typical situation that moves Zoshchenko to humor is a situation of incongruity or discrepancy between the ideal and the real. Comments on some examples of his stories that reflect these situations. Says that the stories represent a series of illustrations of the human fallacy that people can be transformed by government decrees and sermons.

McLean, Hugh. Introduction to *Nervous People and Other Satires* by Mikhail Zoshchenko. New York: Pantheon Books, 1963.
Notes that during the 1920's and 1930's, Zoshchenko was, next to Gorky, the most popular Russian writer. Argues that his technique of creating uncertainty in the reader's mind about the author's relation to his work is adapted from Nikoli Gogol and Nikoli Leskov. Discusses Zoshchenko's use of this technique by creating a distinctive narrator in many of his stories.

Slonim, Marc. "The Condemned Humorist." In his *Soviet Russian Literature: Writers and Problems*. New York: Oxford University Press, 1967.
A short introductory essay on Zoshchenko, commenting on his use of the absurd idiom of the half-educated, his mixing popular speech with bookish terms, and his use of implausible plots based on perfectly realistic incidents.

Discusses his characters and the objects of his satire. Says that he is the only full-fledged humorist in Soviet literature and that his sketches still are significant satirical documents of the post-revolutionary era.

Selected Title

"Adventures of a Monkey"
Mihailovich, Vasa D. "Zoshchenko's 'Adventures of a Monkey' as an Allegory." *Satire Newsletter* 4 (1967): 84-89.
Discusses the attack made on the story in 1946 at a meeting of Leningrad writers. Attempts to explain the reason for the attack on what many feel to be an innocuous children's story by showing that it is allegorical. Argues that the meaning of the story is that ultimately it is better to live in the zoo than at liberty in Soviet society.

INDEX

INDEX